Changing Track

Changing Track

Michel Butor

Translated by Jean Stewart

CALDER

CALDER PUBLICATIONS
an imprint of

ALMA BOOKS LTD
3 Castle Yard
Richmond
Surrey TW10 6TF
United Kingdom
www.calderpublications.com

First published in French as *La Modification* in 1957 by Les Éditions
de Minuit, Paris
This translation first published in Great Britain as *Second Thoughts* in
1958 by Faber and Faber Ltd
This revised translation first published by Calder Publications in 2018

© Les Éditions de Minuit, 1957
Translation © Jean Stewart, 1958, 2018

Cover design: Will Dady

Printed in Great Britain by CPI Group (UK) Ltd, Croydon CR0 4YY

ISBN: 978-0-7145-4570-7

Contents

Changing Track

PART I

I

S TANDING WITH YOUR LEFT FOOT on the grooved brass sill, you try in vain with your right shoulder to push the sliding door a little wider open.

You edge your way in through the narrow opening, then you lift up your suitcase of bottle-green grained leather – the smallish suitcase of a man used to making long journeys – grasping the sticky handle with fingers that are hot from having carried even so light a weight so far, and you feel the muscles and tendons tense not only in your finger joints, the palm of your hand, your wrist and your arm, but in your shoulder too, all down one side of your back along your vertebrae from neck to loins.

No, it's not merely the comparative earliness of the hour that makes you feel so unusually feeble, it's age, already trying to convince you of its domination over your body, although you have only just passed your forty-fifth birthday.

Your eyes are half closed and blurred with a faint haze, your eyelids tender and stiff, the skin over your temples drawn and puckered, your hair – which is growing thinner and greyer, imperceptibly to others but not to you, not to Henriette or Cécile nor, nowadays, to the children – is somewhat dishevelled, and your whole body feels ill at ease, constricted and weighed down by your clothes, and seems, in its half-awakened state, to be steeped in some frothing water full of suspended animalcules.

You have chosen this compartment because the corner seat facing the engine and next to the corridor is vacant, the very seat you would have got Marnal to reserve for you if there had still been time – no, the seat you would have asked for yourself over the telephone, since nobody at Scabelli must know that it's to Rome you are escaping for these few days.

A man on your right, his face level with your elbow, sitting opposite that place where you are going to settle down for this journey, a little younger than yourself, not over forty, taller than yourself, pale, with hair greyer than yours, with eyes blinking behind powerful lenses, with long restless hands, nails bitten and tobacco-stained, fingers crossing and uncrossing nervously as he waits impatiently for the train to start, the owner, in all probability, of that black briefcase crammed with files, a few coloured corners of which you notice peeping through a burst seam, and of the bound and probably boring books stacked above him like an emblem, like a legend whose explanatory or enigmatic character is not lessened by its being a thing, not a mere word but a possession, lying on that square-holed metal rack and propped up against the partition next to the corridor,

this man stares at you, irritated at your standing motionless and with your feet in the way of his feet; he would like to ask you to sit down, but his timid lips cannot even frame the words, and he turns towards the window, pushing aside with his forefinger the lowered blue blind with its woven initials, SNCF.

On the same seat as this man, next to a space at present vacant but which someone has reserved with that long umbrella in its black silk sheath stretched against the green moleskin, beneath that light attaché case in its waterproof tartan cover, with its two gleaming locks of thin brass, a fair young man who must just have finished his military service, dressed in light-grey tweed, with a diagonally striped red-and-purple tie, holds in his right hand the left hand of a young woman darker than himself, and plays with it, passing his thumb to and fro across her palm while she watches him contentedly, raising his eyes for a moment to look at you and dropping them quickly when he sees you watching them, but without breaking off his play.

They are not merely lovers but a young married couple, since they are each wearing a new gold ring, on their honeymoon perhaps, and they must have bought for the occasion – or else been given by a generous uncle – those two big, identical pigskin cases, brand-new, one on top of the other above their heads, with little leather label frames fixed onto the handles with tiny straps.

They are the only ones to have reserved their seats in this compartment; their brown-and-yellow tickets, with big black numbers on them, hang motionless from the nickel rail.

On the opposite side of the window, sitting by himself on the other seat, an ecclesiastic of about thirty, already plumpish, meticulously clean except for the nicotine-stained fingers of his right hand, is trying to bury himself in his breviary, which is stuffed with pictures, while above him a briefcase, the greyish-black colour of asphalt, with its zip-fastener gaping a little like the needle-toothed jaw of a sea serpent, lies on the rack, onto which, straining, like some grotesque athlete at a fair lifting by its ring a huge, hollow cast-iron weight, and using one hand only since your other is still clutching the book you have just bought, you hoist your own luggage, your own suitcase of bottle-green, coarse-grained leather, stamped with your initials, L.D., a present from your family on your previous birthday, which had been really rather smart then and quite suitable for the head of the Paris office of Scabelli Typewriters, and which can still pass muster despite the grease spots revealed by close scrutiny and the insidious rust that has attacked the hinges.

Opposite you, between the clergyman and the graceful, gentle young woman, through one window and another window beyond it, you can dimly make out, in another less up-to-date coach with yellow wooden seats and string racks, in the half-darkness beyond the composite reflections, a man of your own height, whose exact age you could not guess and whose clothes you could not describe with any precision, reproducing even more slowly than yourself the weary movements you have just made.

Sitting down, you stretch out your legs on either side of those of the intellectual, who now wears a look of relief and at last stops fidgeting with his fingers, you unbutton your thick, shaggy overcoat with its shot-silk lining, fling it open to reveal your two

7

knees in their sheaths of navy-blue cloth, the creases of which, though pressed only yesterday, are already spoilt, you uncross and unwind with your right hand your scarf of mottled, loosely woven wool, which with its knobbly texture of straw colour and pearl reminds you of scrambled eggs, you fold it carelessly in three and thrust it into that ample pocket that already contains a packet of blue Gauloises, a box of matches and, of course, shreds of dusty tobacco that have collected in the lining.

Then, violently grasping the chromium-plated handle, the dark iron core of which shows through a tiny crack in the plating, you struggle to close the sliding door, which after a few jerks refuses to move any farther, while at the same moment the window pane on your right reveals a short rosy man in a black waterproof and a bowler hat, who slips through the opening as you had done earlier, but without making any attempt to widen it, as if it were only too certain that this lock and this sliding door would not function properly, and apologizes silently, with a barely perceptible flicker of eyelids and lips, for disturbing you, while you draw back your legs – an Englishman to all appearances, and surely the owner of that black, silky umbrella lying across the green moleskin, which indeed he picks up and lays, not on the rack but below it, on the narrow shelf of rods, together with his hat, the only hat in this compartment so far, a slightly older man than yourself no doubt, his head much balder than your own.

On the right, through the cool pane against which you press your forehead, and through the corridor window beyond it, in front of which a rather breathless woman in a nylon hood has just passed, the platform clock can be dimly made out against the greyish sky, its slender second hand moving jerkily round; it shows exactly eight minutes past eight, so you have two whole minutes' respite before the train leaves, and still clutching in your left hand the volume you bought in the station lobby as you hurried past, relying on the name of the series and having read neither the title nor the author's name, you bare your wrist, hitherto concealed under the threefold sleeve – white, blue and grey – of your shirt, your jacket and your overcoat, and disclose your rectangular watch, fastened by a dark-red leather strap, its figures painted with a greenish substance that shines in the darkness; it shows twelve past eight, and you set it back accordingly.

Outside, an electrically driven truck pushes its sinuous way through the grey crowd of busy, encumbered people, who amid the excitement and confusion of their arguments and goodbyes strain to hear the distorted snatches of speech poured forth by the loudspeakers, then the other train moves noisily off, its green coaches passing by one after the other, and the last of all, as it withdraws like the fringe of a theatre curtain, discloses before you, like an immensely elongated stage, another crowded platform with another clock and another motionless train, which will presumably not start until your own has left the station.

You can hardly hold your eyes open or your head up; you want to sink deeper into the corner, to dig yourself a comfortable hole there with your shoulder, but you twist and turn in vain, and then there's a jolt, and the vibration begins.

Outside, space suddenly expands; a tiny engine draws near and then disappears, moving over a surface patterned with rails; your eyes cannot follow it for more than an instant, nor the leprous backs of those familiar tall buildings, that criss-cross of steel girders, that great bridge over which a milk lorry is just starting, those signs, those catenaries with their posts and bifurcations, that street you notice among rows of streets, with a cyclist just turning its corner, this other street that follows the railway line and is separated from it only by a slight fence and a narrow band of ragged, withered grass, that café where the iron blind is just being drawn up, that barber's shop which still boasts as its sign a horse's tail hanging from a golden ball, that grocer's with its big crimson lettering, that first suburban station with its throng waiting for another train, those great iron keeps where gas is hoarded, those factories with blue-painted windows, that tall cracked chimney, that used-tyre dump, those little gardens with their vine props and their sheds, those little stone villas in their enclosures with their television antennae.

The houses grow smaller, more haphazard in their layout, the breaks in the urban tissue more numerous, with bushes by the roadside, trees shedding their leaves, the first patches of mud, the first stretches of countryside, scarcely green now under the low sky, in front of the line of wooded hills faintly seen on the horizon.

Here, in this compartment, alternately lulled and jarred by the continuous noise, by its deep, constant vibration irregularly stressed by jagged tufts of shrill and strident sound, the four faces opposite you sway in unison without a word, without a gesture, while the clergyman on the other side of the window, with a slight sigh of exasperation, closes his breviary, bound in limp black leather, keeping his forefinger between the pages as a bookmark, while the narrow white satin ribbon hangs loose.

Suddenly all eyes turn towards the door, which is opened wide, with a single, apparently effortless shove of his shoulder, by a red-faced, breathless man, who must have climbed into the coach just as the train was leaving, who flings onto the rack a bulging suitcase and a rough ball of a parcel done up in newspaper and tied with a ragged string, and then sits down beside you, unbuttons his raincoat, crosses his right leg over his left, pulls out of his pocket a film weekly in a colour cover and begins to look at the pictures.

His coarse profile hides the clergyman's, and you can see nothing of the latter but his hand resting on the window sill, its fingers shaking with the general movement, the forefinger tapping gently and mechanically, silently amid the noise, on the long screwed-on strip of metal along which there sprawls, as you know (for you can't really read it, you can only guess roughly what each of those horizontal letters is, so flattened and distorted by perspective do they appear), the bilingual inscription: "*It is dangerous to lean out – E pericoloso sporgersi.*"

Concrete and iron posts, in unbroken succession, like black streaks, sweep swiftly past the whole breadth of the window pane; telephone wires rise, part, fall again, rise again, cross, multiply, combine, their rhythm marked by the insulators, like a complex musical stave, not loaded with notes but indicating sounds and their blending by the mere play of lines.

A little farther on, a little more slowly, the dense woodland, ever more infrequently interrupted by villages or houses, turns on itself, opens up in an avenue, doubles back as though to hide behind one of its own limbs.

The train is now skirting a real forest, or rather passing through it, for beyond the pane against which your forehead is still leaning, beyond the now empty corridor and its row of windows, visible right to the end of the coach, you see the same drab trees, the same tangled undergrowth, growing ever denser.

The railway cuts a deep trench through it, so narrow that you can no longer see the sky, and on either side there rise up tall ramparts of bare earth or of masonry, on which you see for an instant, just long enough to recognize them, the big letters, red against a white rectangle, which you had been expecting of course, but not perhaps quite yet, which you have read many times, which you look out for on each trip if it's light enough, because they tell you either that you're nearly home or that the journey has really begun.

You have gone through Fontainebleau-Avon. Beyond the corridor, a black Citroën 11CV draws up in front of the town hall.

If you had been afraid of missing this train, the motion and noise of which you have grown used to again, it was not that you woke later than you intended this morning, for, on the contrary, your first movement on opening your eyes was to stretch out your arm to prevent the alarm from ringing, while dawn began to show in relief the tumbled sheets on your bed, looking as they emerged from darkness like defeated ghosts, lying crushed on the soft warm surface from which you were trying to tear yourself.

Turning your eyes towards the window you saw Henriette's once black hair, you saw her back outlined against the drab, discouraging early light, faintly at first and then suddenly seen through her white, rather transparent nightdress, becoming more sharply visible as she pushed open and noisily folded back the iron shutters, their slits laden with the fluff and soot of city dust, with here and there a few rust spots like clots of blood.

The cool raw air flooded into the whole room, brushing against your nostrils, and when all six window panes were exposed she turned, shivering, her right hand drawing together the flimsy lace that uselessly adorned her sagging bosom, and went to open the door of the Louis-Philippe wardrobe; the mirror swung round carrying with it the reflection of the ceiling and its mouldings, and that crack which was getting deeper from month to month and which you really ought to have had plastered and hidden long ago (in this diffuse but parsimonious light, which seemed to be filtered through flakes of slate of infinite fineness, the mahogany itself was almost colourless; a single coppery gleam, rust-coloured rather than red, quivered at the edge of the mould-ing); then, hunting among all the garments dangling from their hangers, with sleeves falling straight and insubstantial as if they clothed the stiff and threadlike arms of the ghosts of Bluebeard's former wives, silently swaying in pitiless irony, she took down her grey-and-yellow plaid dressing gown, slipped it on, showing her armpit as she raised her bare arm, and nervously tied the silky cord, looking, thus clad, like an invalid, with her drawn features and anxious, suspicious expression.

There was certainly no tenderness in her glance just then, but, after all, what need had she to get up, when you could quite well have looked after yourself as had been agreed, and as you had often done while she was on holiday with the children; when she's about, she's incapable of trusting you with such details, always assuming that she's indispensable to you and trying to convince you of it...

You waited till she had left the room, closing the door behind her gently so as not to awaken the sleeping boys next door, then, fastening your watch on your wrist (it was barely half-past six), you sat on the bed and thrust your feet into your slippers, scratching your head as you stared vaguely through the window at the dome of the Panthéon, dim against the grey sky, and wondered about your wife's expression, asking yourself not, of course, whether she suspected anything – for that was only too obvious – but exactly what she suspected and, particularly with reference to this journey, exactly how far she had seen through you.

Of course you enjoyed drinking the *café au lait* she had heated for you, but it really was unnecessary, as she knew, since in any case you meant to take advantage of the restaurant car to have some breakfast.

On the landing, you hadn't the courage to refuse her sad kiss.

"You'll only just have time now; though of course there's always room in first class."

How did she know that you hadn't booked your seat this time? Had you really told her yourself, and why? But in any case, one thing she certainly doesn't know is what sort of carriage you're travelling in, and that this journey, far from being requested and paid for by Scabelli, is being made without the knowledge of your bosses in Rome or your own staff in Paris.

She had shut the door of the flat before you started down the stairs, thus missing her last chance of touching your heart, but it's obvious that she had no desire to do so, that if she got up this morning to look after you she did so automatically, from habit, moved at most by a sort of pity strongly tinged with contempt; it's obvious that she is the wearier of the two. Why hold it against her that she did not even watch you leave, after those few words which may have been spoken in irony and to which you neither would nor could reply, whereas it would surely have been better for you both if she had not got up at all nor even opened her eyes, if you had left her sleeping, while the sheets rose and fell with her deep breathing, barely visible in the dark room where you'd have left the shutters unopened.

If you were afraid of missing this train, now smoothly rolling along between bare fields and brown copses, it was because you took far longer than you'd foreseen to find a taxi, and you had to go down the whole length of the Rue Soufflot carrying your suitcase, and it was only at the corner of the Boulevard Saint-Michel, opposite the Café Mahieu, that finally, after several fruitless attempts, you succeeded in stopping a Citroën 11CV, the driver of which didn't even trouble to open the door for you or to help you in with your meagre luggage, so that you had the absurd feeling that he could see by your face that this time you were going to travel third class and not first as usual, and it was particularly embarrassing to realize, suddenly, that, by some disconcerting vagary of your dream-dazed early-morning consciousness, you were reacting as if this was something shameful.

Ensconced in the right-hand corner, just as you are now, you saw the tree trunks go past on the still-deserted pavements, in front of still-closed shops, then the Sorbonne church with its still-empty square, then those ruins that are known as the Thermae of Julian the Apostate, although they are probably older than that emperor, then the Halle aux Vins, the gates of the Jardin des Plantes, the apse of the cathedral to the left, on its island, above the parapet of the Pont d'Austerlitz, among the other spires, and on the right the station tower with its clock showing eight o'clock.

As you were asking the ticket collector which platform you had to go to, you noticed that it was almost in front of you, with its clock face over the entry, whose motionless hands showed not what time it was but what time the train was due to leave, 8.10, and the noticeboard indicating the principal stops of that list that you know by heart – Laroche, Dijon, Chalon, Mâcon, Bourg, Culoz, Aix-les-Bains, Chambéry, Modane, Turin, Genoa, Pisa, Roma-Termini and farther still (this train goes farther still), Napoli, Reggio, Syracuse – and you took advantage of the few moments that remained to you to buy, without choosing it, the book you are still holding in your left hand and the packet of cigarettes which lies, still intact, in the pocket of your coat, under your scarf.

Beyond the corridor, a black Citroën 11CV starts off in front of a church, follows a road alongside the railway, races the train, draws near, moves away, disappears behind a wood, reappears, crosses a little river with willow trees and a deserted boat, drops behind, catches up, then halts at a crossroad, turns off and escapes towards a village the steeple of which soon vanishes behind a fold of land. Montereau station has gone by.

A tinkle pierces through the rumble and you see coming towards you the dining-car attendant in his gold-braided blue cap and his white jacket, whom others beside yourself have been awaiting, for the young couple look up at each other with a smile.

A man, a woman, another woman whom you only see from the back come out of their compartment and go past; a raincoat sleeve brushes the window against which you are still leaning, then a voluminous black nylon handbag with a plastic button knocks against it once or twice.

The temperature has risen perceptibly, and the strip of metal, patterned with diamond-shaped grooves, that runs along the floor between the seats is growing hotter. Your neighbour, the newest arrival, obviously the least well off of all the occupants of this compartment, folds up the weekly he was reading, hesitates for a moment, wondering where to put it, gets up, stows it on the shelf, where it unfolds like a fan, takes off his raincoat, clutching it like a cleaning rag in his great paw, and flings it roughly, crumpled, onto the rack, between his newspaper-wrapped parcel and your suitcase (the horn buckle taps against the metal, then swings at the end of the dangling belt), picks up his paper again, unfolds it and resumes his seat.

Who's the actress whose wedding is celebrated in that photograph, and how many times has she been married before?

You turn your eyes to the right as you hear the sound of the bell again, and for a few moments you watch the white-jacketed attendant going back to his coach to fill pale-blue cups, the colour of an uncertain spring sky over a northern town, with coffee that is neither cheap nor good.

The young woman makes up her mind first, and then her husband; they apologize as they go past you, both blushing and smiling, as if this were their first journey and everything, down to the slightest incident, delighted and amazed them, then half-close the door, which for some little while had been standing wide open, and hurry off.

The man opposite you draws up the blind on his side.

Go along there yourself; thrust that tiresome book into your pocket and leave this compartment; it's not that you're really hungry, since you've already had a cup of coffee, it isn't even a matter of routine, since you are subject to a different timetable; no, it's part of the decision you have taken, and the process that you have started off is taking its course mechanically, almost without your knowledge.

II

Yes, this is the compartment you were in; there's the man with greying hair, now absorbed in a thick book bound in coarse black cloth, who was sitting opposite you, next to that florid, very clean-looking man with small greedy fish's eyes, and there's the clergyman next to the window trying in vain, once more, to bury himself in his breviary.

For the other two, the lovers, the married couple, whom you left four coaches farther on, leaning over their table, deep in peaceful talk, everything is a pretext for speech, a source of fresh contentment; but you are driven back by boredom and loneliness to this pigeon-hole, your home within this train that is carrying you away, identified by that object belonging to you, your suitcase up on the rack to your left.

But you ought to have kept your place below it, the corner seat next the corridor, facing forward, which you had been so glad to find vacant at the Gare de Lyon because it's the very one you always get Alexandre Marnal to reserve for you in a first-class carriage for your business trips; you ought to have left behind that book which is weighing down your coat and stretching your already overloaded pocket, and which you never meant to start reading along there; for now your place is taken by that newcomer who aroused your dislike, as soon as he appeared, by the way he showed off his strength, opening the door with one shove of his shoulder, by his stupid self-assurance, his vulgarity, and who's sitting there still deep in his illustrated weekly, without showing the slightest intention of disturbing himself to give it back to you,

a commercial traveller unmistakably, but in what? Wine, pharma-
ceuticals, lingerie maybe, certainly not typewriters, because he'd
have quite different luggage in that case, unless like yourself he
was running away...

The temperature has gone on rising during your absence, or else
it's because you've been moving about and drinking hot liquid,
you're sweating. Your face, just level with the mirror, is trembling
within the frame because of the motion of the train. You shaved
hurriedly this morning and you notice a number of black specks
near your ears. You pass your damp hand over your chin. Your
skin is not only rough, it's taut; your features are drawn, your
eyes dull, your mouth sullen. You haven't succeeded in waking up
completely yet in spite of that second coffee, although, consulting
your watch, you see it's long past nine o'clock, so that on a normal
weekday you would already be at work in the Avénue de l'Opéra,
striking terror into the hearts of belated typists, and although last
night you went to bed quite early.

This journey ought to be a release, a renewal, a great cleansing
of your body and mind; shouldn't you already be enjoying the
benefit and the excitement of it? Why do you feel so weary and
almost sick? Is it the fatigue accumulated through months and
years, and held in check by an unremitting tension, which is now
taking its revenge, invading you, taking advantage of this holiday
you have allowed yourself as the high tide takes advantage of the
slightest fissure in a dyke to pour its bitter sterilizing waters over
the lands hitherto protected by that rampart?

But isn't it precisely to guard against that danger, of which you
were only too conscious, that you are undertaking this adventure,
isn't it towards the cure for all such first faint cracks, forerunners
of approaching age, that this engine is hastening you, towards
Rome, where rest and recovery await you?

Then why are your nerves so tense, why do you feel benumbed
by such anxiety? Why aren't you more relaxed already? Is it really
no more than a change of timetable that disturbs you so, provokes
such bewilderment and apprehension, the mere fact of leaving at
eight in the morning instead of in the evening as usual? Can it be

that you've already become such a slave to routine? Oh, then it's high time you made this break, for if you'd waited a few weeks longer you'd have been done for, the dreary hell would have closed in on you, and you'd never have found courage again. But at last deliverance is in sight, and years of wonderful life.

In the mean time, take off your coat, fold it and lift it on top of your suitcase. With your right hand you clutch the hand-rail; you have to lean over sideways, a position which is all the more awkward because you have to hold it despite the constant swaying in order to press with your thumb the knobs of the two shiny locks whose catches fly open, releasing the leather lid, which rises gently as though moved by a feeble spring, to grope inside blindly, feeling the pouch of red-and-white striped opaque nylon in which you packed, or rather flung pell-mell this morning, in your haste and irritation, as soon as you had dried the face at which you had been staring in your own mirror in the flat at 15 Place du Panthéon, your still-damp shaving brush, your shaving soap in its grey plastic case, your packet of new blades, your toothbrush, your comb, your tube of tooth-paste, the smooth nylon wrapping that holds them all, with the tiny ring of its zip fastener, then the envelope containing your slippers, the silky stuff of the purple pyjamas that you carefully picked out last night for Cécile's benefit from among the variegated elegance of your store of linen in the bedroom wardrobe, while Henriette put the finishing touches to dinner, and you heard, filtered through the thickness of a single wall, the squabbling of the boys who, at their age, really ought to be able to get on together, then, finally, you find the pamphlet you were hunting for.

The lid drops down with a few limp quivers and you don't bother to fasten it again.

You sit down in the middle of the seat between the clergyman, saying his breviary (how many hours they must spend at it!) in front of the window overlooking the swift fields and the slow, misty skyline, and the commercial traveller bent over his unfolded newspaper, slowly and conscientiously ploughing his way through the story of a star's wedding in front of the pane next to the corridor, along which there passes a plum-coloured corduroy coat that you had noticed a moment ago in the dining car.

You feel the warmth creep through the soles of your two tan shoes, on one of which the broken lace has been mended with a hidden knot that makes the leather bulge slightly like a tiny abscess and presses against your skin, and between which there is another shoe, a black patent-leather shoe facing the opposite way, gleaming in the shadow, fastened over a navy-blue cotton sock that shows under trouser hems of cloth finely striped in two neighbouring shades of grey, against which a slender white thread is untidily spiralling like a shred of cloud driven by the morning wind.

This black foot moves shakily up and to the right, the leg to which it belongs crosses over its twin leg, and bringing your own legs together you begin to examine the square sky-blue cover of the Chaix guide to the south-east region, clutching it with hands that are shaking too, shaking gently like everything else in this compartment as it moves from Paris to Rome.

It's the "Edition of 2nd October 1955, winter service, valid until 2nd June 1956, inclusive", with its advertisements: "Hôtel de la Paix, Nice, open all the year round" (you've never stayed there), "Chabert & Guillot's Nougat", then, in minute lettering, which you bring close to your eyes to try and read it, which is all the harder because of course you can't hold it still in front of them, "The Golden Beehive", curving like a little basket handle above a picture of an old-fashioned hive, a tiny round hut with a thatched roof, with four irregular blobs presumably representing bees (the hum of this train, low-pitched but with an occasional shrill note to remind you that metal is rolling and rubbing against metal), elsewhere: "Verveine du Velay" (you've never drunk any of that; it must be sugary and greenish; you might ask for some in the dining car by and by, they're always offering you liqueurs).

Then you remember the name Le Puy-en-Velay, one of those innumerable towns to which you've never been, one of those French provincial towns which must exude the blackest tedium, in spite of its geological curiosities, its dykes, if that's what they're called, and its cathedral full of paintings, a town in which you've got a member of your staff, Scabelli's representative for the whole of the Cévennes region, where obviously they're in no great need of typewriters – a child who's just passed his School Certificate could have told you that (but of course your network had to cover the whole of France) – and where, as might be expected, the man's not getting on too well, so that only yesterday you had to send him a somewhat threatening letter, although you've never seen him, you don't even remember his name, since Molandon has been given entire charge of this business and visits Le Puy on his annual tour of inspection of the central region.

They ought to have come back long ago, the young husband and his brand-new wife, for they went to the dining car before you and had already been served when you caught sight of them on entering, were already buttering their toast. But of course they're together, they're delightedly discovering things, they're presumably doing this trip for the first time, they've got so much to say to each other that they've no need to spin out the various stages of the journey in order to fill up, as far as possible, its boring vacuum, or slow down the motion of their jaws, as you were doing, in order to use up a few more minutes, because whatever they do takes them a long time and will be done only too quickly, because they're not burdened with the anticipated weariness of all those hours before the journey's end, with which you are only too familiar, all those hours that separate you from Cécile, and which, this time, you'll have to endure in the discomfort of a third-class carriage, which won't in any way detract them from their happiness, so that if, like yourself, they are bound for Rome, you'll see them wake up tomorrow morning exhausted but smiling.

She comes in, gracious and considerate, apologizing to the man on your right, the commercial traveller who has taken your seat, who looks up from the magazine in which he's now trying to solve a crossword puzzle, pressing it against his knee to write with a ballpoint pen, apologizing to the professor opposite (he can't be anything but a professor) who shuts his black book, showing a grimy oval label on the back on which is written in black ink, in thick old-fashioned writing, its catalogue number in, presumably, a university library, apologizing to the Englishman (he must surely be an Englishman), who is sitting very upright, the only one in the compartment with nothing to read for the moment, apologizing to you, who haven't drawn back your leg fast enough; she stumbles, she puts out her left hand, clutching her handbag with the other, a basket-shaped handbag of plaited rush lined with white leather, with string handles, from which peep the tip of a scarf and the pages of a women's magazine folded in two; her fingers lean for a moment on the green moleskin just beside your thigh, her raincoat brushes against your knees. She turns to look back; her lips are just at your eye level; she smiles at her companion who is follow-ing her, clinging with his right hand to the nickel-plated frame of the rack opposite you. She has steadied herself and bends down, deliberately this time, to pick up the two books that were keep-ing their places, a Blue Guide and the Italian Assimil study guide, which she hands to her husband and which he puts up on the shelf.

They must have noticed the rise in temperature too, for they take off their raincoats.

She sits down by the window, slipping her bag into the corner by her side, and clasps her hands between her knees, furrowing her grey tweed skirt. He picks up his books from the shelf and settles down; they look at one another, they look at you, they smile at you; they had recognized you along there while he was crush-ing a lump of sugar in his thick blue cup; a very slight intimacy has arisen among the three of you which sets you apart from the other four, from the mere fact of having eaten that little meal, not together but in the same moving dining room, so that it would be easy for you at this juncture to draw a little nearer them and start a conversation, but as you don't wish to do so he very quickly loses interest, looks away, opens his guidebook, unfolds the map of a town, while she pulls her women's magazine out of her bag and begins turning over pages of dresses. The young clergyman bends his arm again and reverts to reading and wearily muttering his breviary. You can see cows in the fields. Then you start turning the pages of your railway guide once more.

Here are the closely printed pages of regulations, the list of stations in narrow columns, the tables of international connections, and here is the one that interests you: E, Italy, where you recognize the train in which you're travelling: 609, fast train, first, second and third classes (it won't be running next year apparently), a black diamond referring you to supplementary information in the margin, where you discover that certain coaches run directly not only from Paris to Rome but also on to Syracuse, and you wonder whether you mayn't be in one of these, and whether the two lovers, the young couple, aren't perhaps going on there, right on to that town which you don't know, but which from what you've heard tell about it and the photographs you've seen seems to you just the place for a honeymoon, especially at this time of year when even in Rome the weather isn't likely to be good.

The station of Saint-Julien-du-Sault goes by, with its lamp-posts and noticeboards, the inscription in outsize lettering on the side of the building, the church steeple, the roads, the fields, the woods. The young couple talk to one another about some detail he is pointing out on the map. Beyond the corridor there are scattered rabbit warrens and little dells, and a road ahead along which a lorry trundles, moves away, comes nearer again, disappears behind a house, is chased by a motorcyclist who passes it in a fine curve like a slack bow, drops behind him, behind your train, then vanishes from the scene.

This train, which left the Gare de Lyon at 8.10 today, as it does every day, which includes a dining car, as is shown by that tiny crossed knife and fork, the very dining car which you and the young couple have just visited, and to which you will return for lunch but not for dinner, because then it'll be a different one, an Italian one; this train will stop at Dijon and leave again at 11.18, it will pass through Bourg at 13.02, leave Aix-les-Bains at 14.41 (there's sure to be snow on the mountains round the lake), will wait for twenty-three minutes at Chambéry to allow for a connection, and again at the border from 16.28 to 17.18 for customs formalities (that tiny house next to the word Modane is the symbol for customs); it will reach Turin Piazza Nazionale at 19.26 (oh, night will have fallen long before that), depart again at 20.05, leave the Piazza Principe station at Genoa at 22.39, reach Pisa at 1.15 and, finally, Roma Termini at 5.45 tomorrow morning, long before dawn, this train which is almost wholly unfamiliar to you since you always take the other, the one in the next column, the Rapide No. 7, the Rome Express with sleeping cars, which has first and second class only, which is so much faster, doing the journey in only eighteen hours forty minutes, whereas this one, let's see, this one takes twenty-one hours thirty-five minutes – that makes, let's see, that makes two and a half hours more – and which is so much more convenient, leaving at dinner time and arriving early the following afternoon.

If you want further information about the train on which you're travelling (as for the other, the Rome Express, you know its times almost by heart, and when you take it you don't need this square booklet in which, for all your experience, you find your way with some difficulty), you'll have to consult Table 500, in which the itinerary is far more detailed, mentioning all the stations, even those at which the train doesn't stop, then, after Mâcon, where it leaves the main Paris-Marseille line, Table 530, but after Modane you'll need an Italian timetable, for in this one there's only this page with the principal stops: Turin, Genoa, Pisa, whereas there are bound to be some other stops, at Livorno probably, possibly at Civitavecchia.

It will still be pitch-dark. You'll wake up uncomfortably after a broken night, especially if you're forced to stay in this uncomfortable seat in the middle of the row, but still you've quite a good chance of securing a corner seat when one of your present fellow travellers gets out, for surely they can't all be going all the way.

When that time comes, which of the six will still be in this compartment, where probably only the blue night-light will be shining, that little round, dark bulb you see inside the ceiling lamp, nestling between the other two transparent, pear-shaped ones? In the countryside, the lights will be out in all the houses. You'll see the headlights of a few lorries go past, and the lamps of the stations; you'll be feeling cold; you'll rub your hand over your chin, which will be far rougher than it is now; you'll get up and go out, and walk to the end of the corridor to splash a little water on your eyes.

Then, after the oil refinery with its flame and the lights that deck its tall aluminium towers like a Christmas tree, while you're travelling almost the whole way round the dark and sleeping city, in which the clamour of trams and trolleybuses will already have begun, suburban stations will file past you: Roma Trastevere (and you'll catch a glimpse of its reflection in the black water of the river), Roma Ostiense (you'll guess at the ramparts and the pale tip of the pyramid), Roma Tuscolana (then, passing through the Porta Maggiore, you'll make straight for the centre).

And at last it'll be Roma Termini, the transparent station, at which it's wonderful to arrive at sunrise, as you can by this train at another time of year, but tomorrow it'll still be pitch-dark.

Beyond the corridor there is a farm, with a clump of yellow poplars, a deep lane that twists back and reappears behind the bulge of a big field, scored with furrows and speckled with rooks, and on which there appears a helmeted motorcyclist in a leather jacket, who comes towards the railway and then disappears behind embankments under a bridge over which the engine and the front coaches of your own train can now be seen moving. You try to catch another glimpse of him through the window between the clergyman and the bride, but he must be far behind you now.

This journey was planned very suddenly, for on Monday evening when you went home for dinner, leaving your suitcase at your office in the Avenue de l'Opéra, at the corner of the Rue Danièle-Casanova, because you hadn't the car with you, no such thought had entered your head; for although you had certainly been meaning for a long time to find a job for Cécile in Paris, you had up till then taken no positive steps to that end, and it was not until Tuesday morning that, after you had gone through all the current business and read the mail that had accumulated during your stay in Rome, you rang up one of your customers,

Jean Durieu, director of the Durieu Travel Agency, the windows of which you could see from your own window, and asked him in strict confidence if he knew of any situation that might suit a remarkably intelligent woman of about thirty, speaking fluent English and Italian, who was at present secretary to an attaché, a military attaché, if you remembered rightly, at the French Embassy in Rome, who was dissatisfied with her present post and who, in view of her keen desire to get back to Paris, would be content with quite a modest salary.

It was quite possible he might find something, he told you; he'd ring you back as soon as he had made enquiries, which he did that very afternoon, to your great surprise and satisfaction, informing you that he intended to reorganize his own business and that a person such as you had described might prove very useful to him in his new set-up, and offering such very reasonable terms that you undertook to vouch for her acceptance.

When should she take up her new post? Whenever she liked, the sooner the better, but there was no hurry: let her take her own time settling her affairs in Rome, handing in her notice, moving her belongings, finding a home in Paris; he was well aware how many unforeseen difficulties might arise on such occasions; and in his voice, in his politeness, there sounded an unpleasant note of connivance.

At that time you intended to settle everything by letter and not to see Cécile again until your next monthly trip, for the annual general meeting of the directors of Scabelli's foreign branches, and it was only on Wednesday that things came to a head, and that, no doubt, because it was 13th November and consequently your birthday, and because Henriette, who still clung to these ridiculous family ceremonies, had laid particular stress on it this year, being suspicious of you, with even more justification than she knew, and hoping to hold you, to ensnare you in this net of petty rites, not out of love – of course all that came to an end between you long ago (and if there had been some sort of youthful passion once, it had never been anything comparable to that feeling of release and enchantment that Cécile brought you) – but from her dread, increasing daily (how she was ageing!) of seeing any alteration in the order of things to which she was accustomed, not really out of jealousy but out of the haunting fear that some rash step on your part or some violent disagreement might ruin her comfort and the children's, although there was no danger of that, and because she had never really trusted you, or at least had long ago ceased to do so, which was undoubtedly the cause of that rift between you which had grown deeper through the years, and because your undoubted success, to which she owed that handsome flat that meant so much to her, had never really convinced her, so that you were increasingly aware of her mute reproaches and her watchful gaze even before you had given her valid cause.

When you went into the dining room for lunch on Wednesday (through the window the splendid scrolls on the Panthéon frieze were gleaming in a ray of pale November sunlight which soon faded), when you saw your four children standing stiffly, mockingly behind their chairs, when you recognized that smile of triumph on her face, on her lips half-hidden in shadow, you had the impression that they were all in league to trap you, that those presents on your plate were a bait, that the whole meal had been carefully planned to seduce you (how could she fail to know your tastes after living with you for nearly twenty years?), the whole scene set to convince you that henceforward you were an elderly man, sobered and tamed, whereas only recently so different a life had opened up for you, a life which you still led only for a few days at a time in Rome, that other life of which this life in the Paris flat was a mere shadow, and that was why, clinging to prudence despite your irritation, you took pains to play their game, you managed to seem almost gay, congratulating them on their choice, conscientiously blowing out the forty-five candles, but quite determined to bring to an end as soon as possible this unremitting imposture, this rooted misunderstanding. It was high time!

Now Cécile would come to Paris and you could live together. There would be no divorce, no scandal, of that you were and are quite certain; everything would go very smoothly, poor Henriette would keep silence, you would visit the children once a week or so; and you were certain, too, not only of agreement but of triumphant delight from Cécile, who had teased you so much about your bourgeois hypocrisy.

Oh, how urgently you needed to escape from this threatening asphyxia, to take a deep breath of that future air, of that happiness that awaited you, how you needed to tell her the news, to tell it her yourself so that the thing would be settled at last without risk of misunderstanding.

And so, that afternoon, in the Avenue de l'Opéra, you made sure that there was no pressing business, you notified Maynard, your second in command, that you would be away for a few days, from Friday to Tuesday, you sent Marnal to buy the railway guide you are now holding, without asking him to buy your ticket because you did not want it known in the office that you were going back to Rome.

When you told Henriette that evening that unforeseen circumstances obliged you to leave on Friday morning, the Friday morning that is now going by, it was not the actual fact of your journey that puzzled her, since in fact you had, several times already, had to make an extra trip to the head office between two regular journeys, on some urgent business, but it was the unusual and obviously inconvenient time of your departure, chosen so that you could enjoy the whole weekend with Cécile and have lunch with her tomorrow, Saturday, and also, it must be admitted, because there were third-class coaches on this train and you felt that this escapade which, though undoubtedly very important for the future course of your life, was strictly speaking not indispensable and which would obviously be at your own expense, was already going to cost you quite enough, and it was on that very point of the time and train you had chosen that she began to question you, and that you had to invent false reasons, so unskilfully indeed that she could easily counter each of them with the soundest objections, to which you could find no reply, and consequently she only wondered all the more at seeing you so absurdly persistent.

During the dinner that followed, which was painful for everyone, and in the course of which the children never stopped sniggering over their plates, you scarcely spoke to one another except when Jacqueline, whom you had ordered to go and wash her ink-stained hands, went off shrugging her shoulders and you lost your temper violently with her, and her mother, of course, chose to take her side publicly, so that when the child came back, having listened from the bathroom to every word of this noisy conversation, she sat down again preening herself at having at last got the better of you (she, the youngest of them, the one you're fondest of because you've no sort of intimacy with the others, you don't know what they think, you don't understand what they like, the three of them have formed a sort of league against you, except when the two boys are fighting), and, had you still felt any doubts, this scene would have resolved them.

Swallowing your last mouthful, you pulled on your coat, hurried downstairs and off to the garage in the Rue de l'Estrapade to fetch your Citroën 15CV, in which you drove out of Paris and covered nearly a hundred kilometres in the rainy darkness, leaving it parked by the pavement in the Place du Panthéon when you got back after midnight, to find Henriette in bed, not asleep, not saying a word to you but staring at you with a mocking, scornful sort of look in her eyes.

Fortunately things had calmed down the next day, which was yesterday, Thursday, and mealtimes passed quietly, in that bitterly cold weather which is still going on and even growing worse, on that day of hustle and agitation when, before taking the brief holiday you'd ventured to grant yourself until next Wednesday, you'd had to set in order the firm's invariably complicated affairs, but that evening the traffic jam on the Place du Théâtre-Français seemed even slower to break up than usual, and then, at the garage, where you hoped to get your car overhauled during your absence, because it had been unduly noisy all week, you were kept waiting, and finally, at the end of your tether, you'd had to shout before anyone would deign to attend to you, and then, at 15 Place du Panthéon, the lift was out of order and you had to walk up to the fourth floor, and then, in spite of being late, you found dinner not even laid, and you heard Henri and Thomas nagging at each other in their room, and Henriette feebly and ineffectively nagging at them both, and when she came out into the passage to call Madeleine she had that lifeless, exhausted stare of hers, like a corpse's stare, with that flicker of suspicion and resentment when she saw you, that scorn she pours on you as if you were responsible for her all-too-obvious deterioration, and all that half-life seemed to close around you like pincers, like a strangler's hands, all that larval, twilight existence from which you were about to escape at last.

For in your briefcase lay that railway guide in its blue cover which you're holding in your hands and staring at still, without focusing on anything in particular at the moment, and after dinner, just before you lay down alone in the great bed to which Henriette came only after you had gone to sleep, you put it in your suitcase on top of the little pile of clean linen you had packed.

It was your talisman, your key, the pledge of your escape, of your arrival in Rome, city of light, of that process of rejuvenation whose clandestine character enhanced its magical aspect, of this journey which is taking you away from that corpse of a woman still going through the illusory motions of usefulness, that prying corpse from whom you would have parted long ago but for the children, who are drifting further from you day by day so that they seem like waxwork images of themselves, growing more and more secretive about their lives while you grow less and less interested in knowing and sharing those lives, away from that Henriette, divorce from whom is out of the question because she would never agree to it, because in your position you want to avoid any scandal (Scabelli, being Italian, pious and hypocritical, would take a very poor view of such a thing), away from that dead weight of a woman to whom you're fettered, who would drag you down into the suffocating depths of that ocean of boredom, of resignation, of exhausting and stupefying routine, of unconsciousness in which she wallows, if you hadn't got that refuge, Cécile, that breath of fresh air, that source of new strength, that rescuing hand reaching out to you from the realm of happiness and light, away from that oppressive, tiresome ghost whom you're about to shake off for good, towards that enchantress who, with a single glance, can deliver you from this whole horrible caricature of an existence and make you yourself again, in blessed oblivion of all this furniture, of all these meals, of that prematurely faded body and that exasperating family,

the pledge of that decision you've reached at last to break away, to rid yourself of that harness of vain scruples, all that paralysing cowardice, to show your children too how to be bold and free, that decision which has shed its gleam over this whole week, a week given up to figures, regulations and signatures, a week of rain, recrimination and misunderstanding, and enabled you to endure it without being overcome, without abandoning everything, without ruining your life for ever,

the pledge of this journey which is a secret from Henriette, since, although you told her you were going to Rome, you concealed your real motives, a secret from Henriette who knows only too well, however, that there's a secret behind this altered timetable, your secret, and knows, too, that it is called Cécile, so that you cannot really be said to have deceived her on this point, so that your lies to her are not wholly lies, could not be wholly lies since, after all (and you're justified in considering them in this light), they are a necessary stage towards clarifying your relations, towards achieving that mutual sincerity which, for the time being, has become so profoundly obscured, towards Henriette's release too, through separation from you, towards her own salvation in some slight degree,

a secret because nobody at your office knows where you're going, because no mail can reach you there, whereas usually when you arrive at the Hotel Quirinal you find letters and telegrams already waiting for you, so that for the first time in years this brief holiday will bring genuine relaxation, as in the days before you had assumed your present responsibilities, before you had really become successful, a secret because at Scabelli's, on the Corso, nobody knows that you're going to be in Rome from Saturday morning till Monday night, and nobody must discover it while you're there, so that you'll have to take certain precautions for fear of being recognized by some member of Scabelli's obliging, attentive, over-friendly staff,

a secret even from Cécile, now, since you haven't warned her to expect you, intending to relish her surprise.

But Cécile will share this secret with you unreservedly, and this unexpected meeting will be like the sword that is to sever finally all those bonds that entangled you both, that held you tethered so painfully apart.

Last night, woken by the screech of brakes on the Place du Panthéon, you switched on the lamp on your right, in its Empire-style candlestick, and looked at poor Henriette asleep on the other side of the bed, her greying hair spread out on the pillow and her mouth half-open, separated from you by an impassable river of linen.

Outside the window, between the young woman and the clergy-man, high-tension pylons file past along a road on which a huge lorry trailing a petrol drum is travelling towards the railway line, which now makes a sharp turn, high above the fields, after cross-ing a bridge under which the lorry vanishes. The man opposite you can perhaps see it on the other side of the corridor, where another row of high-tension pylons meets your eyes, over ever more steeply undulating country.

The upper windows of the Stazione Termini will be opaque mir-rors under the night when, after trudging along the platform, suitcase in hand, under the fine concrete vault, between the square pillars of polished black marble, amongst the crowd of drowsy travellers hurrying in confusion towards the exit, you hand to the Italian official part of that ticket which you bought this morning at the Gare de Lyon and which now lies, folded in two, in your wallet, next to your identity card, your family-allowance card and all the rest, in the inside left pocket of your jacket; and in the main lobby, where bookstalls and other kiosks will all be closed, you'll catch sight, through the vast sheets of glass and that other ghostly lobby reflected in them, not of the Baths of Diocletian which lie in darkness on the farther side of the square, but of the gleam of street lamps, the blue spark of trams and a few headlights sweeping the ground.

Once you've drunk your espresso in the bar which, if it isn't already open, will be opening just about this time, once you've been down to the Albergo Diurno in the basement to have a bath and shave and change your clothes and, only then, left your suit-case in the cloakroom, the early-morning light will have begun to peep, to glimmer through; but it will be half-past six or even seven before the sun really rises and reveals, in their greys and ochres, all the façades and ruins around the piazza, and by then you'll be slowly savouring a foaming *caffellatte,* with your hands and your mind unencumbered, sitting in comfort to watch the show, so as to gain a firm footing in this new day, to settle into it quietly, reading the newspapers which you'll buy the minute the cyclist delivers them, while the light gains strength, richness and warmth; and when you leave the station at daybreak, while the city appears in all its deep redness, as though the blood of bygone days exuded from all its bricks and stained all its dust, under a sky that's sure to be clear and bright, then, since you'll have nearly two hours to idle away before the time comes to surprise Cécile at the door of her house, to catch her unawares, hurrying towards the Embassy as she does every day of the week, you will plunge at leisure into that magnificent Roman air which will seem like spring regained after the autumn of Paris, you'll go on foot, with nothing to constrain you, nothing to prevent you from exploring the detours that may seduce you, however long, however devious or fantastic they may be.

But roughly, you'll follow the same route as usual, leading first to the Piazza dell'Esedra (Will its 1900 fountain be play-ing yet? Will its lascivious bronze women, those absurd and exquisite figures, be splashed with water or left high and dry?), with this difference, though, that being on foot this time you'll be able to go under the arcades, then along the Via Nazionale, where the shops will be opening and the motorcycles starting off with their usual odious petulance; only, instead of stopping at the still-sleeping Hotel Quirinal, instead of going in there, booking your room and leaving your suitcase, you'll pass by quickly on the opposite pavement, unless indeed, by a somewhat ridiculous excess of prudence, you take some parallel street to hide from the porter instead of seeking out his welcome, his assistance, his obsequious greeting; and you'll make your way down towards the Victor Emmanuel monument, noticing the tunnel as you go, you'll leave the already crowded Corso on your right, you'll skirt the Palazzo Venezia, you'll pass the Gesù, then you'll go on as far as Sant'Andrea della Valle; or rather, no, for it will inevitably be too early still, in spite of all the zigzags, loops and pauses with which you'll have overlaid your journey, like an embroidery, an accompaniment, a commentary to that route the bare bones of which seem so long and often so tedious when you travel along them in a taxi or, in the opposite direction, at night, when you walk back from Cécile's room to your hotel, but which tomorrow will be all too short, however slowly you go, however wearily after your night in the train; no, you'll have to make a longer and better walk of it than that, you'll have to take advantage of being here at this unwonted hour, of seeing things in this unfamiliar light, of this prelude to Cécile's surprise and joy, this prelude to the three days heralding the days that are to come; you must not go straight on like that, you mustn't even reach the Piazza del Gesù, but, on the contrary, you must go round the Capitol, for instance, or better still, go up to the Piazza del Campidoglio and then down again to the Tiber, then across to the Largo Argentina with its medieval tower and the wide central ditch, populated by starving cats, where stand those four ruined temples of Republican date, passing through that broad thoroughfare, whose name you've forgotten, which opens on to the Ponte Garibaldi and which you take when you're going to dine in a pizzeria on the Trastevere; or else...

She won't leave the house before nine o'clock, but you'll take up your post long before then in the Via Monte della Farina, just opposite her tall house with the dingy image of St Anthony of Padua over the door and the rusty plaques of two insurance companies, to watch for the opening of her shutters on the fourth floor, while you smoke one of the cigars you mustn't forget to buy next time you go to the dining car.

Beyond the corridor, between a barn and a clump of trees beside a pond, a motorcyclist appears who turns right and then is suddenly hidden by a great blue coach with its roof loaded with luggage, and then turns left towards a gatekeeper's lodge; the train leaves this behind and then leaves the coach behind, and in the distance you can see a village with its spire and its water tower. The young couple look out of the window, their heads pressed close together, shaking in unison. Joigny station goes by, the whole little town reflected in the Yonne.

You turn back to your railway guide, you close it and, as you are studying the map on its cover, a diagram of the south-eastern region where only the Mediterranean coast and the borders are sketched in to help you find the towns which are shown in their approximate position, joined by straight black lines of varying thickness, like a network of small cracks, like the leaden framework of a stained-glass window whose subject is unrecognizable, the man sitting opposite you gets up, with his raincoat still buttoned up to the neck and tightly belted round him, not presumably because he wants to get off at the next stop – that obligatory first stop for all main trains, the importance and the very existence of which is entirely dependent on the railway, Laroche-Migennes – since he has left his umbrella and his hat on the shelf and his blue-and-green-tartan-covered case on the rack, but merely because he wants to go along the corridor, not realizing that the station is close at hand and that it is forbidden to make use of these conveniences while the train is not in motion, though of course it's true that in this coach the warning to that effect is printed in French and

Italian only, and that he probably can't read either language well, despising foreigners as the English always do, so that it won't worry him.

But there must be exactly the same sort of regulation in his own country, in England, and how do you know that he can't read either French or Italian, that he isn't just as used to this line as you are yourself, or even used to this very train, which is more than you are, indeed how do you know that he's an Englishman, this man about whom all you've got the right to say for the moment is that he looks English, that his complexion, his clothes and his luggage look English, this man who hasn't spoken a single word, and who's trying in vain to close the door behind him?

The train stops and all eyes look up at once, all books are forgotten in the sudden silence and motionlessness.

In the corridor, you see the back of the man who's just gone out as he lowers the window and leans out to see, as if there were anything to see here but that placard of white-enamelled iron, with spots of rust round the bolt fastening it to its post, bearing the name Laroche-Migennes in red, and the grey sky streaked with black catenaries, the black ground streaked with gleaming rails, some wooden trucks and some little old houses.

Then a gust of fresh air comes into the compartment, and the hoarse voice of the loudspeaker is heard uttering unrecognizable syllables of which the conclusion sounds something like "non-stop to Dijon".

The clergyman on your left drums with his fingernails on the black leather of his closed breviary; the man you call the professor takes off his glasses and rubs the round lenses with a chamois leather; the man you call the commercial traveller goes back to his crossword; and in the corridor the man you call the Englishman pulls a packet of Churchman's out of his raincoat pocket, extracts the last cigarette and throws the packet onto the line, then closes the window slowly, turns towards you, strikes a match, begins to smoke, hunts in the pocket of his check jacket for the *Manchester Guardian*, which he begins to read, and then folds up, walks away and disappears.

You feel an urge to do likewise; you get up, slip the railway guide under the lid of your unfastened suitcase, pick up your coat, fumble in the left-hand pocket, under the scarf, to find the novel you bought at the Gare de Lyon just before leaving, which you put down on the seat in the place you've just left, and the unopened packet of cigarettes, of which you tear open one corner.

The two men on either side of the door have stretched out their intersecting legs; you apologize for disturbing them, and you go out.

III

YOU RECOVER THE SEAT WHICH the commercial traveller left a moment ago on seeing a business acquaintance in the corridor, just as the station of Laumes-Alésia, with its shed for disused engines, loomed up in the onrushing Burgundian landscape, with unseen Alise-Sainte-Reine close by, the scene, according to tradition, of Julius Caesar's victory over the Gauls; you leave untouched on the seat beside you the novel you had put down to keep your place, and as one of the windows in the front of the coach is slightly open and sends a thin cold draught across your face, you try to reduce this by tugging at the door, which yields suddenly and shifts a few inches.

After fiddling for a moment with the lid of the ashtray screwed to the window frame, you dip into your right-hand jacket pocket and pull out the packet of Gauloises, which you've torn at one end without breaking the white paper band struck across the middle like a seal, and from which two cigarettes are already missing; you take out a third and light it, guarding the flame with both hands and blinking a little as the smoke gets in your eyes, then after looking at your watch and seeing that it was a quarter past ten, so that you've been travelling for a little over two hours and still have nearly an hour to go before the next stop, Dijon, at 11.12, you flick off the ash and, as you inhale once more through the little tube of white paper filled with shreds of dry leaf, you see two quivering red sparks light up in the glasses of the short-sighted man opposite you, not the Englishman now but once more his neighbour the professor, bent over his thick book with its yellowing pages, two red sparks that flare up and fade with each of your puffs, beside the tiny distorted reflection of the three panes of glass, the chink of the door and a curved landscape flying past, below his prematurely baldish forehead with its three deep furrows.

The lines on his page are dancing about with the motion of the train, but he's trying hard to keep his eyes fixed on them so as to read quickly without missing out anything important, a pencil in his right hand, making a cross in the margin from time to time, because he's got to use this text to prepare something, probably a lecture which isn't ready and which he has to deliver this afternoon, a lecture on law most likely, since, although the title is too unsteady for you to read it upside down, you can still make out the first three letters, LEG, of the first word, which must be "legislation", presumably at Dijon, since there's no other university town on this line before the border.

He's wearing a wedding ring on his slender, shaking finger; he probably goes to give his lectures two or three times a week, or perhaps once only if he's been clever, if he's got a pied-à-terre there or a cheapish hotel that suits him, for his salary's not likely to be princely, leaving his wife in Paris where he lives like most of his colleagues, with the children, if he's got children, who have to stay there for the sake of their education, not because there aren't excellent schools in this town but because they may already have passed their *baccalauréat*, the eldest girl at any rate or the eldest boy (it's a foolish reaction, granted, but you'd certainly rather your first child had been a boy), since, although he's undoubtedly younger than yourself, he may have got married earlier, and his children have probably been more carefully educated and will surely have done better at school than Madeleine, who at seventeen is only just in the sixth form.

He turns the page feverishly; he turns it back again; his conscience isn't easy; he must be sorry he put off to the last minute a task he ought to have finished at leisure long ago, or else some unexpected difficulty has arisen and he's suddenly found himself obliged to revise everything he had in fact prepared, the lecture he thought he wouldn't need to bother about, having cheerfully given it year in year out since he got his job. There's a certain genuine distinction about him and a look of unmistakable integrity.

Far from enjoying a salary which would enable him to escape to Rome as you're doing, he probably wishes, if he could afford it, if the avoidance of unnecessary expense on clothing hadn't become second nature with him, that he could wear other clothes than these almost threadbare ones which, even when they were new, can never have had any claim to smartness, a different coat to this one, which is probably a byword in the faculty by now, this black overcoat with thick buttons which he has kept on, sitting in discomfort unlike everyone else in the compartment, not because he was any less hot than the rest but because he didn't notice it, being so absorbed in his problem; his face, which had looked so pale before, is slightly flushed now, and through the glinting reflections on his glasses you see his eyes blink nervously.

How can anyone bear to live like that, lecturing on law and obviously unable even to afford a car? (And if he doesn't mind that on his own account, doesn't give a thought to it, being probably as modest as he is conscientious, yet his wife and children must feel the lack of it.) But on the other hand how can anyone bear to be Managing Director of the French branch of Scabelli Typewriters? For although it's true that you earn far more money than he does, that you have a car, that you're able to indulge some of your whims, that you're very well dressed, and so is your wife when she chooses – at least she could be if she wanted to – yet even if what he does doesn't interest you, it's quite plain that it interests him, that he's chosen this profession with its semi-penury for that reason, whereas it's equally certain that before going to Scabelli you had the most supreme contempt for typewriters and the sale of typewriters; and then there are of course those wonderful holidays, whereas practically the whole of your time is taken up by your profession, even when you leave Paris for somewhere other than Rome.

They're good machines, granted, quite as good as any others, very fine articles that work beautifully, but that's quite outside your department, your duties or concerns, for you've nothing to do with the production side: you've merely got to see that people buy a Scabelli rather than an Olivetti or a Hermes, and that, naturally, without any really valid reason; it's a game that's quite amusing sometimes, an exhausting game, a game that leaves you hardly any respite, a remunerative game, a game which might destroy you utterly like a vice, but which hasn't done so, since today you're free, since you're going to find your freedom, which is called Cécile; and so no doubt, in spite of your material wealth and his too obvious indigence, you are more to be pitied than he, because he's doing what interests him, because his whole life is centred round what he enjoys, if you hadn't got that splendid love, that proof of your independence, that proof that you've been successful on both planes, since on the one hand you've got nearly enough money and on the other you're still young enough in spirit to be able to make good use of it in a wonderful life of adventure.

You've not got quite enough money, though; you're not independent enough as regards money, otherwise you'd be travelling first, and that would be better still, but, if you look at things from another angle, you can say that you didn't shrink from the discomfort of travelling third, that you've enough sporting instinct to disregard so slight an inconvenience. You feel supremely awake now, alive and masterful.

Your cigarette burns your fingers; it has been smouldering away on its own. The young husband gets up, puts his Blue Guide and his Italian Assimil on his seat, apologizes for disturbing you, goes out and disappears behind you.

You shake the ash that has fallen on your trousers onto the diamond-scored iron floor-heater, near the feet of the professor, who now shuts his book and stands up too, but only to take off his black overcoat, which he bundles onto the rack between his briefcase and the blue-and-green tartan attaché case, and then hastily resumes his research.

You crush out your fag end in the ashtray. A hand taps against the window with some metal object, the hand of the ticket collector with his punch, and you hunt inside your jacket for your wallet, not the black one the children gave you for your birthday on Wednesday and which you left in its box on a shelf in the wardrobe, but the old red one, containing your passport (which will have expired in a month and which you'll therefore have to get Marnal to renew for you before your next trip to Rome for the annual meeting), five thousand-franc notes folded in two, and in one of the pockets two ten-thousand-franc notes, that's to say more than the twenty thousand you're allowed in theory to take across the border, even subtracting the cost of lunch in the dining car, but suppose by some extraordinary chance they should check (which has never happened to you), they're not likely to make a fuss about so small a sum (and if there should be the slightest argument you'd immediately hand over the disputed difference), your rather grubby identity card with your unrecognizable old photograph, a few thousand lire, three Paris Métro tickets and a part-used booklet of bus tickets (and now the clergyman holds out the little cardboard square and puts it back, once it's been dealt with, between the front page and the cover of his breviary), three Italian stamps, your family-allowance card, a snapshot of Cécile and yourself taken on the Corso, your membership card of the Société des Amis du Louvre (which you've forgotten to get renewed) and that of the Dante Alighieri Society, and, at last, your ticket, which you hold out, get punched and put away again.

The ticket collector, as he leaves the compartment, meets the young husband coming in, who, slightly flustered, makes a sign to his wife, hunts in one pocket and then another, finds his ticket at last, is released, and comes in with apologies.

She closes her magazine, lays it down beside her on top of the Blue Guide and the Italian Assimil, straightens a lock of her hair, picks up her bag and stands up, meets and passes her husband between the seats, smiles at you while her silk stocking rubs against your trouser leg and the young man sits down in the place she has just vacated, opposite the clergyman.

The ticket collector has just left the next compartment and is tapping with his punch on the window of the one beyond.

The professor shuts his book with an air of satisfaction, presumably reckoning that he's done enough, that his lecture is ready, that he'll manage now, then puts his pencil away in his breast pocket next to his fountain pen, in front of the handkerchief which he's obviously been using, rubs his hands together, passes a finger behind his ears, then between his eyes and his glasses, gets up, takes his briefcase from the rack, packs away his black book, its pages marked with scraps of paper, and goes out too, whistling an inaudible tune, the rhythm of which you can follow by the movement of his lips and which he taps out with the back of his hand on anything he comes across; he is almost immediately replaced by the young woman who, even before entering the compartment, notices that her husband has picked up her magazine and is turning the pages ironically, the corners of his lips twitching with the regular rhythm of the whole carriage, probably because he's reached the advice column, and who goes up to him saying teasingly: "So you *do* find it interesting too," – the first words, apart from a fair number of polite greetings, uttered aloud in this mobile waiting room since the train left – at which he shrugs his shoulders good-naturedly.

Darcey station has gone by. Some way down the corridor the ticket collector comes out of one carriage to go into the next, which must be the last, then a girl of about Madeleine's age goes past, followed at a little distance by that commercial traveller who'd taken the corner seat you chose on leaving Paris and which you've succeeded in recovering. The young couple are sitting side by side again, but their positions are reversed, he being next to the window and she next to the Englishman. Beyond the corridor you see a long goods train with refrigerated carriages, dirty white-painted wooden carriages with big black letters on them.

If only the weather's fine in Rome, *hic ver assiduum*, so that you don't have to shelter in a nearby gateway from one of those virulent autumn showers they get there, which might prevent you from meeting or catching sight of Cécile or even from running after her as she hurries off to the Embassy in her transparent raincoat, but are able to wait for her quietly in the fresh air, rested and restored after a night which is obviously not going to be pleasant, smoking one of the cigars that you're going to buy presently in the dining car, with your coat tucked under your arm, standing in the shadow but revelling in the sunshine which will be gilding the housetops, at the corner of the Via dei Barbieri, opposite 56 Via Monte della Farina, which is going to be your secret address for a couple of nights.

The shutters on the fourth floor will still be closed when your watch begins, because you know how impatient you are: you won't manage to keep away from your observation post after eight o'clock, in spite of all your detours, and you'll have to wait for a long while and kill time studying that façade and its cracks and the faces of the first passers-by, before her window opens at last, but then perhaps you'll see her appear, leaning out to watch some noisy motorcycle swerving past, tossing back her still-unkempt black hair, the hair of an Italian woman although her father was French, and then perhaps she'll catch sight of you standing there, but as she knows nothing of your arrival, she won't recognize you, merely noticing a certain likeness to yourself in that idle stranger so persistently staring at her.

So then you can watch her, as it were, in your own absence; then she'll vanish into the dark depths of her large, high-ceilinged room in that old Roman house, which she's arranged so cleverly with the divan in the corner, large enough for you both, and the flowers that are always so fresh and so varied, next to the other two rooms which are let to tourists in spring and summer, in one of which you'll officially be staying for these two nights, a fair distance away from the rest of the house where the proprietress Mrs Da Ponte, like Mozart's librettist or the painter Bassano, lives with her family, beyond a very dark little entrance opening directly through a glass door into the huge kitchen.

And so you'll watch for her next appearance at the front door, under the almost invisible image of St Antony in his dusty glass case, and you hope she'll be wearing over her shoulders the great white shawl you gave her, for that's what she looks loveliest in, and her wide-pleated, violet-and-crimson patterned dress, or else, if it's too chilly, her dark emerald-green corduroy suit, with her plaits of black hair rolled above her forehead and held in place by two or three hairpins with heads of iridescent glass, her lips painted, her eyebrows finished with a blue pencil but nothing else on her face, nothing on that wonderful skin of hers.

She'll turn left immediately, towards Sant'Andrea della Valle, for that's the way she usually goes, the way she likes best although it's not the shortest, but this time she can't fail to see you, especially as you'll wave to her, you'll call her if need be, you'd rush after her if that weren't enough, and she'll stop short, unable to believe her eyes.

Then excitement will set her face quivering, like the wind tossing a cluster of gladioli.

You'll burst out laughing. You'll tell her no more than that you're going to be there till Monday night, for you've got to let her surprise increase gradually so as to extract the full delight from it, enabling her to enjoy it drop by drop without losing a single one of its elements; you'll make her alter her route, bringing her back to the Largo Argentina to have coffee with you, in spite of her protests, her dread of arriving late at the Embassy, which isn't going to matter any longer, reassuring her and kissing her, then taking her in a taxi (there are sure to be some by then, looking for fares along the Corso Vittorio Emmanuele) as far as the Piazza del Palazzo Farnese, a gesture of pure extravagance since the distance is too small to make the saving of time appreciable, and promising, as you say goodbye, to pick her up there at one o'clock.

All the rest of the morning you'll be by yourself, like a tourist in Rome, with no settled home and your suitcase still at the station, and you'll take advantage of this freedom, of this holiday, to revisit a museum to which you haven't been for years, not since you knew Cécile in any case, one of the few places in this city, except for the firm's office and those of its business connections, that you've never been to with her, primarily because it's only open between ten and two and closed all day Sunday, namely, the Vatican.

You've never been to St Peter's together, either, because she hates popes and priests as much as you do, and in a far more virulent and emphatic way than yourself (and that's one reason why you love her so much), although this doesn't prevent her from taking the keenest delight in baroque fountains, cupolas and façades, and you yourself have certainly no desire to return tomorrow morning inside that gigantic architectural fiasco, that immense and opulent confession of poverty.

The first thing you'll have to do, since the few thousand lire you've got with you will be almost exhausted once you've paid for this evening's dinner on the Italian dining car, is to go and draw some money on your account in the branch of the Banco di Roma on the Corso, opposite the Palazzo Doria, then you'll take a bus as far as the Piazza del Risorgimento, and as you'll still have a fair way to go on foot along the impressive ramparts, it'll be well after ten o'clock when you reach the gates, which will be open.

You'll pass quickly through those endless passages, where antique statues, pillaged from here, there and everywhere, are lined up so stupidly without the slightest concern for quality or for period, that conglomeration of mediocrities with an occasional outstanding masterpiece on which they've stuck an utterly idiotic head, ludicrous arms or feet that rob it of any dignity (and is there nobody within that long-decaying Vatican City to protest against this scandalous confusion, against these fakes?), you'll have a quick look round the Stanze, you'll spend a little time in the Sistine, then you'll come back at leisure through the Borgia Apartments.

Cécile will be looking out for you this time, when she comes out at one o'clock onto the Piazza del Palazzo Farnese, and it's during lunch, at the Tre Scalini restaurant for instance, in the Piazza Navona, the former Claudian circus, while you sit admiring Borromini's cupola and the elliptical spires that stretch up as though carried away by the general movement of that elongated space, and the water spurting from the fountain with its four great rivers, Danube, Nile, snub-nosed Ganges leaning back in amazement, Rio de la Plata with hidden face, barely emerging from the veils enfolding him, those four white stone giants that seem, with their gestures, to be moving spirally around the rock on which stands the obelisk of rosy granite, and meanwhile rolling your tagliatelle on your fork, that you'll tell her the reason for your journey, you'll explain that this time you've come not on Scabelli's business but solely for her sake, that you've found her a job in Paris, that you're not stopping at the Albergo Quirinale but that you're going to stay all the time with her, and therefore you'll have to go first of all, early in the afternoon, to fix things with Mme Da Ponte, then get your luggage from the cloakroom, before you can go off together, unhurried, with your arms round one another like young lovers, and enjoy the spaciousness of Rome, its ruins and its trees, and its streets, through all of which you can pass freely, even the Corso and the Piazza Colonna, because the office will be shut by then, except through the Via Vittorio Veneto, near the Café de Paris, where Signor Ettore Scabelli is liable to sit for hours.

When the sun sets you'll go back to the Via Monte della Farini to fetch your coats, and then Cécile will probably want to go for dinner with you to some local pizzeria, studying the cinema programmes on the way, but only for the following evening, because tomorrow you'll be feeling the aftermath of the weary, broken and uncomfortable night you'll have spent, the weary night you're about to spend, and so you'll go to bed very early in her room, and this time you won't leave it till next morning.

Beyond the corridor, the clouds seem unwilling to lift. The Englishman crosses one knee over the other. Through the window you see a slow, tremulous swell of hillside covered with leafless vines.

Before you knew Cécile, even though you'd seen most of the sights of Rome and enjoyed its atmosphere, you hadn't this love for the place; it was only with her that you began to explore it in some detail, and your passion for her colours all its streets so thoroughly that when you dream of Cécile in Henriette's presence, you're also dreaming of Rome in Paris.

Thus, last Monday morning, when you got back on the Rome Express at nine o'clock, having certainly spent a better night in your first-class carriage than the one awaiting you this time, while a little early-morning sunshine filtered through the windows of the Gare de Lyon, instead of leaving the station immediately and taking a taxi home to 15 Place du Panthéon for a shave and a bath before going to the garage in the Rue de l'Estrapade to fetch your car and drive to the office, you looked about to see if there wasn't, in the main hall, the equivalent of an Albergo Diurno, and you managed to find some sort of public baths, where you washed in a bathtub of dubious cleanliness; then, as you don't usually get to your office before half-past ten when you've been to Rome, you took advantage of the time you thus had over to stroll about a bit, like a Roman tourist in Paris, as if Rome was where you usually lived and you only came to Paris from time to time, every two months or once a month at most, on business.

You left your suitcase in the cloakroom, telling yourself you'd send Marnal for it later in the day, you walked as far as the Seine, you crossed it by the Pont d'Austerlitz, and as it was really rather a fine day for November you unbuttoned your coat as you walked along by the Jardin des Plantes, then crossed over to the Île Saint-Louis where you had a *café au lait* with croissants, in spite of having drunk tea and nibbled rusks in the dining car as usual, an unsatisfying breakfast that you always had to supplement at home by some substantial snack, which must have been waiting ready for you last Monday as on all previous occasions; then you walked almost the whole way round the Cité, one hand in your trouser pocket, the other holding your briefcase and swinging it to the rhythm of a song by Monteverdi which you hummed to yourself, and it must have been ten o'clock when, in front of Notre-Dame, you climbed back on to the 69 bus that took you to the Place du Palais-Royal.

In order to prolong the feeling that you hadn't really come home yet you decided to lunch out, but not wanting to cause Henriette unnecessary anxiety you rang up the flat – Danton 25 30 – only to learn from the maid Marceline that Madame had gone out and the children, of course, were at school; so you asked her to let Madame know that you wouldn't be back until the evening.

Half an hour later she rang back:

"Can I speak to Monsieur Delmont?"

"Speaking... Hello, how are you? I'm awfully sorry I shan't be able to get home for lunch."

"You'll be home to dinner, I suppose?"

"Of course."

"And tomorrow?"

"Is anything special happening tomorrow?"

"No, nothing; Wednesday's your birthday..."

"Yes, of course, how sweet of you to remember."

"Did you have a good journey?"

"Just as usual."

"See you tonight then."

"See you tonight."

On the other side of the Rue Danièle-Casanova, in the first window of the Durieu Travel Agency, there were posters inviting you to visit Burgundy: the polished tiles of the hospice at Beaune, September vineyards laden with clusters of black grapes among variegated leaves, the ducal tombs at Dijon; in the second window, overlooking the Avenue de l'Opéra, everything suggested winter sports: skis, ropes and thick boots with red laces, great photographs of cable cars, of dazzling snow fields streaked with ski tracks, of champions in mid-air with arms outstretched, of chalets with roofs covered in thick white fur, shining and glittering in the sunshine, and wooden balconies glistening with damp, of girls in tight trousers and patterned, roll-necked sweaters, pictures of a very different Savoy from the one you'll be crossing through presently, still dark and misty, with a few patches of dirty snow; the third window was devoted to Italy, with the star-spangled interior of the cupola of the Holy Shroud at Turin, the staircase of the Palazzo Balbi at Genoa, the Tower of Pisa, a flautist from Tarquinia, the square of St Peter's with the obelisk from Nero's circus brought there by order of Sixtus Quintus, and pictures of a number of other towns you don't know: the church at Lucca, the Arch of Trajan at Benevento, the Olympic Theatre of Vicenza; the fourth window welcomed you to Sicily.

After crossing the Rue des Pyramides, leaving on your right, between the arcades, the golden horsewoman softly gleaming against a background of clouds, while on the other side of the avenue other travel agencies repeated the word "Italy", you turned right at the Place du Théâtre-Français, you waited till the green light turned red and stopped the stream of traffic like a sudden dam, you crossed the Rue de Rivoli, plunged through the turnstile and emerged on the other side facing the broad, restless, mother-of-pearl sky over the Tuileries. As you passed between those three bad statues representing the sons of Cain hidden in their garden square and the triumphal arch of the Carrousel, you caught sight of the grey needle of the Obelisk rising between this archway and the distant one at the Étoile.

Cars were parked close together like books on a shelf, and there were two or three coaches in front of the entry of the Pavillon Mollien; some American women, armed with cameras, sat on the stone benches waiting for their guides and glancing at maps.

Without paying more attention than usual to the sarcophagi or to the bronze copies of antique statues from the Vatican, you went up the staircase leading to the Victory of Samothrace, going where fancy led you without any clearly defined sense of direction; you started along the Egyptian rooms and then took the small spiral stair going up to the eighteenth-century rooms.

You glanced rapidly over the Guardis and Magnascos in the first of these, over the Watteaus and Chardins in the second, over the English school and the Fragonards in the third; only in the fourth did you pause, and then it was neither for Goya's sake nor for David's. The pictures you had come so far to see and which you now scrutinized so lovingly were a pair of large paintings by a third-rate artist, Pannini, representing two imaginary art collections displayed in high, well-lit rooms, in which people of fashion, nobles and clergy, were walking about amongst the sculptures, between the landscape-hung walls, making gestures of admiration, of interest, of surprise and bewilderment, like visitors to the Sistine, with this peculiarity, that there was no perceptible difference between things supposed to be real and things supposed to be painted, as though he had wished to represent on his canvas the fulfilment of that dream shared by so many artists of his time: to produce the absolute equivalent of reality, so that a painted capital was indistinguishable from a real capital, except for the frame surrounding it, just as the great illusionist architects of Roman baroque paint in space and offer to the imagination, thanks to their marvellous system of signs, their clusters of pilasters, their voluptuous curves, buildings as impressive and as magical as those immense, authentic ruins of antiquity which they had perpetually before their eyes, putting them to shame; systematically, they integrate the details of their ornamentation into the very basis of their language.

And it is precisely this weighing of the new against the old, this endeavour to take up the challenge – for so it seemed from the sixteenth century onward – made by the old Roman Empire to the existing Church, which is stressed in these two symmetrical paintings: a gallery of views of modern Rome to the right of the window overlooking the Cour Carrée, a gallery of views of ancient Rome to the left of it, in which you amused yourself recognizing the Coliseum, the Basilica of Maxentius, the Pantheon, as they looked two hundred years ago, about the time when Piranesi engraved them, those three white capitals barely rising above ground level, which are those of the temple of Mars Ultor in the likeness of Augustus in the latter's forum, which nowadays stand high on their splendid columns, the portico of the temple of Antoninus and Faustina with the façade of the church which had been built inside it and which has not yet been destroyed, the triumphal arch of Constantine and that of Titus, which were then embedded amid houses, the Baths of Caracalla in the open country, and that mysterious round temple, called the Temple of Minerva Medica, which you see from the train as you're coming into the station.

Outside the window, among the vines under a darkening, lowering sky, you see the steep roof of a church with shiny yellow diamond-shaped tiles rising above a neatly clustered village. On the hot strip of metal between the seats, the grooved lines interlace like tiny rails in a marshalling yard.

It was two years ago, or rather more since it was still summertime, late August, you were sitting in a third-class compartment like this one, in the same place next to the corridor and facing forward, and opposite you was Cécile, whom you barely knew, whom you had just met in the dining room, travelling home after her holiday.

It was definitely later in the day than it is now, it was mid-afternoon, in a train which left in the morning like this one and reached Rome at dawn, the same train as this one no doubt, but with some slight difference of timetable, and which you'd had to take on this occasion because of some last-minute difficulty – you can't remember exactly what – until lunchtime you had, of course, been travelling first, in an Italian coach with coloured photographs of famous paintings, probably from Rome, the allegory of the two loves from the Villa Borghese for instance, which is one of those most frequently reproduced.

When you saw her for the first time, you were already sitting at the table next the window for the second service. Dijon had gone past long ago, so had Beaune, Mâcon, Chalon and even Bourg; now there were mountains to be seen instead of vineyards.

She was wearing a reddish-orange dress, cut low over her sun-tanned bosom, her black hair plaited and rolled round her head, fixed with gold-knobbed hairpins, and her lips painted almost violet.

The dining car was gradually filling up, but it so happened that the two of you were alone at your table and, as it was very warm, your first remark was to ask her if you might open the small glass vents over the window; then, seeing her take a railway guide out of her black handbag (it wasn't a pale-blue guide like your present one but light green, like the paint below the rack) and having none yourself, you asked her when the train would reach Aix-les-Bains.

"Lunch will be over long before you get there."

"That's not where I'm stopping. I'm going on to Rome, not on a tourist visit unfortunately, but on business."

At first only a few polite remarks passed between you, separated by long pauses, then gradually a continuous conversation developed, chiefly about the meal, about the wine you made her taste and the dishes you were served with, until the time came when, reading her bill, she realized that she hadn't kept enough French money.

"He's sure to accept lire."

"Yes, but only at a most unfavourable rate of exchange; I'll buy a thousand from you at the Paris rate."

Then she began to talk to you about herself, telling you that she was on her way to Rome too, that she worked there too and had done so for a number of years, at the Palazzo Farnese, that she loved the city and her life there and her job, but felt rather lonely, and was just returning rather regretfully after a month's holiday in Paris, that her mother was Italian and she herself born in Milan, but that she was of French nationality and had finished her schooling during the war at the Collège Sévigné.

As soon as the borders had reopened she had gone back to stay with her mother's family, she had married a young engineer from Fiat who had been killed in an appalling accident on the *autostrada* only two months after their marriage, just as they had made their home in Turin. She still shuddered with horror at the memory, and that was why, wanting to escape from everything that recalled it, she had moved farther south.

Almost all the travellers had gone back to their carriages by now; the waiters were folding up the tablecloths; you left the dining car together, you went past your first-class compartment, but you wanted so badly to talk to her about yourself that you accompanied her to her own carriage and took a seat opposite her. The train, just then, was travelling along the side of Lamartine's lake.

You were still talking when you crossed the border, and that evening you went along to the Italian dining car together. Outside, the wide craggy landscape of Piedmont was bathed in sunshine; darkness was gathering in the valleys, but the grey wooden roofs gleamed on the hillsides. The sweat was trickling down your back, and yet you felt the air was growing cooler. She was listening to you, looking at you admiringly and laughing. Time went by, night fell. There were only three other people in her compartment when you went back there: an old Italian woman dressed in black and two French tourists, brother and sister.

You had reached the tunnels of Genoa; you watched the lighted shop windows and the moon reflected in the water; you had stopped talking; somebody asked for the lights to be turned off. Then there was only the little blue lamp in the ceiling, but the blinds over the corridor windows hadn't been drawn. She'd thought, for a moment, that you were going to leave, and indeed you'd considered doing so, but then you'd intercepted that flicker of regret on her face! You stayed sitting there, facing forward just as you are now, and she was opposite you, in the seat where the professor was sitting a moment ago, and she began to smile, and leant back, a little to the left, and let sleep overcome her while you kept watch, giving a little start from time to time, stroking the window frame with her hand, parting her lips occasionally to breathe out a sigh, with the tips of her teeth just showing against her lower lip; her features grew tense for a moment, and then the motion of the train took hold of her again and lulled her like a spell.

You feel your feet scrape against the iron floor-heater. Outside the window you see the rain, which has been threatening all day, beginning to fall gently in thin drops that streak the window pane with tiny lines, like hundreds of eyelashes.

The picture on the other side is called: *Gallery of Views of Modern Rome*. Michelangelo's *Moses* has pride of place there, and all Bernini's fountains hang there framed; your eyes roam from the Fountain of Rivers in the Piazza Navona to that of the Triton near the Palazzo Barberini, from St Peter's Square to the staircase of the Trinità dei Monti, through all those spots that are haunted for you by Cécile's face, made vivid by Cécile's interest – Cécile whom you taught to love them better, and for whose sake you learnt to love them better.

Beginning to feel hungry, you looked through the windows into the Cour Carrée, where it was raining, and saw that the clock on the central pavilion showed half-past twelve.

You went down the little spiral staircase and hurried through the Egyptian rooms, but on reaching the Victory of Samothrace you turned left instead of going straight on down, you passed through the Seven-Metre Gallery, hurried through the main gallery and threaded your way between the many groups of foreigners till you came to the Poussins and the Claudes: two Frenchmen who belonged to Rome.

You try to recall the arrangement of their pictures, but you can't quite reconstitute it; of course you know that on the right-hand wall there was the small painting of the Forum in the seventeenth century, with the three pillars of the Temple of the Dioscuri half-buried in the ground, and the Campo Vaccino, that wasteland, that cattle market which was once the main thoroughfare of the world's capital, and then there was *Ruth and Boaz*, so like a tapestry, with the two figures with their spreading gestures recalling harvesters in an Egyptian bas-relief, and the cornfield robbed of its brightness by time and varnish, and then, but you aren't quite certain of the next, was it the *Plague at Athens* or the *Rape of the Sabines*, in any case one of those pictures that are so closely akin to Pompeian painting that it is hard to accept the evidence that the artist cannot have known Pompeii, that he has merely, by some miraculous intuition, rediscovered the spirit of it through the medium of the *Aldobrandini Wedding*, that second-rate work of which he made the curious copy to be seen in the Palazzo Doria; but what's on the other side? A bacchanalia, to be sure, but what else? Ulysses handing over Briseis to her father? A seaport at sunrise? Cleopatra landing at Tarsus? All three?

You gazed at the figures which are painted with such simplicity that the mind of the beholder is impelled to inspire them with life, so that you actually began to make up a sort of story about each of them, imagining them before and after the scene depicted, before that single fixed gesture in the midst of their voyages over the waters, imagining their adventures among the streets of those magnificent sea-coast towns, among the halls and colonnades, among the great trees of the gardens surrounding those splendid dwellings, those fantastic creations imbued with Virgilian echoes which are so much closer to antiquity than all the foolish architectural reconstructions which generations of pedants have thrust upon us and will go on indefinitely thrusting upon us.

Your stomach, punctual as a clock, one sign of growing old, so they say, roused you from this reverie, but even then you might have gone downstairs and out faster than you did, you might have gone straight through the Van Dycks and found, immediately on your left, the stair leading to the Medieval Sculpture rooms; instead of which you retraced your steps through the groups of ecstatic tourists, through the Seven-Metre Gallery, past the Victory of Samothrace, and then you couldn't help casting a rapid glance at the mosaics of Antioch, the portraits of Roman ladies of Nero's time and the statue of the latter as a child, round-faced and solemn in his toga.

The rain was falling so fast as you crossed the terrace on which the monument to Gambetta once stood that the Carrousel arch was almost invisible, and the Obelisk, of course, completely so.

There was the same crowd of cars along the Rue de Rivoli as half an hour earlier, but now the wipers were wagging on all the windscreens.

At a restaurant in the Rue de Richelieu, where you had often been before for business lunches, you asked for *spaghetti bolognese*, but either the dish they brought you was unworthy of the name or else the loneliness that suddenly overwhelmed you prevented you from enjoying it, from appreciating its real quality. As for coffee, whereas the waiter smilingly promised you an espresso, it was a filter coffee that he brought you a few minutes later, a very good filter coffee to be sure, but you hadn't the heart to wait till your cup was full to drink it, while paying the bill. If that was how you were going to feel about your food, had it really been worthwhile not going home, and complicating and embittering your relations with Henriette still further by a useless lie?

You still had one cigarette in your packet of Nazionali, but the rain outside was so violent that it went out and you threw it down on the pavement. It was only half-past one, and you had no desire to get back to your office twenty-five minutes too soon, particularly as if you'd been alone you'd probably have fallen asleep: however used to train journeys you are you find them invariably and increasingly exhausting, even in the comfort of a first-class carriage.

From next time onward, things will be better, because you've already raised the point with Scabelli more than once, and they've at last agreed to pay for all your journeys in a sleeping car henceforward; but today you're not even travelling first, and at the thought of the practically sleepless night awaiting you, you begin to regret that thrifty instinct, left over from the days when you weren't so well off; why, no, you correct yourself, it's not from stinginess that you've chosen to travel under these conditions but from sentiment, from romanticism: it's because the first time you met Cécile on the train two years ago, at the end of August, you left your own compartment and went into hers, which was just like this one, and sat down opposite her in the very seat you're occupying now; it's because every time you've been with her you've travelled third;

but here again you're forced to admit a touch of meanness, for you've been paying for her journeys lately and you didn't want them to cost too much, because you were always afraid of being short of money for your home 15 Place du Panthéon, and for your family, and because you dreaded Henriette's enquiries about your expenses. Oh, if only you'd managed to break free sooner from such petty inhibitions, which are absurd now that you're a rich man, you'd long ago have been living all the year round with Cécile, enjoying the life which hitherto you've only sampled on brief visits to Rome.

So, having half an hour to kill, and unwilling in such bad weather to spend it strolling about the streets, you crossed the Avenue de l'Opéra and walked up it on the left-hand pavement, following in the opposite direction the route by which, a short while back, you'd gone from your office to the Louvre, passing on your left the windows of the bookshop with its Blue Guides of Rome and Paris, passing those of your friend Durieu, who hadn't been such a particular friend of yours before but to whom you owe such a debt of gratitude, since Cécile is going to work for him, since it's he who has made it possible for her to come to Paris, he who, without realizing it, has set you free: his Sicilian window, his Italian window with the obelisk from Nero's Circus in the middle of St Peter's Square, the Tarquinian flautist, the Tower of Pisa, the staircase from the Palazzo Balbi and Guarini's great starry cupola, his Alpine window and, in the Rue Danièle-Casanova, his window about Burgundy, the very province you're crossing now, nearing its capital (that city of gourmands, once the home of invention and discovery, but now, ever since Paris took the lead, essentially a place for retreat and enjoyment), with coloured photographs of the courtyard of the hospice at Beaune and its roofs where the shiny tiles form interlacing patterns, of Roger van de Weyden's *Angel of the Last Judgment* and Melchior Broederlam's *Flight into Egypt*, and the *Well of the Prophets* in black and white, and painted posters displaying bunches of grapes, vineyards and bottles; then, on the other side of the street, passing your own window, which has such an Italian look about it with the name Scabelli in big black letters, which by night are not neon-lighted but cast their shadows on the great curved sheet of illuminated, frosted glass, with the window pane reaching right down to the ground, the walls covered with mosaics, the typewriters and calculating machines suspended from bundles of coloured threads stretched here and there, and each lit up by its individual spotlight (of course Olivetti had done that sort of thing before you), and then the door beside it, the original house door, through which not only the staff but all important customers have to pass to get to your office on the floor above, and which you'd been wanting to get altered for a long time, in spite of the reluctance of your Roman bosses to spend money on improving premises which they could never own, this staircase being common to all the upper stories; then passing Brentano's bookshop and the Italian shipping company.

You took the Boulevard des Capucines as far as the Rue Caumartin and went into the Bar Romain, which is so crowded in the evenings and would be crowded that same evening when you went back to it later, wanting to postpone as long as possible your return to 15 Place du Panthéon and your meeting with Henriette and the children, crowded with painted women perched on high stools, swinging spiky heels at the end of their squat legs, fastening their little diamanté buckles and fingering long cigarette holders, but which at this time of day was practically empty, except for a few old gentlemen: the Bar Romain, with its "atmosphere of ancient Rome", as different as possible from the bars of the Italian capital today, but which would not have been out of place in late-nineteenth-century Rome, with its voluptuous vulgarity, its armchairs upholstered in crimson velvet, its collection of coins, and its highly spiced, dark-coloured paintings of *Messalina in a Venerium, Nero's Triumphal Entry into Rome,* and other such scenes characteristic of that showy but vague licentiousness, that grandiose immodesty which, to the restricted Parisian rakes of the *belle époque*, its bourgeois respectability discarded, seemed the unfettered and magnificent realization of their dreams; but you were well aware that, however Roman it might be, that bar could not provide you with the espresso you were longing for, and you had to make do with sipping another filter coffee, with a sidelong glance at two old gentlemen whispering to one another behind their newspapers, until you noticed that it was five minutes to two, and that you had only just time to get to your office when it opened after making a detour to buy yourself some Gauloises; and when, at half-past six that evening, you came out of the office, locking up as you were the last to leave, while in the darkness a thin drizzle was falling, shimmering with the light of all the shop windows, all the headlights, all the luminous advertisements, you waited for a while on the pavement, hailing every taxi in sight but finding none free, clutching your suit-case which you'd sent Marnal to collect from the cloakroom that afternoon, and which seemed too heavy to lug about the underground passages; then, having resigned yourself to taking the Métro after all, you'd gone back to your den, your control room, where everything was dark and deserted and, through the windows of the silent rooms, you could see the flickering lights and shadows of the wet world outside; you left the case lying on your desk and then, unencumbered, you walked as far as the Bar Romain, now crowded with women and with younger men than on your midday visit; you only stopped there for about a quarter of an hour, long enough to drink a pot of very strong tea, because you were cold, and weren't afraid of being kept awake by it at home, after a night in the train, and then you went to the Madeleine to take your train, threading your way through the wet throng hurrying along the Boulevard; you changed at Sèvres-Babylone to the Gare d'Austerlitz line and emerged into the open at the Odéon, where students of all races were pouring down the steps,

not that this was the quickest way home, because if you'd been in a hurry to reach 15 Place du Panthéon you'd have done better to take a bus, but because you wanted to spin out a little longer that Roman route through the streets of Paris which you'd been following all that day, intentionally going past those buildings that reminded you of Rome, of the Roman buildings whose interest had been enhanced for you by Cécile's presence, those fragments of Rome in Paris that revived for you, as you studied them, Cécile's eyes and voice, her laughter, her youth, her cherished freedom,

because you wanted to go on foot, deliberately, like a tourist, along the Boulevard Saint-Germain and across the Boulevard Saint-Michel, then turning right to walk up the left pavement of the latter, in order just to go past (not to examine: you don't want to linger in the rainy dark, and besides, what is there to examine?) those walls of brick and stone, the remains of the Thermae that Julian the Apostate knew, and the only significant relics of his "beloved Lutetia", which amply justifies the attribution of his name to them.

The Place du Panthéon was almost deserted, as it always is at this time of the evening, although you've usually got home by this time, and have got there in your car, which that Monday evening was still in the garage in the Rue de l'Estrapade, to which you took it back yesterday; overshadowed by the sombre bulk of the church with its unseen dome, it seemed interminably long to cross, while the headlights of a passing car lit up for an instant the rain-swept statue of Jean-Jacques Rousseau.

When you pressed the button, the door swung open with a faint buzz, and through the closely curtained windows of the concierge's room on the left only a faint red glimmer showed; you switched on the light and took the lift to the fourth floor where, in the lobby, Henriette came up to meet you, wiping her hands on her grey apron.

She waited for you to kiss her as you'd always done, but you felt unwilling to keep up the farce any longer and began to unbutton your coat, and then she asked you:

"What have you done with your suitcase?"

"I left it in the office; I didn't want to be bothered with it as I hadn't got the car. Everything all right here?"

"Dinner will be ready in a few minutes. Have you had a good day?"

"Very good. I'm a bit fagged out, of course."

She went off to hustle Marceline, and you proceeded to look in at the boys in their room; they both leapt up with that guilty, insolent look on their faces, Henri having obviously been lying on his bed reading a cheap thriller which he'd just had time to hide, not very successfully, under his pillow, and Thomas wiping his hands surreptitiously on his corduroy shorts, with his mother's gesture, in front of the brimming washbasin where little paper boats with coloured sails were slowly sinking, the ashtray on the big table, presumably stolen from some café by one or other of them, overflowing with scraps of burnt paper and cigarette ends, and *Gaffiot's Dictionary* lying on the carpet with a lot of other schoolbooks which must have been used as missiles.

As you closed the door you heard the sound of their stifled laughter; then, looking into the girls' room (Jacqueline's dolls' pram stood in a corner, crammed with a jumble of small garments, and the lamp in the middle of the room shone down on a pile of unfinished needlework), you found Madeleine sprawling in an easy chair, immersed in *Elle*.

"Where's your sister?"

"Mother sent her to do her homework in the dining room."

Really they're at the worst possible age: they've lost the grace and charm of small children whom you can play with in the evenings like enchanting toys, and they're all too young still, even Madeleine, to be talked to like grown-ups, like friends; you can't take a real interest in their studies because of your job, your responsibilities and other preoccupations, yet you have to put up with their noise, which irritates you, and that in turn prevents them from trusting you, so that they've become strangers to you, bold little barbarians in league against you, quite aware that something's gone wrong between their mother and yourself; they watch you both, and even if they don't discuss the matter amongst themselves, which would really surprise you, they must surely have thought about it, must know that they've been lied to, and no longer dare come and ask you questions.

If you had wavered so long about your love for Cécile, it was on their account, to be sure, but obviously the solution was not to let the rot go on slowly spreading; on the contrary, the thing to do was to show them quite frankly that what they'd guessed at was the truth, a surgical operation which would hurt them a little perhaps, but which would deliver them from the infection that was beginning to poison their minds, and thus to show them the example of a man courageously obeying his feelings, for which they'll be grateful to you in the long run; so really it's on their account that you must no longer waver, that you must come out into the open.

You won't be deserting them in any way: you'll still be there to provide for them, to see that they lack nothing, and, above all, now they will be able to approach you without that sort of mistrust, that sneering smile; your relations with them will be purified.

In your bedroom, you opened the window and stared out at the dark bulk of the Panthéon, which you guessed at in the rain above the wet lights of an occasional car; of all historic buildings in Paris this is the one (together with Julian's Thermae) which most infallibly reminds you of Cécile, not only because its name naturally recalls that of the temple dedicated by Agrippa to the twelve gods, but also because the frieze of garlands, just at the level of your flat, is one of the most successful of all attempts at classical decoration, in its imitation of the finest Roman ornaments; then you closed the shutters and went into your dressing room to wash your hands, and seeing your shelf empty under the mirror, you realized how stupid you had been not to bring home your suitcase, and wondered how you were going to manage to shave next morning, since your sons were too young to own such things as shaving brushes, etc.; and as you could not possibly appear with a twenty-four-hour-old beard in front of the Misses Capdenac, Lambert and Perrin, the only solution would be to go to a barber's after you'd had breakfast.

The same thought must have occurred to Henriette when you came home, for she has an amazingly keen awareness of such details, but she had chosen not to mention it; she had preferred to let you find it out for yourself, the better to humiliate you, to make you feel that you still needed her, not in the sphere of love – it was too late for that – but in the sphere of these petty material details. She still pursues the same policy to prevent you from taking action, to avoid shocking the children, the same timid, petty-minded policy, whereas in her heart of hearts she's as anxious for a separation as you are, but she's afraid of it, she's afraid of her friends' pity and of what the children's schoolfellows might say to them; that's what she dares not face, that's why she does all she can to postpone the explosion, hoping that in course of time your passion and your resolution will cool and that nothing will happen.

She schemes to that end unremittingly, but if ever she should succeed, what would she gain? The pitiful advantage of having finally defeated you, the morose pleasure the damned feel at dragging somebody else into their slimy slough of despond, the miserable triumph of getting back a man who'd been incapable of resisting her war of attrition and whom, consequently, she could only despise even more profoundly than she does now, while the battle's still on.

And then, indeed, you would become unbearable to her, and her antagonism would turn into hatred, for she'd know that she had held you against your will, through your sheer weakness and through her own contagious fear of those stupid women; ah, what bitterness would cloud her reproachful face! How could she ever forgive you, or forgive herself, for having irrevocably exposed your cowardice, for having destroyed in you everything that she might still have loved?

With what systematic relentlessness she seeks to drag you down, from motives which, to an outsider, she might plausibly represent as generous, till both she and you shall be irretrievably lost!

You sat down in the armchair in the drawing room, near the window from which you could see in its full beauty the illuminated frieze of the Panthéon, and listened to some of Monteverdi's *Orfeo* on the wireless; you had only switched on the iron standard lamp; through the glass door you could see Marceline laying the table in the dining room; you gazed at the two big Piranesi etchings on the opposite wall, one of the prisons and the other of some buildings; then, from the little library of Latin and Italian authors which you've been collecting ever since your liaison with Cécile began, you picked out the first volume of the *Aeneid* in the Guillaume Budé edition and opened it at the beginning of the sixth book. Just then Jacqueline came in, with black stains on the first and second fingers of her right hand, and sat down in the armchair on the other side of the fireplace, next to the big bookcase of French books, folding her hands and looking a little embarrassed.

"Did you have a good journey, Daddy?"

"Yes, darling, and I hope you've been a good girl?"

"Did you see that lady again?"

"What lady?"

"You know, the one who came here once."

"You mean Madame Darcella?"

"Oh, I don't know her surname. The one you called Cécile."

"Yes. Why do you want to know?"

"Will she be coming back soon?"

"I don't suppose so."

Henriette, opening the glass door to tell you dinner was ready, gave Jacqueline such a look that the child blushed, burst into tears and fled to the bathroom to scrub her hands.

What could be the underlying significance of that little scene? Could it be merely a harmless coincidence? Did those blushes, those tears, that flight mean simply that she had been disconcerted by her mother's behaviour and your own? Or had she, on the other hand, been questioning you deliberately to seek confirmation for the hypothesis she'd been forming in her childish mind, to extract information which she should be the first to possess; or else – and of course this was where the question became so painful, this was what made it impossible for you to go on thus, to keep up this useless deceit and equivocation, to feel so revoltingly ashamed of yourself and of your hope of salvation – wasn't there, in the attitude of this child, who had loved you so much a few years ago, who had just come up to you so sweetly, who must surely still be very fond of you in spite of the grown-up airs she tries to put on in assiduous imitation of her sister Madeleine, a touch of mockery?

That's what you wondered as you lay in bed, since the three cups of very strong tea that you'd drunk at the Bar Romain in the late afternoon prevented you from sleeping in spite of the fatigue of your journey.

Outside the window the rain is falling with increased violence, lashing the pane with great drops that run slowly down in slanting streams. The Englishman folds up his newspaper and pushes it back into his pocket. Beyond the corridor, underneath the quivering confusion of the telegraph wires, you can still make out the blurred shape of an occasional house or tree on the slopes covered with leafless vines.

Well, it's done now; the die is cast, and so you're free!

Of course there are still a good many details to arrange, and it'll be several months yet before the situation's really settled, but you've crossed the threshold.

On Sunday morning, the day after tomorrow, when you wake up at about nine o'clock on the fourth floor at 56 Via Monte della Farina, the sun will be shining through the slits in the shutters and the voices you hear will be Italian voices.

First of all you'll leave Cécile's room; she's sure to be up before you, and she'll hand you a jug of hot water, and you'll go through the communicating door into the room where you're officially supposed to be sleeping, to rumple the bed and to have a wash.

Then you'll go out together into the Roman street, and if it's fine enough, you'll go somewhere outside the city for lunch, to Hadrian's Villa for instance, since you've never seen it in the autumn, or to a beach if she'd rather; whatever she chooses, for this is to be her day; if it looks like rain, she'll probably take you to revisit the first Roman secret she ever revealed to you, Pietro Cavallini's *Last Judgement* at Santa Cecilia in Trastevere, to which a Jesuit father, by special permission, admits visitors at eleven o'clock every Sunday.

Since night falls quickly, even in Rome, at this time of year, you'll go home early so that she can cook something for dinner, because she likes to show off her skill in the kitchen, and thus you'll be able to go to bed early once again.

The next morning, Monday, she'll have to leave at nine to go to the Palazzo Farnese, and for many mornings after that, until she's had the letter from the Durieu Agency offering her the job, and has sent in her resignation and had it accepted; you won't be meeting her until noon, and you'll spend the morning visiting some museum or some building by yourself, knowing that soon she won't be there to see them with you, so that when, later on, you come back to Rome and revisit them you'll be, as it were, solemnly celebrating, commemorating the beginnings of your love; the Thermae Museum, for instance, opposite the station, with Livia's dining room, that consecrated orchard full of birds; or even the Vatican, if you haven't managed to see all you wanted to see there; and just because Cécile has never been there with you, it'll be for her sake that you'll go and examine more closely those rooms which she has never seen, partly because her timetable didn't allow her and partly from deliberate choice, so that you can convey to her the real meaning of the works of art that stand there, freed from the ugly and misleading matrix that encloses them.

Moreover, if you go to the Vatican tomorrow morning, and again on Monday to complete your visit if need be, it will be the first occasion on which you've gone sightseeing in Rome without Cécile, and thus the first of many occasions in the future when you'll have to go without her, because she'll be living with you in Paris and will no longer be there to welcome you in the Via Monte della Farina; and so this visit to the Vatican will be, as it were, a ceremony in anticipation of her absence.

And besides, if you don't take advantage of these two mornings for it, it'll probably be a very long time before you have another opportunity, for you obviously can't often treat yourself to a four- or five-days escapade, and when Cécile's no longer in Rome you probably won't want to.

You're afraid that the "Eternal City" will seem very empty to you henceforward, and that you'll find yourself pining for the woman who drew you thither and who kept you there. It's highly probable, indeed, that henceforward, when you're in Rome, your sole wish will be to take the first train back as soon as you've done your business, without even spending the weekend there, and that if you're there on a Saturday, you'll leave by the 1.38 p.m. train, travelling first or, so you hope, in a sleeper, the same train that you took last Sunday, which is much faster than the one you've chosen for Monday night for the sake of its third-class carriages.

That afternoon, then, you've decided, you'll go for a walk through that part of the town where the ruins of the old imperial city are thick upon the ground, and where indeed there's little else to be seen, the modern city and the baroque city having, so to speak, withdrawn so as to leave these ruins in their immense solitude.

You'll cross the Forum, you'll climb the Palatine Hill, and there almost every stone, every brick wall will remind you of some remark of Cécile's, of something you'd read or learnt so as to tell her about it; from the Palace of Septimius Severus you'll watch evening fall on the stumps of the Baths of Caracalla as they rise up amidst the pines; you'll go down again by the Temple of Venus and Rome, and you'll stand inside the Colosseum while dusk draws to a close and night thickens there, then you'll go past the Arch of Constantine, and along the Via San Gregorio and the Via dei Cerchi, skirting the old Circus Maximus; in the darkness, you'll make out the Temple of Vesta on your left, and on the other side the Arch of Janus Quadrifrons; then you'll come to the Tiber, and you'll walk beside it as far as the Via Giulia to get to the Palazzo Farnese, and then you'll probably only have a few minutes to wait before Cécile comes out.

Beyond the corridor, unrecognizable under the driving rain, a long goods train goes past, coal carriages first then others loaded

68

with long girders, with the unpainted bodies of unfinished cars propped up against one another like the shards of dead pinned insects, then cattle carriages with their barred windows, then petrol carriages with their little ladders, then flat carriages full of rusty flints for making other railway lines, and then the last of all, with its turret and its lamp, not close to the window but a little behind it. The young couple, sitting silently absorbed in their books, have stretched out their legs underneath your seat. The professor is standing in the corridor now, leaning against the brass rail and smoking. A station goes past, but you can't make out its name.

The clergyman on your left gets up, shuts his breviary, puts it away in its black cover, lays it down to keep his seat, apologizes as he goes past you, opens the sliding door a trifle wider, edges past on your right and disappears behind you. It's eleven now; the train's due to stop at Dijon in eleven minutes, is that where he's going to? He must be about thirty-five; he seems vigorous, even impetuous; he was beginning to look bored, ensconced in his corner as if he'd still a long time to spend there. Has he finished reading his service, or has he merely had enough of it? What a perfect disguise a cassock is! True, it proclaims a certain number of things, but how many alternatives may lie concealed behind this label! How can you tell whether he's a Jesuit father for instance, a schoolmaster, a country priest or the curate of an urban parish? The black folds of his garment, which indicate that he belongs to some church, and that he almost certainly recites a certain number of prayers every day and says Mass, don't give you the slightest hint about the kind of life he leads, the way he spends most of his time, the sort of people with whom he comes in contact.

Where's he going to? Farther than Dijon, probably, to judge by his actions, but not much farther, since his only luggage is that black briefcase; and why is he travelling? Not, presumably, to meet a woman, like yourself; he may have gone to visit his family, to see an old mother for instance; they must surely take a holiday from time to time like other men; they must surely be allowed to travel for pleasure, sometimes, although at this time of year... It can't be for his job, or rather for that side of his life which corresponds to what your job is for you; there seems no reason why he should have to go from Paris to Dijon, unless he's an intellectual who's come to town to give a lecture or to consult some document in the Bibliothèque Nationale, in which case you might have passed him last Monday in the Rue de Richelieu without noticing; but he scarcely looks like one.

The law professor turns round and comes in again; he sits down; he consults his watch; he takes off his glasses, pulls out of his pocket a case from which he extracts a chamois leather and begins wiping them again.

You can generally recognize university dons and rummagers after old learning by their clothes, the books they read, their gestures and manners, even when their faces don't give them away as this man's does; but with priests, everything is hidden by their dress, their unctuous manner and their prayer books.

Although it's unlikely he's going to Rome this time, he may have been there already, or perhaps he hopes to go there some day to see his Pope and mingle with the crowd of cassocked figures that swarm through the streets like garrulously buzzing flies, plump ones and bony ones, young and old; the Rome he knows, or will know some day, must be very different from the Rome that Cécile has revealed to you during the course of these two years.

The young husband looks up from his Italian Assimil and notices that the seat opposite him is empty; the young wife at his side has stopped reading her magazine; she's looking through her Blue Guide; she's unfolding a map; you recognize it: it's a map of Rome.

You tuck in your legs so as to allow the clergyman to get back into the compartment; he picks up his breviary from the seat, but doesn't open it again; he stuffs it into one of his pockets and stares out through the rain.

What can be the cause of that discontented look on his face, that nervous tension that makes him clench those muscular fingers? Some deep latent dissatisfaction, a wave of misgiving about all that his cloth stands for, of regret at having chosen a path which, though he daren't quite admit it to himself, he feels is not the right one for him, or even, quite simply, is a blind alley for anyone, or else is it just the effect of transitory and unimportant difficulties, of some shadow which has suddenly crossed his mind, which would fit in perfectly with the hypothesis that he's been to Paris to visit a sick relative, unless he's in fact a Parisian and is going to Bourg or to Mâcon to visit this sick relative?

It may be that the nervous strain he's feeling is due not to remembrance but to apprehension, and the shadow that darkens his face is not that of the past but of something that is to come; it may be that he, too, has to make a decision, and that at this very moment, or rather a moment ago, when instead of going back to his breviary as you expected, he thrust it into his pocket with a look of disgust, he has taken a plunge which is even more important than the one this journey implies for you, he has made up his mind to renounce his cloth and his prayers, and is about to face a liberty which hitherto has terrified and appalled him, and will leave him destitute but a new man.

He looks quite calm, he's merely sulking; he'll wear his soutane to the end of his life; he must be a teacher in some minor school; he must spend his days doling out punishments to lads of your sons' age, who respect him because he's good at football.

The professor opposite you, who was looking through the pane on his left, must have recognized some premonitory sign; he gets up, puts on his coat again and tucks his briefcase under his arm, while the Englishman puts on his coat too, takes his suitcase and goes out; you'd be willing to bet he's the agent for a London wine merchant and has come down here to do a deal over the new vintage.

Rails and telegraph wires grow denser; the first houses of Dijon come into sight.

You want to stretch your legs. The novel you bought on the platform at the Gare de Lyon is lying still unopened on the seat, to the left of where you were sitting; you push it along to keep your place.

PART II

IV

Y OU'VE COME BACK, CHILLED TO THE BONE from the damp cold that met you when you got off the train, you've confirmed, from the metal placard hanging outside the coach under the corridor window just behind you, that it's bound for Dijon, Modane, Turin, Genoa, Rome, Naples, Messina and Syracuse, and you wonder if Syracuse is where the young honeymoon couple are going; they have let down the window opposite you and are leaning out to look at the rails and watch another train move slowly off into the distance, through the pelting rain.

He lifts his head; drops of water are glistening on his hair, fine dry hair the colour of the wood of your dining-room table at home; she shakes her locks and runs her fingers through their November sunshine, just as Cécile does when she replaits her jet-black, snaky tresses, and as Henriette used to years ago, when she was still a young woman.

The clergyman has pulled out his breviary from its case, which now lies on the seat, as though he'd tossed it away, near the novel which you'd put down to keep your place and which you now pick up and, before laying it on the shelf, flick through the pages with your thumb without reading it, just as you used to do with those little flick books when you were a schoolboy, only now it's not in order to see pictures moving but merely to listen, through the hubbub in the train and on the station, to the slight rustle it makes, like the sound of rain.

He's still sitting solidly there in his black dress, its folds now hanging motionless like those of a figure carved out of lava, averting his gaze from the rainswept landscape of railway lines and bridges, too familiar or too depressing for him maybe, and keeping his thick forefinger thrust between the red-edged pages of his book, bending them back; his eyes meet yours for a moment while you take your seat, only it's not at you he's staring but at the man sitting opposite you, where the professor was sitting before he left the train; this man must have got in while you were on the platform studying the placards; he hasn't yet discarded his light-grey overcoat, which is only slightly damp; you can tell he's an Italian not only because he's just pulled *La Stampa* out of his pocket, but chiefly because his pointed shoes, on the floor-heater with its diamond-shaped ripples, are black and white.

The young couple draw up the window and sit down again.

A woman comes in, dressed all in black, a worried little woman with a lined face, in a hat trimmed with net and big round-headed hatpins, holding in one hand a straw suitcase and a shopping basket, and leading with the other a boy of about ten years old carrying a hamper covered with a tomato-red handkerchief, and once they're both settled in between yourself and the clergyman, she heaves a long sigh.

You hear the voice distorted by loudspeakers finishing its harangue: "...Chambéry, Modane and Italy; take your seats please; the train is about to leave", and the dull thud of the last door banging; you're off.

There are a few round, very obvious, splashes of mud on the white leather of those shoes; they must be the only pair he brought with him when he left Italy one day when the weather was fine, last Sunday perhaps like yourself.

Here comes the dining-car attendant in his cap and white jacket, offering blue tickets for the first lunch at twelve o'clock, which the young couple take, and pink ones for the second lunch shortly after one, which you choose, as does the Italian, who looks about the same age as yourself, is probably less well off than yourself, and who maybe travels in his own country, for some Dijon firm, arranging imports of mustard or champagne.

The scarf he's still wearing round his neck is exactly the same shade of cobalt blue as his travelling bag up on the rack, just where the dark-red ink-stained briefcase had stood from which the professor of law took out the books bound in coarse black cloth which he must have borrowed from his faculty library.

What sort of personal belongings does this man travel with? An electric razor no doubt, a thing you've never been able to get accustomed to, and at least one pair of pyjamas, some of those very smart shirts they only make in Italy, leather slippers in a silk envelope such as you see in shop windows on the Corso, and then of course files, papers, typed sheets in several colours, plans, estimates, letters, bills.

The lady in black next to the clergyman, who'll probably be getting out soon (they make an odd couple, their darkness contrasting with the brightness of the young couple opposite) lifts the handkerchief covering the basket sandwiched between her and the small boy on your left (he looks like Thomas a few years ago), who's already growing restless and clapping his dangling feet together.

There goes another station: Gevrey-Chambertin. In the corridor, you catch a glimpse of the attendant's white jacket as he leaves one compartment and goes into the next; and on the other side, through the window, which is once more covered with big raindrops that stream slowly, hesitantly down in a sheaf of irregular slanting lines and mingle jerkily, you see a ghostly milk lorry move off into the distance among dimly seen shapes that are merely dark blotches against the blurred, dun background.

When Cécile comes out of the Palazzo Farnese on Monday evening and looks round for you, and catches sight of you standing there beside one of the bath-shaped fountains, listening to the sound of streaming water and watching her come towards you in the darkness across the almost deserted square, the traders will all have gone from the Campo de' Fiori, and you'll have to go as far as the Via Vittorio Emmanuele with its noisy tramways and its neon signs to find the light and bustle of the great city; but as you'll have an hour to spare before dinner, you probably won't take that overfamiliar route but will make your way slowly, deliberately, windingly along dark little streets, your arm round her waist or over her shoulders, walking just as this newly married pair will walk through Rome, if that's where they're stopping, or through Syracuse, if they're going so far, just as all those precocious young Roman couples do every evening; you'll feel your youth renewed as you wander through the scattered crowd of lovers; you'll go and walk along the Tiber, leaning from time to time over its parapets to watch the reflections trembling in the low black water, while the sound of mediocre music, mellowed by the breeze, drifts up from the landing stages where there is dancing; you'll wander as far as the Ponte Sant'Angelo, where the statues that look so white by day, with such purity in their twisted lines, will appear to you like strange, solid blots of ink; then you'll go through other dark streets until you reach once again the hub of your Rome, until the Piazza Navona, where Bernini's fountain will be luminous, and you'll sit down at the Tre Scalini restaurant, not on the terrace, which will be too cold by now and from which the tables will probably have been moved in, but as close to a window as possible, you'll order a bottle of the best Orvieto and you'll tell Cécile, in the greatest possible detail, all that you've done during the afternoon, so that she can feel utterly certain that you've come here for her sake alone, even though you've spent most of the day apart from her, that you've not just taken advantage of a journey imposed on you by Scabelli, because it's absolutely indispensable for the new life which you two are about to begin together that there should be no falsehood, not even a suspicion of falsehood, underlying it, and also so that you can talk to her once more, for the last time, about Rome in Rome.

And indeed, now that she's going to leave, and as soon as the decision has been taken, the dates are fixed and all arrangements made – that's to say not next Monday, perhaps, but within a few weeks at most – let's say at the time of your next trip to Rome, which will probably be the last time you'll see her there, you'll feel almost as if she'd already left Rome, for she'll now begin revisiting the things she knows in that city so as to anchor it more firmly in her memory, without attempting to deepen her acquaintance with it.

And so henceforward you'll be the more Roman of the two, and you're anxious that Cécile should give you the utmost benefit of her knowledge before absence and life in Paris have blurred it, and that moreover she should make use of her last weeks here, of this brief delay (if needs be she might take a few days' holiday after she has left the Embassy) to become acquainted with the things that you love and that she has not yet seen, notably the things that are of real interest, whatever she says, in that Vatican Museum which hitherto she has refused to visit, not only on account of her general dislike of the Catholic Church (an insufficient reason), but also because, ever since she met you, that city has represented – and with some justification, however sincerely you asserted your independence of mind – all that prevented you from leaving Henriette, all that prohibited you from starting life afresh, from sloughing off the old man which you were fast becoming.

But now, by making this decision, by taking this journey for her sake alone, you'll have proved to her that you've broken off all fetters of that sort, and consequently she need no longer consider these pictures and statues as an obstacle which she must skirt in order to reach you, a barrier which she must overthrow in order to release you; so that she can and must visit them now, in spite of all the irritation which this city, with its guards and its visitors, will certainly arouse in her, so as to strengthen still further your shared feeling for Rome, your shared experience in Rome, that soil in which your love is rooted – a love which is going to grow and blossom elsewhere, in that city of Paris which you both consider as your inalienable home.

Beyond the corridor, through the pane shrouded in a tissue of raindrops, you can guess from that gleam of aluminium that the object looming up, meeting you and vanishing was a petrol lorry. A slightly sharper jolt makes a sleeve button clink against a metal bar. Outside the drowned window, amid a landscape like the reflection of a landscape in a pond, shadowy triangular shapes wheel past: rooftops and a church spire.

When you left the Tre Scalini restaurant after lunching there with Cécile, the day was marvellously fine; but for the coolness of the air, it might have been August; the streaming water of the fountain glittered in the sunlight.

She complained because you were about to desert her and she would have to spend that Sunday afternoon all alone; you tried to soothe her, explaining why you had to be at your Paris office next morning, why you couldn't possibly send a wire to say you'd not be back till the following day, why it was no good for her to try and detain you: you'd still have to go on the later train, the 11.30 p.m. (the one by which you'll be travelling home next Monday).

"But I'd drop everything if I could only go to Paris with you and see you every day, even if only for five minutes, even if it had to be in secret. Oh, I know, I'm only your Roman lover, and I'm crazy to go on loving you and forgiving you like this, and believing you when you tell me I'm the only one that matters, in spite of all the proofs you give me to the contrary."

And so you assured her that you were doing all you could to find her a job, that as soon as the opportunity arose you'd bring her home with you, you'd separate from Henriette, without any to-do, and then you and she could live together.

But although, by now, you have in fact come to a decision, made enquiries among your acquaintance and secured the offer you were hoping for, although everything you said to her has now become true, yet at the time when you said it you had still taken no steps in that direction, it was all still a vague plan which you put off realizing from week to week, from one trip to the next.

She was quite aware of this as she looked at you with that sad smile you thought so unfair, and therefore she made no reply but merely set off towards the taxi rank opposite Sant'Andrea della Valle because it was getting late and you had to collect your suitcase at the Albergo Quirinale.

At the Stazione Termini you climbed from the new *marciapiede* into a first-class carriage, you chose a corner seat next the corridor, facing forward, and reserved it by putting down the newspapers and the Italian thriller you had bought in the great transparent lobby just as the clock said half-past one, you lifted your briefcase and your suitcase onto the rack above, and then you went back on to the platform to kiss Cécile, who asked you once more, in an endeavour to change your answer (and it's true that the answer has changed now, but at that time you didn't know; you were still unable to comfort or satisfy her):

"Well, when are you coming back?"

To which you replied by telling her what she already knew and what you had told her a score of times during your stay:

"Not before the end of December, I'm afraid," which has now proved untrue; then suddenly, as if she had a presentiment of what was going to happen, of what is now happening, she shook off all her melancholy, broke into a laugh and called out to you as the train started off:

"Goodbye then, have a good journey and don't forget me."

And you watched her dwindle in the distance.

Then you settled down in your compartment opposite a coloured photograph of one of the details from the Sistine Chapel, a damned soul trying to hide his eyes, above the seat that stayed empty all the way to Paris, and you immersed yourself in the letters of Julian the Apostate.

The sun was sinking as you reached Pisa; rain was falling over Genoa while you had your dinner in the restaurant car, and you watched the raindrops multiplying on the other side of the pane; you crossed the border about one in the morning, then the light was put out and you fell into a comfortable sleep from which you only awoke at 5 a.m. Lifting the blue blind on your right you saw the still-intense blackness of the night broken by the lights of a station, the name of which you made out as the train slowed down: Tournus.

Outside the rain-smudged window, intruding on the regular series of pylons like a somewhat sharper than expected tap, a chequered signal swings round a quarter-turn. A slightly violent jolt shakes the ashtray lid under your right hand. Beyond the corridor, outside the pane, which is streaked with a sheaf of tiny streams like the track of very slow, hesitant particles in a Wilson cloud chamber, a tarpaulin-covered lorry splashes through the yellow puddles on the road.

This time you won't need to go to the Albergo Quirinale, nor yet to hurry after your meal, since you'll be going back to spend the evening at 56 Via Monte della Farina, in the room which Cécile will soon be leaving, and which, consequently, you'll only be seeing once or twice more.

Then you'll start talking about plans for your future life together, about where she's to live in Paris – a point which isn't really settled yet, and that's why you prefer not to raise it until the last moment, although you have certain possibilities to suggest to her: for instance, there's that attic room available at 13 Place du Panthéon, which might do at a pinch, as a temporary measure, in spite of the extreme awkwardness of having her so close; or a hotel, which, though not at all the sort of thing you'd hoped for, might be considered for the first few weeks; then at the beginning of January the Martels, who are going away to America for a year, would certainly allow you to use their flat, only you'd have to be rather careful with them and only let them partially into the secret because, though they'll ostensibly give you their wholehearted approval, you don't know what they'll really think; and eventually, though not before February, you can have Dumont's little place when he leaves to settle in Marseille; it's rather poky and badly situated, but in the absence of anything better you could make it quite tolerable.

That's what the situation is, the problems facing you are those of a young married couple, but it's quite likely that within the next few days other possibilities might occur; you're going to keep an eye on the advertisement columns and, if you should see anything suitable, you'd snap it up immediately, you'd even get the decorators in so that everything should be ready for when she comes.

You'll lie side by side on her bed, under the photographs of the Obelisk and the Arc de Triomphe, you'll caress one another, and meanwhile, in spite of the uncertainty of your plans, you'll discuss furniture and kitchen equipment, with many pauses between your remarks, between your words; and soon, far too soon, it'll be time to go and settle the bill for the room next door, in which you won't have slept, only rumpled the bed on these two mornings, and then you'll make your way towards the station, not on foot, because of your suitcase, though you tried to make it as light as possible, but in a taxi for which you'll probably have to wait a long time in front of Sant'Andrea della Valle or on the Largo Argentina, since they pass much less frequently towards eleven at night.

In the luminous station, after climbing into a third-class carriage on which there'll be a placard: "Pisa Genova Torino Modana Parigi", and trying to reserve a seat like the one you're in now, a corner seat next to the corridor and facing forward, you'll go back to Cécile on the platform, and she'll ask you perhaps: "Well, when are you coming back?" But it'll be in a very different tone and with a very different intention, and (since not even parting can prevent this night from being a happy one) you'll be able to answer: "Not before the end of December, I'm afraid", using the very same words as last Sunday afternoon but uttering them quite differently, laughing at them yourself, convinced that your happiness is close at hand, that you're going to be reunited for good, without this constraint and irritation.

You'll stop with her till the last minute, kissing her, for this time you need have no fear lest any prominent member of Scabelli, even if by some fantastic chance one should be standing close by you, should recognize you travelling at this late hour and in such an inconvenient train. You'll climb the steps just as the whistle blows, then you'll pull down the window and lean out to watch Cécile running and waving to you till she's forced to stop, panting, flushed with effort and emotion, you'll watch her dwindle in the distance while the train leaves the station; then you'll settle down for your uncomfortable night, only you won't read for a while because your mind will be so full of her that you'll see her eyes, her lips smiling at you on the faces of all your fellow travellers and of all those waiting for other trains on the platforms of suburban stations, Roma Tuscolana, Roma Ostiense, Roma Trastevere.

Then someone will ask for the light to be put out.

Through the corridor window, a little clearer now that the rain has lessened, you catch sight of a car rather like your own, a black 15CV splashed with mud, its wipers fluttering, soon driving off and disappearing behind a barn, between vineyards; and now the dining-car attendant is coming along the corridor, waving his bell. The station of Fontaines-Mercurey has gone by.

The young couple look up quickly, but he, the more experienced traveller of the two presumably, declares that they've got plenty of time: they can wait till they hear the bell coming back.

You look at your watch: it's 11.53, four minutes before the train is due at Chalon, and more than an hour before your lunchtime.

The small boy on your right is munching a bar of chocolate that has begun to melt and run over his fingers, so that the woman in black (Henriette will look like that in a few years' time, except that she'll be a little smarter, and she'll wear grey clothes almost as dark and gloomy as that black) pulls a handkerchief out of her pocket and wipes the small hand, with an exclamation, then takes from the hamper a packet of biscuits wrapped in silver paper, which she tears open, and gives one to her son, her grandson or nephew or whatever he is; he drops a piece of it onto the hot, vibrating floor.

The clergyman looks up from his breviary, represses a yawn and lays his left hand on the window sill, tapping with one finger on

84

the metal strip with the inscription: "It is dangerous to lean out", then he rubs his shoulders against the back of the seat, sinks back, sits up again and starts reading once more as the first houses of Chalon come into sight.

The man who, earlier on, had taken your seat comes back into the compartment and slips on his black raincoat, swaying between the two seats as if he were tipsy; he loses his balance and just manages to save himself by clutching at your shoulder.

There follows a moment of stillness and silence, broken only by a few shouts and scattered sounds of creaking and grating; the raindrops on the window panes hang motionless, and no fresh ones have fallen there.

Effortlessly, the commercial traveller lifts his suitcase down from the rack: a cheap reddish-brown imitation-leather case, reinforced at the corners, in which he must keep his samples – brushes, tinned foods, polishes?

Generally they don't travel so far afield on business: they go from town to town in short stages and make their base close to the region they're prospecting. None of Scabelli's representatives in the provinces would have to undertake journeys of this length for the firm; their job never brings them to Paris: on the contrary, you send your inspectors out to see them; and this man is certainly not an inspector for any sort of firm. Perhaps he works for one of those small inefficient concerns that produce third-rate stuff and distribute it more or less haphazard, unless he's been on a holiday (surely not at this time of year!) or visiting his family, or perhaps he's been to see a woman too – you can imagine what sort of woman, in some low hotel in a backstreet.

As for the parcel done up in newspaper, which may have food in it, the remains of last night's dessert perhaps, he can't carry that about with him all day when he goes to see his customers, nor leave it in the cloakroom; it wouldn't be accepted. But after all, why shouldn't it be accepted? And besides, he may have friends here, he may live here with his wife and children (yes, he's wearing a wedding ring like yourself, like the young husband on the other side of him, like the Italian opposite you), his wife whom he thinks he's deceiving very cleverly, but who's actually well aware of what brings him to Paris, and who lets him go on lying most of the time without contradicting him for the sake of a quiet life, but blows up every now and then.

Now another man of the same sort appears in the doorway, carrying an identical suitcase, a slightly older man, redder in the face and more broadly built, to whom he calls out that he's just coming: undoubtedly the man he'd recognized in a nearby compartment and beside whom he'd gone to sit, giving you back your favourite seat.

The small boy bites violently into a hunk of bread cut in two from which a sliver of ham protrudes.

A young soldier in a wet, hay-coloured greatcoat comes in, looking lost, hoists up the painted wooden box that contains his belongings and sits down next to the Italian.

You hear the whistle blow; you see the posts and benches on the platform start to move; the clatter and the swaying begin again. Now you're out of the station. Cars are waiting at a level crossing. Those are the last houses of Chalon.

People start filing past, coatless, their blue tickets in their hands, to get their meal in the moving dining room, while the tinkling bell is heard returning.

The young bride gets up first, puts down the Blue Guide to keep her seat, tidies her hair in the mirror and, when she's done, goes out with her husband.

The widow has taken a piece of Gruyère out of the hamper and is cutting it into thin slices; the clergyman has closed his breviary and slips it into its cover.

The station of Varennes-le-Grand has gone by. In the corridor you catch sight of the back of the attendant in his cap and his white jacket. Outside the window, which is becoming blurred with rain again, you see some children scampering out of a schoolhouse.

There were two other people in the compartment, asleep with their mouths open, a man and a woman, while up above, in the globe light, the little blue bulb was glowing watchfully; you got up and opened the door, and went into the corridor to smoke an Italian cigarette. Everything was dark in the countryside after Tournus; the carriage windows projected onto the embankment squares of light in which the grass went gliding by.

You had been dreaming of Cécile, but not happily: the face that had haunted you in sleep had worn a look of mistrust and reproach, the look she'd had when she said goodbye on the platform of the Stazione Termini.

Now, if you felt so urgently impelled to get away from Henriette, wasn't it above all on account of that perpetual air of accusation that pervaded her least words and gestures? And were you henceforward to be greeted by the same thing in Rome? Would you no longer be able to find peace there, to immerse yourself and renew your youth in the free and open atmosphere of a new, unclouded love? Had age already begun to corrode that part of you that you thought safest? Were you now to be tossed to and fro between two reproachful and embittered creatures, each accusing you of cowardice? Were you going to allow that thin, ominous crack to spread till it corrupted and brought to dust the whole of that life-saving fabric which you had watched growing in strength and beauty on each of your journeys? To let that lichenous growth of mistrustfulness which made that other face so hateful to you spread over this one too merely because you dared not wrench it away with a rough movement of liberation?

True, you shrank from removing that huge insidious canker that now hid Henriette's former features like a horrible mask – hardening her mouth so that she was almost speechless (every word she uttered seemed to come from beyond a wall that grew thicker from day to day, beyond a wasteland bristling with thorn bushes that grew daily denser and sharper), and so that the lips that took your kisses out of pure habit felt as cold and rough as granite, hardening her eyes, coating them with a distorting film – but that was because you dreaded hurting her to the quick and seeing, like a surgeon when he withdraws his lancet, all that old agony suddenly gush forth.

But such a cleansing is needed if this deep, horrible, suppurating wound is to heal, and, were you to go on waiting, the gangrene would spread further and deeper still, the infection would grip you more closely, until Cécile's very face was entirely devoured by the leprous blight...

Already, it was clouded with the ominous shadow of resentment. It was high time to choose between these two women, or more precisely, since your choice was not in doubt, to face the consequences of that choice, to proclaim it openly, never mind about hurting Henriette or upsetting the children, since this was the only possible way to cure her, to cure them, to cure yourself, to safeguard Cécile's health; but how hard the decision was to take, how the knife shook in your hand!

Oh, you'd have put things off again till another week, till another trip, if you hadn't been overwhelmed by all that dreary muddle of petty vexations in Paris; you'd have tried to hedge, you'd have been the coward that Henriette thinks you and that Cécile was beginning to think you too, only she won't think so any longer now that you've taken the decisive step; you'd have gone on thus postponing the advent of your own happiness, in spite of that voice that haunted you, in spite of those reproaches that harried you, in spite of that face that had tormented you in your dream and that you could see now against the flying grass on the embankment in the squares of light cast by the carriage windows, that face from which you had tried to avert your thoughts in spite of the siren wail of anguish that had begun to sound in your heart and which you strove to silence.

You turned for help to the memory of her final laughter on the platform, but in vain, for now you seemed to hear it ring out more bitterly on your next journey in December and then turn into sarcasm on your subsequent partings.

To drive it away, to blot it out, to stifle it in the distance, you stared into the dark night, where the even darker masses of trees and houses sped by like great herds, close to the ground, you fixed your attention on the successive stations with their lights and placards and clocks: Sennecey, Varennes-le-Grand, the long empty platforms of Chalon at which the train didn't stop, Fontaines-Mercurey, Rully; then, exhausted, hoping you could fall asleep again, you went back into your first-class compartment and closed the door; pushing aside the blue blind that hid the pane on your right, you saw the lights of a station, and as the train slowed down once more you could read the name: Chagny.

Outside the window, spotted with smaller raindrops now, a village goes by which must be Sennecey. The clergyman gets up, takes his briefcase off the rack, unfastens the zip, thrusts in his breviary and sits down again. On the floor-heater a biscuit crumb is trembling in the middle of one of the diamonds, between the shoes of the lady in black and those of the young soldier, who now unbuttons his coat, spreads out his knees, leans his elbows on them and stares into the corridor.

In the third-class compartment in which you awoke, Cécile was asleep opposite you, while the blue light glowed watchfully over-head, and there were three other travellers dozing there.

Then, in the early-morning light, you saw by your watch that it was not yet five o'clock; the sky was absolutely clear and each time you emerged from a tunnel it seemed a lighter green.

Between two hills, on the other side of the corridor, you caught sight of Venus, and as the familiar station of Tarquinia appeared the people next to the window shook their heads and stretched their limbs; one of them unfastened the blind, which rose up slowly on its own, and the light, gradually growing rosier, cast a glow on Cécile's face and showed her features in clear relief; then she began to stir, sat up, opened her eyes, stared at you for a while without recognizing you, wondering where she was, and then smiled at you.

You remembered the drawn features and tangled hair of Henriette in bed beside you yesterday morning, whereas Cécile's wreath of black hair, which she had not unplaited, lay almost intact, merely a little looser from being rubbed and shaken during the night, and lay resplendent in the new light round her forehead and her cheeks like a halo of the richest, most voluptuous shadow, sending a shimmer over the smooth silken glow of her skin, her lips and her eyes, which for a moment had fluttered in dazed bewilderment, but had already resumed all their vivacity with something added, a sort of trustful gaiety that hadn't been there yesterday, and for which you felt yourself responsible.

"What, are you here still?"

Rubbing your hand over your rough chin, you told her you'd be back in a moment, then you walked up the train against the direction of travel to the first-class compartment, now empty, in which you had left Paris, you lifted your case down onto the seat and pulled out the nylon bag in which you keep your toiletries, so as to have a shave, then you came back through carriages where almost all the blinds were up, almost all the travellers already awake, back to Cécile, who meanwhile had also washed, had adjusted her plaits and reddened her lips – Cécile, whose name you did not yet know.

After Roma Trastevere and then the river, after Roma Ostiense with the Pyramid of Cestius shining in the morning sun, after Roma Tuscolana and then the Porta Maggiore and the Temple of Minerva Medica, came Roma Termini, the great transparent station, where you helped her to get down, you carried her bags, you walked through the lobby with her, you bought her breakfast, gazing through the great glass panels at the ruins of Diocletian's building lit up by the magnificent young sun, you persuaded her to share your taxi, and that was how you arrived for the first time at 56 Via Monte della Farina, in a district you hardly knew at all.

She hadn't told you her name; she didn't know yours; there had been no suggestion of another meeting; but as the taxi drove you back to the Albergo Quirinale through the Via Nazionale, you already felt convinced that some day or other you'd see her again, that this couldn't be the end of such an adventure, and that you would then introduce yourselves formally and exchange addresses and arrange to meet somewhere, and that soon she'd admit you not only into that tall Roman house into which she'd disappeared, but also into the whole of her district, into a whole section of Rome that was still unknown to you.

Her face haunted you all day while you were walking and talking, all night while you were asleep, and the next day you couldn't resist prowling about in the neighbourhood of Via Monte della Farina and even standing for a few minutes in front of No. 56, as you're going to do tomorrow, in the hope of seeing her look out of a window, then, afraid of making a fool of yourself (it was a long time since you'd behaved like that) and particularly of annoying or embarrassing her if she saw you, of getting snubbed for your importunity, afraid of bungling everything, of defeating your own ends by your impatience, you resigned yourself to going off, you tried to forget her, resolved in any case to let fate arrange the next meeting.

The soldier's shoe crushes the biscuit crumb against the floor-heater. The clergyman pulls his purse out of his pocket and counts his wealth. Outside the window, on which the spots of rain are now sparser, you see a church and a village drawing near, and you know that's Tournus.

The little blue lamp was glowing on the ceiling. The air was hot and heavy, and you could scarcely breathe; your two fellow passengers were still asleep, their heads rolling from side to side like fruit tossed by a strong wind, then one of the two awoke, a thickset man who got up and staggered towards the door.

When you strove to drive that haunting face of Cécile's from your mind, the faces of your family in Paris rose up instead to torment you; then, when you tried to drive these away too, faces from your office; there was no escaping from this triangle.

If only the light had come on again you could have read, or at least stared at something attentively; but you dared not disturb the woman who was still asleep in the dark – about whose looks you knew nothing, neither her eyes nor her features, the colour of her hair or of her clothes, whom you might perhaps have seen coming in the night before but whom you'd forgotten, that blurred shape huddled in the corner next to the window facing forward, sheltering behind the armrest which she'd lowered, breathing regularly and a little hoarsely.

Through the half-open door a strip of yellowish light, full of dancing dust, lit up your right knee and lay on the floor in a trapezium, which the burly man's shadow broke up as he came back to lean against the sliding door; you could see his right leg, his right sleeve, the soiled edge of his cuff and its ivory button, and his hand diving into his pocket to pull out a packet of cigarettes, not Gauloises but Nazionali; then as you watched the skeins of smoke rising, twisting, drifting into the compartment and finally spreading out, a more violent jolt told you that you had reached Dijon.

In the silence, broken by scattered sounds of grinding and rattling, the woman, who had woken up, unfastened the blind beside her and drew it up a few inches, letting in a thin bar of grey light, for the darkness outside was already less intense, and gradually, when the train had started off again, this bar grew broader and paler, although without the brightness of dawn.

Presently the blind was up and you could see the cloudy sky, while raindrops printed tiny rings on the window panes.

The blue lamp had gone out overhead, as had the yellow lamps in the corridor; one by one doors opened and people came out, trying to widen eyes still clogged with sleep; all the blinds were going up.

You went along to the dining car for a cup of coffee, not Italian coffee, that precious, concentrated, life-giving drink, but a black watery fluid in a thick pale-blue earthenware cup, with those odd rectangular rusks done up in threes in cellophane, which you've never met with elsewhere.

Outside, in the rain, the forest of Fontainebleau went by, its trees still hung with leaves which the wind tore off as though in handfuls and which fluttered slowly down like swarms of crimson and tawny bats, those trees which in the few days since have lost all their glory, and on which, when you passed them just now, only a few dark shreds were quivering at the tips of bleak branches, vestiges of the pomp that had been so prodigally lavished that glades and copses were teeming with it; and you seemed to see the figure of an immensely tall horseman come riding through thickets and groves, causing all this stir, clad in the tatters of a splendid habit with ribbons and gold braid fluttering loose like a comet's tail of tarnished fire, riding a horse whose dark skeleton, like damp charred beech boughs, could be glimpsed through the loosely floating flesh and fibre, the strips of skin flapping to and fro – the figure of the Great Huntsman – and you even fancied you could catch that famous wailing cry: "Do you hear me?"

Then came the outskirts of Paris, the grey walls, the signal boxes, the maze of rails, the suburban trains, the platforms, the clock.

Outside the window, ever more sparsely spotted with rain, things are more clearly visible than they were; under a clear patch of sky you see houses, posts, earth, people going about, a cart, a small Italian car crossing a bridge over the line. Two young men come along the corridor; they've put their coats on, they're carrying their cases. Senozan station has gone by.

The clergyman has taken his ticket out of his purse, which he puts back into the pocket of his cassock after counting his wealth. Then he buttons up his black coat, wraps a knitted scarf round his neck, tucks his bulging briefcase under his arm after vainly trying to make it shut, while the first streets of Mâcon disappear behind him; then, clinging to the metal rail and lifting his heavy shoes up high, he makes his way past the lady in black, between the soldier and the small boy, between yourself and the Italian, who's turning the pages of his newspaper, then goes out and stands motionless in front of the corridor window waiting for the train to stop.

What has he got inside that cheap leather case, apart from his breviary? Other books? Textbooks, perhaps, if he's a master in some school, to which he's going back to have his lunch in a few moments and, at two o'clock, to teach a class of young rascals like Henri and Thomas, or else exercises to be corrected, dictations streaked all over with red pencillings: poor, very weak, 0/10, exclamation marks, underlinings; grammar preps "to be signed by your parents", compositions – "Write a letter to a friend describing your summer holidays" (no, that was too long ago, they always set that subject at the beginning of term: "Imagine that you are the Paris representative of an Italian typewriter firm, and write a letter to your director in Rome to explain that you have decided to take four days' holiday"). "Ideas, but no plan", "Careful of your spelling", "Your sentences are too long", "Irrelevant", "You'll never convince your Italian director with reasons of that sort." Or else: "Imagine that you are Monsieur Léon Delmont, and write a letter to your mistress Cécile Darcella to tell her you have found her a post in Paris." "It is obvious that you have never been in love. But what can he himself know about it?

Perhaps he's consumed by it; perhaps he's torn between his longing for the thing he knows can save his life on earth, and his dread of a divorce from the Church, which will leave him so bereft.

"Imagine that you want to leave your wife; write her a letter explaining the situation." "You should show more sympathy with your character." "Imagine that you are a Jesuit priest; write a letter to your superior announcing your intention of leaving the Society."

Somebody has opened one of the corridor windows and the loudspeaker can clearly be heard reciting: "…Chambéry, Saint-Jean-de-Maurienne, Saint-Michel-Valloire, Modane and Italy; take your seats, please…"

These coatless, luggage-less passengers must be on their way back from the dining car after the first lunch; yes, here come the young couple, just as the guard on the platform slams the carriage doors and the train starts off; the bride sways from side to side like a young birch tree in the wind.

The widow picks out a rosy apple from her hamper, peels and quarters it and hands pieces to the small boy, one at a time, laying the peelings carefully on a piece of newspaper spread on her lap, which she folds up when she's finished, crumples into a ball and throws under the seat, after using it to wipe her penknife, which she then closes and puts away in her handbag; then she slides along to the corner seat next to the window, where the clergyman had been, and the little boy moves away from you, licking his fingers and munching his fruit; the place is full of the smell of apple.

Pont-de-Veyle station has gone by. In the corridor, two young men leaning against a brass rail in front of the window light one another's cigarettes. On the floor-heater, the young husband's foot in its light-brown crêpe-soled shoe has almost completely hidden the light-brown stain made by the fragment of crushed biscuit.

One evening, more than a month after your meeting in the train, when you had almost forgotten her, after a September or October day of lingering heat and superb sunshine, you had dined alone in a restaurant on the Corso, where you'd paid an exorbitant price for a very poor wine; as you'd had to cope with a number of somewhat thorny questions at Scabelli's, you went for relaxation to see some French film or other at the cinema at the corner of the Via Merulana, opposite the Circus of Maecenas, and there, in front of the box office, you met her; she greeted you with perfect simplicity, and you went in with her, and were given seats next to one another by the usher, who understood that you were together.

A few minutes after the film began, the ceiling slowly swung open, and so you stared, not at the screen, but at that blue strip of widening night sky full of stars, among which an aeroplane passed with its red and green tail lights, while light puffs of air drifted down into the cavern where you sat.

At the end of the film you asked her to have a drink with you, and as the taxi was taking you past Santa Maria Maggiore, along the Via delle Quattro Fontane to the Via Veneto, you told her your name and your address in Paris, and where you could be got hold of in Rome; then, under the exciting spell of the bright, fashionable throng, you asked her to have lunch with you next day at the Tre Scalini.

That was why the next morning, on your way to Scabelli's head office, you called in at the post office to send Henriette a wire letting her know you wouldn't be back in Paris until Monday; then, shortly before one o'clock, sitting at a table on the terrace, you watched Cécile coming towards you across the piazza, where small boys were bathing in the Fountain of the Rivers, looking minute beside those dazzling giants, and if at that time you'd known Cavalcanti's poetry, you'd have said that she made the air shimmer with light.

She sat down opposite you, laying her bag and her hat on a cane chair beside her, laying her long hands on the snowy cloth, where flowers stood between your glasses, stirring faintly in the delicious shade that surrounded you, the protective, kind, encouraging shade that fell from the tall old houses, cutting what had been an emperor's circus into two distinct regions.

Together you watched the spectacle of the crowd crossing the threshold of sunlight without interrupting their talk or their gestures, while the colours of their garments lit up or faded, while unexpected glints shone suddenly in black hair, in the folds of black dresses, and what had been a blaze of whiteness revealed a prodigiously varied iridescence.

Together you praised the piazza, the fountain, the church with its two elliptical spires, those embryonic songs, and for the first time you talked to one another about Rome and its buildings, those of the seventeenth century to begin with; and then Cécile, wishing to show you her favourite corners, took you that afternoon for a long walk past all the Borromini churches which were still unknown to you; and tenderness soon crept into your companionship.

On the floor-heater the ball of newspaper rolls over as far as the Italian's feet. The young soldier, whose hay-coloured coat is dry now, gets up and goes out. A man walking up the train thrusts his head in, then, realizing his mistake, goes off again.

The train was crammed, although it was wintertime; it was somewhere in this district, between Mâcon and Bourg, and about this time of day; you'd had the first lunch and were hunting for your two third-class places; Henriette insisted it was farther on, and she was quite right, and yet you kept opening doors (with the greatest of ease, as you were stronger then than you are now), thrusting your head in and withdrawing it on realizing your mistake, just as that man has done.

You nearly did the same thing when you came to your own compartment, because all the occupants were different; they included now a family with four children who had taken possession of the seats you had left, carefully tidying away on the rack above them the books you had left to keep those seats.

You had waited in the corridor, looking out at the fields, the dark woods and vineyards, the low gloomy sky above, the snow which began to fall at Bourg, snowflakes flattened against the pane, clinging to the frame of the window, until you got to Chambéry where you managed to sit down again, Henriette next to the window and you beside her, just like the honeymoon couple, only facing the other way.

The snow had stopped falling by then; under a milky sky, it covered all the mountains and trees and the roofs of houses and stations; you had to keep wiping away the steam that condensed on the icy pane.

That night, after you'd crossed the border, the carriage was badly heated and you sat huddled in your coats; she went to sleep with her head on your shoulder.

Another man, walking down the train in the direction of travel, thrusts his head through the door and then goes off. The young soldier comes back and sits down. With an unintentional kick he sends the ball of newspaper rolling back under the seat.

Before your next visit, you had written to let her know you were coming – the first letter you'd ever written to her, very different from today's letters, for since then "Dear Madame" has given way to "Dear Cécile" and now to lovers' pet names, *vous* has become *tu*, and polite phrases have been replaced by kisses.

You found her answer waiting for you at the Albergo Quirinale, as you'd suggested; she asked you to collect her at the gate of the Palazzo Farnese so that she could take you, if you liked, to a little restaurant she knew on the Trastevere.

It soon became a habit; you saw her again each time; soon autumn came, and then winter; you'd talked about music, so she got you concert tickets; she studied cinema programmes for your benefit, took to organizing all your leisure hours in Rome.

Unconsciously, unintentionally (you discovered it together while you explored your Rome for one another's sake), she had dedicated your first walk together to Borromini; since then you've had many other guides and patrons; for instance, as you'd been one day in a little antiquarian bookshop near the Palazzo Borghese (the very shop where not long after Cécile bought you for your birthday those prints of *A Building* and *A Prison* which now hang in your drawing room at 15 Place du Panthéon) and had spent a long time there looking through a volume of Piranesi depicting the ruins of Rome – almost the same subjects as those of the imaginary paintings in Pannini's picture – that winter you visited and studied all those piles of brick and stone, each in turn.

At last one evening – you'd been up on the Appian Way, you'd felt very cold there because of the wind, you'd been caught out by dusk near the tomb of Cæcilia Metella, from which you'd been gazing at the city and its ramparts wrapped in a dusty, reddish haze – she made a suggestion which, for several months now, you'd been hoping for: she asked you to have tea in her flat; and so you crossed the threshold of 56 Via Monte della Farina, you climbed up those four steep stairs, you went through the Da Pontes' apartment with its black sideboards, its armchairs with lace antimacassars, its promotional calendars (there was one from Scabelli) and its religious pictures, and then you went into her room, which looked so different and so fresh, with a bookcase full of French and Italian books, photographs of Paris and a brightly coloured striped bedspread.

There was a big pile of wood by the fireplace, and you told her you would light the fire; but you'd got out of practice since the war, and it took you a long time.

Then at last it was warm in the room; sunk deep in an armchair, you began to drink her tea, which was wonderfully comforting;

you felt a delicious weariness creep over you; you watched the bright flames and their reflections on glassware and pottery and in Cécile's eyes, close to yours; she'd taken off her shoes and was stretched out on the divan, leaning on one elbow, buttering a slice of toast.

You could hear the scraping of the knife, the muttering of the fire; the smell of toasting bread mingled deliciously with the smell of wood smoke; once again you felt as timid as a youngster; you knew that you had to kiss her, that there was no escaping from your fate; you stood up suddenly and she asked you: "What's the matter?"

You looked at her without answering, unable to take your eyes from hers, you went slowly up to her, feeling as if you were dragging an immense weight behind you; as you sat beside her on the divan, your lips still had a few terrible inches to go, your heart was as tight as a wet cloth being wrung.

She dropped the knife she was holding in one hand, the bread she was holding in the other, and you did what lovers do.

On the floor-heater, you watch an apple pip jumping from one diamond to another. In the corridor the dining-car attendant comes along again, tinkling his bell. Polliat station has gone by.

The young soldier gets up and carefully lifts down the walnut-stained plywood box with a metal handle which is all he's got by way of luggage, and goes out, soon followed by the Italian, who goes off in the opposite direction and is hidden a minute later by two women from another compartment who move off after him, while the first houses of Bourg come into sight; so that there's nobody opposite you now but the young married couple, with their big twin cases above them, made of fine, pale leather, each bearing a label on which is doubtless written the name of the town they're going to, in Sicily maybe, where it's almost summery now, the place you'd like to go to if you could take a pseudo-honeymoon with Cécile.

Besides her toiletries and all that complicated apparatus women have for doing their nails, she's sure to have in her case some light sleeveless dresses in which her bare arms can turn golden in the sun, although she'd kept them strictly hidden in Paris, which she left at the same time as you did, and will do so until the end of the journey, even if she and her husband stop off in Rome, even if they spend a day there and travel on by the evening train, to endure twenty-four hours more of a slower, noisier progress than this, more ruthlessly tossed about, more violently and frequently jolted than they are now, and arrive at last, exhausted, at Palermo or Syracuse; but as soon as they set foot there, either in the evening or in the morning, they'll see the sea, resplendent and golden like a Claude painting and full of green and purple depths, they'll breathe the delicious fragrant air, and they'll feel so wonderfully cleansed and relaxed that they'll look at one another like two champions who've just performed a great exploit; they're sure to have packed swimsuits and big bath towels with which they'll dry themselves that evening, or that morning (it'll be Monday or Tuesday, and by then you'll already be on your way home, you'll have passed the border at Modane again), before stretching out on the sand.

The woman in black has finished her lunch now, for the small boy is sucking a peppermint drop; she opens the window, on which only a few raindrops are left, to throw out the wrappings, while the almost deserted platforms, the wooden carriages, the wires overhead and the rails that echo them on the ground stand motionless now against a background of little grey huts.

Hearing the tinkle of the bell on its way back you stand up, take a deep breath of the moist air, glance at the labels on the two suitcases which, as you expected, are inscribed "Syracuse", and at the photographs in the four corners: mountains, boats, the citadel of Carcassonne and, over your own seat, the Arc de Triomphe; then you take from the shelf the novel you'd bought at the Gare de Lyon, put it down to keep your place, and go out.

V

A s you go in, you crush out the butt of the cigar you
have just smoked in the ashtray fixed to the window frame,
you bend over to pick up the book that was keeping your place
under the photograph of the Arc de Triomphe, you seize it clumsily
with two fingers of your left hand and then let it slip as a sudden
jolt sends you lurching, and you grab at the seat to steady yourself.

You hadn't thought that half-bottle of Mâcon would have had
such an effect on you; true, you've also had a cigar and a brandy,
and that glass of port before dinner that you couldn't resist asking
for, a thing you never do normally when you're by yourself; and
of course you're overtired after that shortened week in Paris,
when you had to cope with all Scabelli's current business even
more rapidly than usual, and brace yourself moreover to take this
all-important decision about your future way of life, while saying
nothing about it at home but trying to keep up appearances for the
benefit of your family – and far from attaining that indifference
you'd hoped for towards things which you knew weren't going to
last, you've found that family even more unendurable since being
practically certain you were going to leave it.

The pages of your book are soiled and creased from lying on
the iron floor; you smooth and dust them with your hand, while
that nice little boy Thomas watches you with his round eyes.

There you go again, playing your favourite game of giving
names to your fellow passengers; but this one's not really right
for the small boy wriggling in his set, who's so much younger
than your son; better call him André, for instance; the woman

who has taken him by the hand to lead him out can be Madame Polliat; as for the young couple, let's have no literary allusions, just Pierre and, let's see: Cécile is out of the question, but Agnès would do very well, Sant'Agnese in Agone, Borromini's church on the Piazza Navona.

You close your book again and put it back on the shelf, then you sit down just as the Italian comes back, much redder in the face than he was; let's give him one of those classical names they're so fond of — Amilcare? That's very un-Roman. Nerone? Traiano? Augusto?

And how do you know he's a Roman? What would you like to bet that he gets off at Turin, where his wife will be keeping dinner hot for him (he's wearing a wedding ring too), pasta, Chianti (or perhaps he's been deceiving his wife, he's told her he won't be back till the next day, and he's going to meet somebody else), or at any rate at Genoa at bedtime. You remember the Romanesque tympanum in the cathedral there, with the martyr on his gridiron; and at Turin, too, there's that cupola of Guarini's on crossed arches, which is dedicated to St Laurence; so Lorenzo would do very well in either case.

Here comes Madame Polliat, bringing back her nephew; she sits him down beside the hamper from which she extracts the bag of peppermints, almost empty now.

You can imagine her a native of some dank, gloomy town in the Alps where her father, a cashier in the bank, used to come home worn out and in the evenings, was unfaithful to his wife with café waitresses, and where the whole family went to the Protestant church on Sundays and sang hymns through their noses; you can imagine how she passed her *brevet élémentaire*, practised scales for years on an upright piano, visited Lyon with her mother for the first time at eighteen, went to a dancing class in the town hall run by the music master, and then, at a New Year's ball, met a medical student home for the holidays who invited her out to a café; and how they met again, how she went to the station to see him off and took a platform ticket, and watched the last coach disappear into the distance;

and how she then began writing to him secretly, and the family found out, and there was quite a little scene in front of the piano, and they made enquiries about the young man which proved so satisfactory that the correspondence received official sanction;

and how she took to reading novels, which made a different girl of her, and bought a lipstick which she kept in her bag like a talisman, and from time to time experimented with make-up in the privacy of her bedroom.

When he'd finished his studies they became engaged, and when he'd done his military service they got married; they went to Paris for their honeymoon.

He got his practice all right, but then the war came and he died, leaving her childless; since then she hasn't left her home town except to go to Bourg to visit her eldest brother who's a bank clerk, hoping to become cashier, and who's got two boys and three girls; André, the youngest, hasn't been very well, and as the doctor has said he needs rest, they're sending him to stay with his aunt.

Chindrieux station has gone by. Beyond the corridor, through the pane from which the few remaining raindrops are evaporating, you see the lake outspread like a sheet of platinum under the low grey sky.

You'll be travelling along close to the seashore, and when somebody asks for the light to be put out, if you've managed to find a corner seat somewhere, you may be able, by raising the blind beside you a little, to catch sight of the moonlight reflected in the waves under the night sky, which is sure to be clear after such a lovely day.

You'll have said and done all you had to, you'll have settled everything; even the dates will be roughly fixed; you'll be completely reconciled, oh, far more than reconciled: you'll be more closely united than you could ever be before; you'll be free from that gnawing anxiety that still persists in spite of all your reasons for hope.

Weary, but with quite a different sort of weariness, feeling utterly relaxed after your stay there, you'll fall asleep easily in spite of the discomfort, even if all the seats are taken, whereas tonight you know your sleep will be troubled.

The train will stop at Civitavecchia, and perhaps you'll guess in the darkness when it passes through Tarquinia station, then your eyes will close and you'll enjoy a foretaste, free from nightmare, of the life that awaits you, made possible by this journey; in your dreams you'll explore that country whose border you've crossed thanks to this hard decision.

At Genoa the hubbub in the station will wake you before day; you'll go along the corridor to shave, you'll have breakfast in the dining car and you'll be back in your seat when the train reaches Turin.

Then you'll gradually climb up into the Alps, whose peaks will be dazzling with snow lit up by the full brilliance of the morning sun, you'll cross white forests on the sides of great precipitous valleys, and the whole compartment will be flooded with reflected light, clear and fresh, steeping all the travellers in its grave gaiety, even those who've slept worst, but among all those faces none will show such serene joy, such release and triumph as your own, and the very customs officers at Modane will seem human to you.

On the downward slope, to be sure, the sky will be cloudier, and while you eat your lunch, you'll probably see snow falling or you'll pass through clouds, the windows will be blurred with steam and then, as you go lower, it'll turn to rain, the forest will be black once more, and the sky will grow greyer and greyer.

Soon you'll be back in this part of the country again, you'll skirt this lake in the opposite direction; but the suitcase over your head will be full, not of clean smooth linen, which by then you'll be wearing, but of soiled and crumpled things, the things you have on now.

Outside the window, from which the raindrops have all disappeared, you see Aix-les-Bains station draw slowly near and then stop, and you watch the engine and all the coaches of the Rome-Paris train go past in the opposite direction – the very train you'll have taken on Monday night and which will be passing here on Tuesday afternoon just at this time.

Last Sunday, when you looked at that same suitcase open on the table of your bedroom in the Albergo Quirinale, overlooking the noisy Via Nazionale, whose creaking trams and clattering Vespas had already woken you several times that morning, when you noticed hanging out of it the crumpled sleeve of the shirt you'd worn during the journey from Paris to Rome, since you had no clean one to put on, since the one you were going to wear was the same that you had taken off the night before on your return from 15 Via Monte della Farina, lying with the rest of your clothes on a chair beside your bed, you said to yourself, as you'd already done on several previous occasions, that on your next journey you'd have to bring a second spare shirt; and once again you've forgotten to do so.

The sun was already lighting up the two top floors of the house opposite; you folded up the unruly sleeve and shut the lid, so that you wouldn't have to spend more than a moment in the hotel when you came to collect it on your way to the station.

You had stayed very late with Cécile the evening before, unable to leave her, although you knew you couldn't spend the night there (but all that seemed so absurd to you just then), so that it was nearly ten o'clock when you went out into the street.

Cécile, you were sure, would have woken up much earlier than you, she'd have had her breakfast, tired of waiting for you; that was why you went into a bar for a *caffellatte* and one of those cakes stuffed with jam that they call croissants in Italy, taking your time over it, so that it was nearly eleven when you reached 56 Via Monte della Farina; all the Da Ponte family were at Mass, and you found Cécile alone, very annoyed because she'd got everything ready for you, tea and toast and so on, since you'd told her the night before that you'd like that... But you'd told her so many things the night before, so many whispered things, that you'd forgotten all about it.

On the floor-heater a couple of apple pips are lying still beside your left foot.

One Sunday evening rather more than a year ago, a little earlier in the season, you'd been having tea very leisurely, with the windows and shutters wide open and part of the cornice of the house opposite lit up by the fading red light of the setting sun; you were sitting side by side on the divan, both leaning against the wall, the smell of toast hanging in the air, her head resting on your shoulder, her hair touching your neck, your arm lying round her waist.

Gradually the noises in the street grew clearer, the piece of sky above the rooftops flushed to a darker pink, and then, between dishevelled clouds, the first stars appeared.

There was plenty of time still before the 11.30 p.m. train that you were both going to take, since she'd at last made up her mind to travel to Paris with you, but the coolness of the night air made you suddenly shiver.

By the light of the lamp above the small stove and washbasin in the closet which serves as her kitchen, you dried the plates and cups as she washed them; then you closed the window while she finished packing her case; you'd had your own taken to the cloakroom.

The Corso Vittorio Emmanuele was as busy as ever, but beyond it the streets were amazingly quiet, the Piazza Navona almost deserted, the Fountain of the Rivers playing in darkness, and all the tables had been moved in from cafés and restaurants.

In a third-class compartment like this one, in a corner seat next to the corridor facing forward, you watched her fall asleep, with her head on your shoulder, as soon as the light went out, as though the train were as familiar to her as her own room, since you were there with her, and next morning you breakfasted together at a table where, by good luck, you were alone, and you talked about your first meeting.

On the heated floor strip, in the space between your feet and those of the Italian opposite you, the two apple pips lie crushed in a groove, a little of their white pulp oozing out through the slits in their thin husks.

On the little round table, just level with the divan and its splendid, brightly striped cover, which you had bought her on a previous visit and which had been so smoothly spread, but which she had crumpled when she flung herself upon it, drawing up her knees, leaning back against the wall, her hair pressed against the photograph of the Arc de Triomphe, and looking like a black fine-spun cloud against the high pile of white clouds crowning that dull Napoleonic monument, kicking off her slippers with the tips of her toes and displaying bare feet, with traces of yesterday's red varnish still visible on the nails, against the many-coloured cloth (but she can't do that in Paris at this time of year),

on the little, low table, covered with a damask cloth bearing the initials, not of her former husband who was not rich enough to afford a whole new set of household linen, but of her parents or even her grandparents, as she'd explained to you over breakfast at this same table on some other occasion (you've forgotten the details),

there stood the polished silver teapot, which you knew was half-full of cold tea, with the milk pot of turquoise earthenware, the glass sugar bowl, the two big cups of fine china, one of which had a stain at the bottom, a persistent pale-brown mark with a few black specks, the flower-patterned plate on which lay four slices of toast, the nickel toaster in which these had been made, the salad plate with butter in it, the bowl full of jam,

and on the metal of the teapot a brilliant gleam of sunshine like a star in the duskiness of the room, for the shutters were barely ajar and only a single sunbeam thrust in.

"It's all cold now. Shall I go and heat some water?"

But as she sat there stiff and unsmiling, it was clear that she had no intention of bestirring herself, and in any case you didn't want tea.

"I know I'm late; I thought you'd have put everything away; I've had some coffee."

You flung open the shutters wide, and everything on the table began to glitter, and so did her nails; from where you sat the glass on the two photographs of Paris above the bed had turned into mirrors.

Outside the window, Aix-les-Bains station moves away and disappears.

Then, after travelling alongside the Lac du Bourget, in the middle of the brief late-November afternoon, you'll recognize that station, Chindrieux, as you go past. The sun, or rather the daylight, for you won't see the sun again after you've crossed the border, will be fading fast; at Bourg it'll be dusk already, at Mâcon the sky will be black, and you'll probably see nothing of all these towns and villages but their lights, their street lamps and electric signs, and then only through windows blurred with rain.

You'll see nothing of Burgundy, then; the damp chilly darkness will have settled heavily over everything, and you'll feel it pervade your own being as you draw nearer to Paris, where there awaits you an even more exacting week than last week, for now that things have been definitely settled you'll have to keep as quiet as possible about them till they can be realized; you'll have to go on living with that woman, with Henriette, in the midst of your family, as if nothing had happened, wearing a mask of silent serenity while you wait for Cécile's arrival in Paris.

What, are you really so weak then? Wouldn't it be better to tell her everything, quite honestly, as soon as you get back? Is your resolution so frail as to be at the mercy of complaints and recriminations, and of the attempt to seduce you that you know lies behind them?

No, it's not of Henriette's tears that you're afraid; will she even shed any?

Surely not: her reaction will be a far more insidious and more terrible one: there'll be that silence, that contempt, not only in her eyes but in her whole body, in her slightest gestures, her slightest attitudes; after a while she'll ask you: "How long are you staying here?", and you'll have to go.

Then there'll be that lonely life in a Paris hotel, the thing you dread above all others, and in such a situation you'll be vulnerable to the least of her attacks, the meanest of her ruses, and God knows that they'll be subtle, that she's well acquainted with the flaws in your armour and your personality.

After a few weeks of it you'd be back like a beggar before her, finally defeated in her eyes, in your own eyes, in the eyes of Cécile, whom you wouldn't even dare to see again.

No, any premature disclosure would jeopardize the success of the escape you've so elaborately planned.

It's indispensable for your success that you should be fully aware of the extent of your weakness, that you should take the utmost precautions to protect yourself against it, and consequently there's only one solution: to keep up this silence, to live this lie for weeks and possibly months more; for to imagine yourself strong would be to ensure your own ruin.

But how hard it is, how humiliating, to accept this decision dictated by prudence for the ultimate victory of love, so hard that you badly need to strengthen it still further, and above all, next Tuesday night, the nearer you get to Paris, the more firmly must you bear in mind these unwelcome but irrefutable arguments, since, intoxicated by the feeling of strength and courage you'll have gained from these few days with Cécile, you're quite capable of being carried away by the wish to make an end of things once and for all.

You'll have to prepare yourself to face those weeks and months of lying, you'll have to strengthen your determination to wait in silence, you'll have to foster and watch over your inward flame, and organize all your secret resources for your long defensive battle, while you eat your dinner in the restaurant car, while you look out through dark panes bewilderingly spangled, maybe, with thousands of raindrops, and see the banks under their blanket of rotting leaves emerge from pitch darkness as the windows of the lighted train sweep past, and the innumerable tree stumps of the forest of Fontainebleau, amongst which you catch a fancied glimpse of the immense grey tail of a ghostly horse, like a floating scarf of vapour torn to shreds by the bare and prickly branches, while above the rattle of the wheels you seem to hear the galloping

hoofs and that wail, that appeal, that objurgation, that temptation: "What are you waiting for?"

Beyond the corridor, through two panes on which the rain has
dried in smears, you no longer see the sky but only the hillside,
with terraced houses here and there and a cyclist riding at full tilt
down a little winding road, the tails of his grey raincoat flying
out behind him. Voglans station has gone by.

Madame Polliat gets up, straightens her black hat at the mirror,
thrusts a jet-headed hatpin through her hair and asks Pierre to
help her lift down her straw suitcase; he hands his Blue Guide to
Agnès, who keeps her finger between the pages as she closes it so
that he can easily find his place near the end of the book, while
the two narrow blue ribbons dangle unused, swaying gently as the
whole train rocks in a light insistent rhythm stressed by the jolts
at each interruption of the rails.

Madame Polliat has collected all her luggage on the seat, in that
corner next to the window and facing forward where she'd sat
since the clergyman left, buttons her unresisting nephew into his
coat, pulls his little scarf tight and takes a comb out of her basket
to tidy his hair, thus concealing from you Agnès's face and that
of Pierre, who has sat down and must have picked up his book
again, or rather, to judge by the movement of his left arm, which
is all you can see of him, must be leaning across his wife's knees to
look through the smeared window at the first houses of Chambéry.

How did they get to know one another? Did they meet in the
train, like you and Cécile, or were they fellow students like you
and Henriette? No, that's highly unlikely, he was probably at some
engineering college and she at the Arts Décoratifs or the École du
Louvre, or preparing her *licence* in English, and they met for the
first time at a party given by mutual friends; they danced together,
not that he was a very good dancer himself, but he succeeded in
making her shed that shyness, that lack of self-confidence that
paralysed her, and everybody noticed it; she made a joke of it
herself; people began to tease her about it; she tried not to blush,
but each time she felt her cheeks growing hot.

Next time he saw her, it was summer; he noticed that the minute he came into the room she started violently; he took her off into a quieter room; they went out on to the balcony, overlooking a Parisian boulevard; beneath them cars mingled their headlights and the shivering leaves of plane trees made a rustling sound that rose at times into a sigh. Oh, she knew she was in love, right enough; she'd walked straight into that realm she'd so often seen shining afar, in books and films, and thought inaccessible, and she wondered if it were really possible that she'd won him, that splendid young man, Pierre, when there were so many girls who, like herself, only wanted to be his slave; she dared not quite believe it, she wanted to guard against too cruel a disappointment, and stood silent, not even looking at him, while he felt quite at a loss.

How familiar it all seems: they went to clubs and film-society meetings to watch, with pious reverence, the very films you used to see at your local cinemas with Henriette; he took her to nightclubs and restaurants once or twice; they told their parents about it; they got married in church yesterday; they were worn out by the evening; there had been so much bustle in the flat and so many friends to be greeted.

But now everything's all right, they're feeling rested in spite of last night's lack of sleep, and those chaotic rooms seem very far away,

and how earnestly, in the depths of their hearts, they're vowing to be faithful to each other! How long are these illusions going to last?

Oh, if they knew why you're travelling, if you were to tell them what you too were like at their age, when you took that journey with Henriette, how you too imagined that your harmonious relationship would last for ever, and how, when the children came, you thought they'd make another bond between you, and then what happened, how it all deteriorated, and why you're here, and the decision you've had to take to make an end of things, to free yourself, wouldn't your face, your slightly hunched-up motionless figure strike terror into their hearts?

Oughtn't you to disturb that quietude of theirs, oughtn't you to tell them that they mustn't imagine they've won; that you had thought so too once, with all the sincerity of which you were then capable; that they must start right away to prepare for their parting, must uproot all their prejudices, which are due to an environment like your own, and which, when difficulties like your present one arise, will hold up their moment of decision, of deliverance, when what happened to your Henriette has happened to his Agnès, when that inexplicable contempt has overrun all her being and turned her into the mere corpse of a woman, when he too has to turn to another woman so that he can make a fresh start, another woman who seems quite different, like youth preserved?

The train has stopped. Madame Polliat lowers the window briskly; the platform is on that side. She entrusts her luggage to Pierre, asking him to pass it to her when she's got out, leads off her nephew André, shuffling apologetically between your feet and those of Signor Lorenzo.

Two boys of about sixteen and eighteen, standing in the corridor, let her pass and then come in; they're wearing leather jackets with zip fasteners and carrying students' briefcases.

You catch sight of the widow's hand reaching up for the straw suitcase and the shopping basket and the hamper from which so much food had emerged, that bony clutching hand. You can't see the small boy beside her, who may not be her nephew after all: she may not be a widow, her name's not Madame Polliat, and it's very unlikely that he's called André.

The two brothers settle down in the seats they had occupied, the younger next to the open window, with their briefcases above them in the rack, they unzip their jackets, and Agnès, looking at them, wants to have boys like that, lively and good-looking, and says to herself: when Pierre is as old as that gentleman who's watching me, when we're an old married couple, then I shall have sons like these, only they'll be even more smartly turned out, for we'll have managed to give them a far better education than these boys can have got at some school in Chambéry.

Two Italian workmen, talking noisily, unload their knapsacks and lay them on their knees; now all the seats are taken.

Three conversations in two languages mingle in the air, and you make no attempt to disentangle them, while through it all there sounds the unintelligible voice of the loudspeaker announcing that the train is about to start.

And the familiar noise begins again, and the swaying movement, and the rush of the outside world towards you, towards that far-flung line that passes through your seat and beyond which things become invisible; now the wind sweeps in and dries up the air suddenly. Pierre shuts the window.

Just as you are leaving the town, the ticket collector taps on the pane with his punch. Everybody gets busy in silence.

The station of Chignin-les-Marches has gone by. Outside the window the hillsides are covered with denser and darker forests on which there's a little snow already.

Leaning out, in the lovely sunshine of that autumn morning, you looked down at a heavy cart loaded with charcoal turning a corner with difficulty. It's true that winter comes even in Rome, and that most likely next weekend the weather won't be as mild as the previous one; the room in which you're theoretically going to live will be icy, and in Cécile's room next door there'll be a good fire blazing almost all day.

You felt her hand stroke your head, which is already growing a little bald; leaning on her elbows beside you, she was saying:

"D'you know, it's all really too idiotic! What a pity that you feel obliged to take a room, each time you come, at that ridiculous Albergo Quirinale, and go back there every night as if you were a boy at boarding school or a soldier in barracks who has sneaked out but has to be back for roll-call next morning.

"And honestly it's rather like that, in spite of all your protests. How can you keep up this lie with her, if indeed it really is a lie as you insist, if it's not rather your whole relation with me that's a lie?

"Don't protest: I'm quite aware that you love me and that you're being sincere when you tell me that you find it increasingly hard to bear her; I know all about it, don't tell me, I know by heart all you're going to say to me, that in this case it's nothing to do with her but with your firm, with Scabelli, who wouldn't tolerate... Oh yes, you've explained it all to me already, and I'm only scolding you to tease you, to be revenged on you for your lack of courage, for which I've really quite forgiven you.

"But if only you could get free from it all one day; well, I heard this morning that the tenant of the room next to this, through that door with the huge old-fashioned bolt, is leaving the house this week; I've only got to ask the Da Pontes to let you have it; they're sure to agree (you're my cousin, aren't you?), and we should have such peace together.

"I heard him go out a short while ago and I'm sure he hasn't come back, we'll just have a peep."

She drew the bolt, which was rather stiff; the hinges creaked as she opened the door.

The shutters were still closed; you saw the big iron bed, still unmade, a suitcase standing open and all sorts of ties and socks scattered about on the chest of drawers, next to the enamel washbasin on its three-legged stand, with its jug and pail.

And you began to imagine the thing that's going to happen tomorrow, without suspecting that your dream was so soon to be realized, without even intending to realize it; you imagined it as a remote possibility with which you toyed for a moment to suit Cécile's whim: your own belongings scattered untidily about the furniture, on those old red-velvet armchairs, the bed made up for you under that quilt and those blankets with clean sheets which you would not soil, which you won't soil but merely rumple to look as if you've slept in them, and the door standing open all night long.

On the floor-heater, amidst the muddy footprints left by the damp shoes of people coming in from outside, like threatening snow clouds, you stare at the constellation of tiny stars of pink paper or brown cardboard which have just been clipped out of the tickets.

The ticket collector had examined yours; you had gone back into your compartment with Cécile. You were sitting side by side like Pierre and Agnès, in silence; you were reading a book, as he is, a book which you'd put down to keep your seat and picked up again when you came in; you don't know exactly what it was, but probably a book about Rome, and from time to time you pointed out some passage to her.

But soon your eyes strayed from the lines, and while you stared through the pane at the very landscape through which you're travelling now, watching the mountains go past in the opposite direction, you asked yourself: why can't things always go on like this? Why do I always have to leave her? We've taken one great step forward: I've succeeded in having her with me elsewhere than in Rome; our life together has succeeded for once in breaking out of the narrow limits within which we were forced to restrict it; on all my other journeys we had to part, to say goodbye at the Stazione Termini; we've at last managed to shift that frontier; and during the whole of her stay in Paris, where usually it's such anguish to me to be so far from her, with all those miles and all those mountains between us, I shall know that she's there, that I'll be able to see her from time to time.

Of course this gave you great happiness and a sense of victory, but your joy was mingled with the sadness of knowing that this was only a first step, that you hadn't the least idea when the others could be taken, that your parting was only temporarily postponed, the frontier crossed only this once, that on the next journey everything would begin again just as it was before, and you'd have to part from one another at the Stazione Termini, that this was only an exception and nothing was really changed.

Up till then you had never envisaged making such a drastic change; you were satisfied with your double life; in Paris you dreamt of your existence in Rome, but it hadn't seriously occurred to you that you might change your existence in Paris.

And now your mind was dominated by that possibility which had at first appeared as a crazy, terrible temptation, which then slowly infiltrated into all your thoughts until you've gradually grown accustomed to it, which haunts you continually, which has made Henriette so hateful to you.

How rash you'd been to undertake that journey from Rome to Paris together! Until then things had gone on so calmly, and now you felt their inadequacy, and you knew she felt it too, that she was going to do her utmost, with consummate art, to make of your relationship something, if not permanent, at least as enduring and constant as your social and professional position would allow, that she too was haunted by the possibility of dominating you unchallenged, of reaching and enabling you to reach that state of magnificent uncorrupted love, that new freedom of which your affair had only, hitherto, offered an unworthy reflection, always interrupted, always piecemeal, never involving more than a part of yourself.

And now, after a year, that possibility is going to be realized: that's what you've decided to do; that's what you are actually doing.

You left Chambéry; you watched Voglans go past; you stopped at Aix-les-Bains; you went out into the corridor together to look at the lake.

A man thrusts his head through the doorway, looks right and left, sees that he's in the wrong compartment, moves off and disappears.

One winter morning before daybreak, rather less than three years ago, in the days when you'd never visited the Via Monte della Farina and Rome still meant solitude for you, you arrived at the Stazione Termini (that frontier where your life with Cécile was usually cut short, and which, a year ago, you had provisionally crossed with her); your companion on this occasion was a travel-weary Henriette, whom you still loved or at least whom you were not conscious of loving less, since there was as yet nobody with whom to make a comparison; Henriette, already growing older and harder and more withdrawn under the destructive influence of her contemptuous feelings, who had nevertheless forgiven you everything for the sake of this journey, so many times postponed, which she'd so longed to repeat, for the sake of this city which she'd so longed to revisit, where she sought, as you are seeking now, a renewal of youth which was not to be granted her, where she hoped to pick up the thread of those days before the war when she'd seen it for the first and only time, that thread which since then has grown so tangled and so badly frayed,

you took a taxi to the Albergo Quirinale, where you'd reserved a double room for the occasion, larger, better and more comfortable than any of the single rooms you've had there since, and which you've remembered with a certain longing every time you've got your key from the porter, so that the hotel has become, as Cécile noticed (but you've only just become aware of this), a sort of citadel of Henriette's within Rome, surreptitiously and unobtrusively obliging you, every time you set foot in it, not so much when you go back at night but in the mornings when you wake up there and gradually become conscious of your surroundings, to turn your thoughts towards her, if only with hatred against her for thus pursuing you.

She signed her name besides yours, happily. You asked for breakfast to be sent up. The shutters were still closed. It was very cold outside, but for once the room was well heated. She took off her shoes and lay down on the bed, and you waited for daylight together.

She had looked forward so eagerly to this long-postponed visit, she had expected so much from it, hoping to regain that contact with you which she'd been gradually losing, day by day, over the years, and to close the gulf between you which grew more marked after each of your journeys, since each time you became more bitterly conscious of the difference between that freer, happier life which the air of Rome promised you and the oppressive burden of life in Paris which weighed her down, and since each time you seemed to her to be losing more of your integrity in Paris, in that job of yours which was increasingly remunerative, although within certain irksome limits, and to the absurdity of which you tried increasingly to close your eyes; thus, every time you brought some new business connection to dinner, you dropped a little more of your former pride and judgement, you gradually came to imitate their vulgar laughter, their moral and immoral clichés, their way of referring to their staff, their competitors and customers, degrading yourself, grovelling before that system which, formerly, you'd known how to criticize, with which, formerly, you'd only compromised, maintaining a certain detachment, at least in your remarks, and then, for a while, at least in your remarks to her, but now surrendering to it more and more blindly, each time protesting that it was for her sake, so that she might have a better home, enjoy this handsome flat, so that the children might be more smartly dressed, so that she should have no cause to reproach you, as you used to tell her, ironically in the old days, but gradually drifting further and further away from her and from your real self.

And she was well aware that the streets of Rome with their gardens and their ruins were linked in your mind with a vision whose hold on you was growing prodigiously, the vision of all that you had given up in Paris, that Rome was the place where you felt genuine, that a whole side of yourself had developed there in which she played no part, and it was to this radiance that she so longed to be introduced by you.

The only pity was that it was all, at that time, merely a dream and a spell, still vague and unexpressed: you couldn't recognize anything; you had studied nothing; you'd brought no enthusiasm to it; you were incapable of explaining anything about it.

Oh, she'd imagined that your acquaintance with this city was incomparably deeper, that your love for it was based on that knowledge which only Cécile has enabled you to acquire; that was why, as you walked about the streets with her that winter, you could give no reply to the many questions she put to you, making you aware at every step of your own insufficiency, of the fragility of that refuge you'd thought you had built for yourself; as she walked beside you, trying to understand, asking for your help, abandoned by you, she soon came to represent for you the impossibility of ever attaining the thing which the streets of Rome usually seemed to promise so infallibly, of ever being able to verify or even hear

properly the message they were telling you, which you felt must
be so easy to interpret, like a Latin translation at which one casts
a casual glance, intending to examine it at leisure.

Faced with your silence, your powerlessness, she gave up; suddenly she began to hate everything that she too had once loved so
much, and by the end of that first day you knew by the strained
look in her eyes that she wanted to go away, and you wished she
were away so that once more things would seem easy for you in
Rome.

The snow began to fall, the first and only time you've seen it in
Rome, not in big flakes like the snow now blurring the mountain
landscape but melting as it fell, lying as slush in streets suddenly
silent and deserted save for a few figures hurrying by, muffled in
their coats.

She caught a cold and was forced to stay in bed the whole of
Sunday, while you had to spend the following day almost entirely
at Scabelli's, so that she was reduced to going out by herself and,
not knowing where to go, wandered in utter boredom from church
to church, telling a few beads in each of them.

She wanted at all costs to see the Pope, which you refused to
do; you didn't try to prevent her; and when she came back she
seemed ill at ease, but her eyes had a fanatical glitter. You met
only for meals, just as in Paris, and at night; the end of the visit
came as a relief to both of you.

If only this journey with Henriette hadn't taken place so stupidly in the depths of winter, in the middle of a cold spell, merely
because it had been postponed so long, because you'd decided on
it in a fit of irritation, just to get it over with... But mightn't it
have been possible to discover something wonderful there, even
amidst all that snow and fog and rain, if only you'd known Cécile
then, if she'd already shown you how to explore Rome and that
side of yourself that Rome fostered?

But would you have loved Cécile herself much if there hadn't
been, before you met her, this unfortunate journey? But if you'd
already known Cécile then, would you have drifted apart from
Henriette, would you be travelling in this train now?

Of course everything would have happened quite differently, and perhaps you'd have long ago...

An old Italian with a long white beard casts a glance through the door.

There was a thin mist over the lake, and then the clouds thickened and the rain began to fall more densely, blurring the windows.

You went back to your seats again, you took up your book and she leant against your shoulder; but you were unable to start reading again because you felt that not only was this crossing of the frontier only temporary, but also that it was far less effective than you'd imagined, that in the coming fortnight you'd be far less with Cécile than you could be in Rome, that you'd only be able to see her from time to time, and far more furtively, that the frontier, even on this occasion, was not abolished but only moved back a little, that your parting would take place in Paris instead of in Rome, at the Gare de Lyon actually, on your arrival, instead of at the Stazione Termini on your departure.

You had closed your book; Cécile was deep in hers, bending over it to see because the light was bad, with rain falling over the Jura and dusk falling over Burgundy, her body was no longer touching yours. Neither of you spoke.

Oh, already (you realize it now; at the time there was only that uneasiness, that feeling of unaccountable anguish that crept over you as though something, some demon of weariness and cold, were concealing your real self from you; only now do you realize it, for you'd put it out of your mind since then, you'd been careful during these last weeks to avoid recalling memories of that sort, for you hadn't had the time, you were fully occupied by too many cares at once; and it's taken this pause in your life made by a clandestine journey, a journey which for once has not been undertaken on your firm's behalf and on which business problems no longer trouble you; it's taken this respite for them to come back and harass you, for you'd been unwilling, lately, to give a thought to anything that might in any way shake your faith in the existence, the reality of the solution which you've at last determined to reach, of the imminence of that new and happier life),

already things were proving precarious, they were beginning to break up, to loosen, to spoil; your separation had already begun, and not only had the frontier not been crossed even provisionally, not only had it merely been shifted, but it had been shifted far less than you persisted in believing: instead of a swift goodbye at the Stazione Termini your parting was being dragged out through the whole journey, you were being wrenched from one another slowly, painfully, fibre by fibre, without clearly recognizing what was happening, and although you were still sitting side by side, each of the stations you came to, Culoz, Bourg, then Mâcon and Beaune, meant, as on every other occasion, a further widening of the distance between you.

You were a helpless onlooker at this betrayal of yourself; and just as within your compartment talk in Italian had gradually given place to talk in French with intervals of silence, so within your head the vision of the streets and houses of Rome, the Roman faces that filled them, with Cécile's face always in the centre, lost ground with every mile you travelled, giving place to other faces with those of Henriette and of all your children in the centre, to other houses centring round your own flat, 15 Place du Panthéon, and to other streets.

When, after Dijon, you went to dine in the dining car together, there was in your eyes that pathetic appeal of those who already feel themselves swept away to a lonely doom, far apart; by your brief expressions of enthusiasm, your studied protestations of happiness you sought to avert or cover up that feeling of disloyalty, that sense of exile which had crept between you, a barrier of ever-increasing opacity, but already you were like a lover vainly clasping the dead body of his mistress, her illusory presence only enhancing the pain and the certainty of her loss, already Cécile had begun to change into that ghost that she was to be for you during the whole of her stay in Paris.

Standing at the window of the corridor, while the rectangles of dim light shed by the lights of the train swiftly disclosed tree trunks, banks and dead leaves, you talked to her, hoping thus to exorcise the shadows gathering round her, you talked without a pause, hardly waiting for her answers, as if the slightest silence that occurred might precipitate her disappearance, leaving you face to face with a different, unknown woman to whom you had nothing to say, and in particular you told her the legend of the Great Huntsman who haunts the groves and dark rocks uttering his unvarying cry that echoes far and wide – the meaning of it is obscure, as if he spoke with the accent of far-off times, probably: "Where are you?" – and you kept this up till you reached the station.

On the floor-heater, Lorenzo Brignole shifts his left foot, disturbing and partially concealing the tiny cluster of pink and brown stars and sending the ball of newspaper, which its complicated journeyings under the seat have brought into your neighbourhood, beyond the groove of the sliding door, the frontier of your compartment.

Stop thinking about that past journey to Paris with Cécile; only think about tomorrow and Rome.

"Even if I could arrange to come here just to see you, for if I'm to settle in here it would really have to be without the firm's knowing…"

"Why, how can they object to your staying with friends once in a while? Are you afraid of their checking up on your address to see if your lodgings are respectable?"

"They're quite capable of that, and they might contrive to do it without either of us knowing, but even that's not certain, and I want to avoid such a situation at all costs… Even so, the Da Pontes—"

"Come now, don't make them out to be more naive than they are, in a city where it's so easy for them to salve their Catholic consciences by going to mumble a few prayers next morning in one of those innumerable nearby churches that deal out indulgences *toties quoties*, the Gesù for instance... Did you honestly believe we'd completely taken in those shrewd old eyes? They know all about us, and they've given us their blessing. You can be quite sure they've sent one of their grandchildren to follow you and find out where you work and where you live. All they ask is that certain appearances should be kept up, but of course they insist on that; if a neighbour comes to see them while we're out, the old grandmother or her sister will show her the whole apartment, particularly our two rooms, and she's got to be able to explain that you're my cousin and that you've slept in that bed, and the look of the place must be consistent with her story, for the visitor's likely to be shrewd and nosey too, and all ready to gossip. They want us to deceive them as far as we can, so that they can be sure all precautions have been taken.

"Oh yes, I'm quite sure they'll agree, provided we go on behaving as we've done up till now; far from being a nuisance they'd keep watch over us, all of them, even the grandchildren and nephews who only come from time to time, who wouldn't be told anything of course but who'd all guess, who'd feel the situation in the air – they all know how to hold their tongues as well as they know how to talk – and they'd protect us and envy us."

You were both standing in the doorway between the bright room and the dark room, and she was whispering these words not in your ear but against your mouth, with her lips touching yours from time to time.

"I've lived here for years now, and they've always been kind to me, but in spite of their friendliness, in spite of the long wearisome harangues they feel bound to make me, one after the other, there are a good many aspects of their minds, particularly as regards their religious beliefs, about which I've not yet formed a clear opinion.

"Anyhow, whether they realize it or not (but I think they do realize it and that's why I feel so much at home with them), their brand of Catholicism is poles apart from that dispensed by those regiments of priests that wander like huge flies over the face of Rome.

"In any case, they know (that's obvious; if you knew them as well as I do you'd realize it from the way they look at us when we go out and I wave to them through the glass door into their kitchen), they know we've got a clear conscience, or at least they believe we have (no, I'm not reproaching you: I'm well aware that you believe it too or that you try to believe it, and I'll quickly add, to stop you looking vexed with me, that you sometimes succeed in believing it – I wish I could say you often do; well, it's true: you've made some progress, I've been some use to you during these two years we've lived together at such rare intervals; I've really helped you, admit it, to be more like the free, honest man you want to be, in spite of your position and your wife and children and your flat in Paris), they believe we've got a clear conscience, and they don't care whether it's thanks to their indulgence or in some other way. Oh, how much you'd gain from their deep, wise complicity!"

Then, as though in utter weariness, she kissed you, she moved away to close the door, and the hinges creaked again; she pushed the bolt.

"But of course in a few weeks' time, if you've not made up your mind, if you don't ask them to keep it for you, they'll let it to somebody else, in a few weeks or even a few days..."

"When is he leaving?"

"Thursday, I believe, or Friday. Oh, I know I've been talking crazily; I let myself be carried away, which doesn't often happen to me. Of course I know that on your next trip you'll have to leave me again every night and sleep at your hotel, while on the other side of the wall there'll be somebody or other new. I think it's time we went out for lunch."

The Corso Vittorio Emmanuele was as busy as ever, the door of Sant'Andrea della Valle stood open, and the little streets beyond the Corso were swarming with people coming back from Mass, girls in white frocks, young men in light-blue suits, old ladies in black, bustling seminarists with sashes of every colour.

On the Piazza Navona, now bare of all the tables you had seen there the last time you crossed it, countless groups stood about arguing, while around them all three or four Vespas each carrying two or three riders chased one another with shouts and laughter, thus restoring the huge oval space to its original purpose as a circus.

The Fountain of the Rivers streamed and glittered in the sun. But for the coolness of the air it might have been August. You went into the Tre Scalini.

Through the thickening steam cloud on the window, you're aware of snow still falling, a little less densely. A station goes by but you can't read the name.

You straighten your aching limbs, feeling tired already, and thinking that you've still got to endure a whole night on this hard seat. You look at your watch: it's only half-past three, there's still an hour to go before you reach the border, and fourteen hours before you reach Rome. Now you're passing through a short tunnel.

One of the boys wants to go out, the older of the two, Henri, for that's what Henri will be like in a year or two, but better-dressed, smarter-looking, for you'll have given him a far better education, not quite as strapping to be sure, but that won't matter with all the awards he'll have won, and the fact of your being separated from his mother won't prevent you from going on seeing him when you like, whenever you both want to, instead of that oppressive obligatory meeting at supper each evening, instead of the irksome, noisy propinquity of family life, won't prevent you from keeping an eye on his studies, from helping him on in life later on, from giving him all the support you can,

won't prevent him from visiting you when you're living with Cécile, from coming to have lunch with you, from taking you to see how he's fixed up his room at 15 Place du Panthéon one day when he knows Henriette has gone out;

the fact of being separated from his mother won't prevent you, after some little while, you know it can't prevent you, from going to see her sometimes; you'll keep it secret from Cécile.

Now you're passing through another rather longer tunnel.

You've got to keep your attention fixed on the things you can actually see: this handle, that shelf, the rack with the luggage on it, that photograph of mountains, that mirror, that photograph of little boats in a harbour, this ashtray with its lid and its screws, this rolled-up blind, that switch, that alarm bell,

on the people in your compartment, on the two Italian workmen, on Signor Lorenzo Brignole, on Agnès and Pierre, who have begun to yawn a little and are taking up their books again bravely, after giving one another little kisses on the forehead, on that boy, the younger of the two, who's wiping the steam from the window with his sleeve,

so as to put an end to this inward tumult, this dangerous brooding and mulling over memories;

you must think not of Henri, but of that young man who's just gone out, or of his brother sitting next the window, to whom Thomas will certainly bear no resemblance in a few years' time, and whom you can call André now that the widow's nephew has left and the name's available, Sant'Andrea della Valle, a name you've always liked and you'd have certainly given it to your third son (only after Jacqueline you didn't want any more children), of these two lads who must be going back to their village in the mountains after spending the week at a technical or rather a commercial school in Chambéry, a week which has ended at midday this Friday – why? Has something happened at home? Have their parents sent for them by telephone? Or perhaps they go home every night, and today, one of their teachers being ill, their afternoon classes are cancelled.

Now the train is passing through yet another tunnel; the light goes on in the ceiling.

The Italian workman beside you unfastens the strings of his knapsack and pulls out a case, which he opens to show his friend a necklace of black glass beads, a present for his wife or for his lover? You try to follow their conversation, but it's in a dialect to which you're not accustomed.

Here's the older lad coming back. There is no more landscape now; there are only window panes that turn black with shiny lights when you go through a tunnel, then white like snow.

Go and smoke a cigarette in the corridor, occasionally wiping away the steam from the window with your sleeve, and look out.

You take up the unread novel from the shelf and put it down on the seat.

VI

YOU HAVE TO GO BACK; the French police are passing through.

As you crush out your fag end in the ashtray you notice that you've only eight cigarettes left, then you pick up the book off the seat and replace it on the shelf. All your movements are nervously jerky.

Signor Lorenzo's passport is green; Agnès and Pierre have brand-new ones in blue cardboard covers; those of the two Italian workmen who are now sitting in the boys' places are somewhat shabbier; but yours has undoubtedly seen most service, an old-style passport in a thin cover which you've had since 1950, having already had it renewed twice.

As the train has stopped, the heat has become more oppressive. You know you're at Modane, but the windows are so thick with steam that you can see nothing of the landscape, which must be covered with snow.

When the preoccupied French customs official moves off, Agnès and Pierre exchange glances of relief. The Italian official, wearing a grey-green uniform and boots stained with icy mud, makes the two workmen open the bags they had left in the seats they had been occupying, and you watch them unpack shirts, socks and small presents, while Signor Lorenzo looks on with an air of disgust, fanning himself with his open passport, inside which you catch intermittent glimpses of his photograph and manage to read his name upside down: Ettore Carli.

The workman sitting next to the window is called Andrea, but you haven't time to make out any more; the other's surname ends in —etti.

When the formalities are over, after a slamming of doors and blowing of whistles the train starts off, then stops with a violent jolt, and then really gets going into the Mont-Cenis tunnel.

Suddenly the light goes out; there's complete darkness now save for the red glimmer of a cigarette in the corridor with its almost imperceptible reflection, and silence, against a background of deep breathing like that of sleepers, and the rumble of wheels reverberated by the unseen vault overhead.

You look at the marks and hands of your watch glowing green; it's only 5.14, and what's liable to ruin you, as you realize with sudden terror, what's liable to ruin the splendid decision you'd reached at last, is the fact of having to spend another twelve hours or more, except for the briefest intervals, in this henceforward haunted place, self-pilloried, twelve hours of inner torture before reaching Rome.

The light is restored, the talk starts up again, but you are more and more cut off from it as though by a barrier of noise and migraine; the windows grow gradually greyer, then all at once turn white.

Suddenly, through the clear patch which Pierre has rubbed in the middle of the window pane with his handkerchief, you catch sight of the corner of a station going by and you know it's Bardonecchia, while beyond the corridor, too, you begin to make out something, though the thickness and opacity of the condensation diminish the shapes of the mountains outlined against the sky.

Next Tuesday, when, exhausted by your third-class journey, you've let yourself into your flat at 15 Place du Panthéon, you'll find Henriette waiting for you and sewing, and she'll ask you what sort of trip you've had, and you'll answer: "Just as usual."

And that's when you'll have to take care not to betray yourself, for she'll be watching you terribly closely, and no doubt it's useless to hope that she'll believe such a remark; isn't she well aware already that this was no usual journey? Will you be able to conceal your smile of triumph from her, to leave her in sufficient ignorance and uncertainty of what exactly has happened, of what you'll have decided? You must; you ought to; it would be much safer so.

Next Tuesday, when you're back in Paris at 15 Place du Panthéon, she'll know as soon as she sees you that her fears, that your wishes are going to be realized; it won't be necessary to tell her, it won't be possible to conceal it from her, and then she'll do her utmost to extort particulars from you; she'll ask when Cécile is to come, but that you don't know yourself, and you won't know it even then; you'll tell her that you've no idea, which will be the honest truth, but she won't believe you, she'll pester you with questions, spoken or silent, and there'll only be one way out for you, to explain to her in detail how things happened.

Of course it would have been better if she'd known nothing, if she'd suspected nothing until Cécile was actually there, but since she's sure to know already...

Next Tuesday, when you find Henriette waiting for you and sewing, you'll tell her before she even has time to ask you anything: "I've lied to you, as you must have guessed; it wasn't for the firm that I went to Rome this time, and of course that's why I took the 8.10 train instead of the other faster, more comfortable one which has no third class; it was solely for Cécile's sake that I went to Rome this time, to prove to her that I've definitely chosen her rather than you, to tell her that I've at last succeeded in finding her a job in Paris, to ask her to come so that she may always be with me, so that I can enjoy that wonderful life with her which you haven't been able to give me, nor I you; I admit it: I'm to blame towards you, agreed; I'm ready to accept and confirm all your reproaches, to plead guilty to whatever faults you like if it can help in the slightest degree to comfort you, to lessen the shock, but it's too late now: the die is cast, I can't change anything, I've made that journey, Cécile is going to come; you know I'm no great loss, it's not worth bursting into tears like that..."

But you know quite well that she won't shed any tears, that she'll merely look at you without uttering a word, that she'll let you run on without interrupting you, so that you'll stop of your own accord from sheer weariness, and that you'll realize then that you're in the bedroom, that she's lying in bed sewing, that it's late, that you're tired after your journey, that it's raining outside...

Next Tuesday, when you go into her bedroom, you'll tell her all about your journey and you'll say to her: "I had gone to Rome to prove to Cécile that I chose her rather than you; I had gone intending to ask her to come and live with me for good in Paris..."

Then your own voice cries out within you in a wail of terror: ah, no, that decision which cost me so much to take cannot be allowed to disintegrate so; am I not in this train, travelling towards my wonderful Cécile? My will and my desire were so strong... I must put a stop to such thoughts, get a grip on myself, reject all these fancies which assail and threaten me.

But it's too late now, the chain of your thoughts, forged more firmly by this journey, rolls on as relentlessly as the train itself, and in spite of all your efforts to break free, to turn your attention elsewhere, to concentrate on that decision which you feel escaping you, you are caught up and fettered by it.

The man you call Pierre, whose real name you hadn't time to read on his passport just now, has stopped looking through the window, for you're going into a tunnel and the noise of the great train that's carrying you along is dulled once more as if it were something happening inside your own body; the window now discloses nothing but the blurred reflection of things and faces.

It was twenty-five minutes to three; the sun poured into the Stazione Termini from the left; it cannot possibly be as warm and bright tomorrow or the day after tomorrow or Monday. That was a last oasis of summer, belatedly glorifying and gilding the splendid Roman autumn, now about to fade.

Like a swimmer plunging into the Mediterranean after years of absence, you immersed yourself in the city; carrying your suitcase, you made your way on foot to the Albergo Quirinale, where smiling obsequious servants welcomed you.

You weren't on holiday this time: you had an appointment at Scabelli's at three o'clock, and you had to stay there till after half-past six, and then you couldn't refuse to go out for a drink to some open-air café on the Via Vittorio Veneto, as it was such a lovely evening; Cécile meanwhile was expecting you, for this time, as on all your ordinary journeys, you had let her know you were coming and arranged to meet her as she left the Embassy, in the little café on the Piazza Farnese as usual, only usually you were there by six o'clock, before her.

When you got there at last of course it was empty. No, there was no message for you; and the lady with whom you usually came had been, but she hadn't stayed long, and they didn't know which way she'd gone.

There was a light in her window in the Via Monte della Farina. Old Madame Da Ponte opened the door and called up at once: *"Signora, signora, e il signore francese, il cugino."*

"Oh, there you are at last; I wondered what had happened, whether you'd had to put off your journey."

She had not taken off her coat; you went down straight away, kissing one another in the dark stairway.

Cécile knew where she was taking you, to a small restaurant on the Trastevere about which her colleagues were raving and which she wanted to try, but you went by way of the Tiber Island, which was obviously not the quickest route, and then you lost your way among backstreets, so on the way back you didn't go up to her room with her.

Now you've come out of the tunnel, and the noise of the train has grown clearer, but night has fallen almost completely, and through the panes, now almost clear of condensation, you begin to see little lights shine out at different levels on the mountainside. On the iron floor-heater the diamond-shaped pattern seems to you to form a grille through which the hot air from some hidden furnace is rising.

It was just about this time of year; night had fallen, and it was raining; you went out of the Gare de Lyon together in silence, for you were tired and cold after so long a journey.

The pavement was so crowded that you had to wait for some time for a taxi. This was so very different from the joyous welcome you'd hoped for from your city, that city from which she, particularly, expected so much, which she longed so ardently to see again, and of which she considered you the ambassador and almost the prince, that she could not help feeling disappointed on seeing you suddenly lost in the crowd, battling with those trivial difficulties which prove so intolerable in the long run, and from which she had hoped your mere presence would protect her.

You took her to the hotel you had chosen for her in the Latin Quarter, not too near the Place du Panthéon, of course, so that Henriette should not often meet her, a very quiet, fairly comfortable hotel in the Rue de l'Odéon.

The plan had been that she should go up to her room to tidy herself a little, then come down and collect you, so that you could finish the evening together in some pleasant café near Saint-Germain-des-Prés, but she was tired out, and you yourself had overestimated your strength and energy, so you said goodbye in the street, arranging to meet the next day for lunch, outside your office this time.

You went home on foot, carrying your suitcase, along the Rue Monsieur-le-Prince, and you felt as though you had landed in a strange town where you knew nobody, in search of a lodging, and this took you back a great many years to the time when you were neither rich (in so far as you can be said to be rich now) nor married, as though suddenly the very foundations of your life, your solidity, your personal appearance even had deserted you; the street seemed extraordinarily long. You did not breathe freely nor recover your self-confidence until you had crossed the empty Place du Panthéon and were in the lift.

Henriette, on hearing you turn the key in the lock, came out of the drawing room where she was sitting sewing.

"Was your train late?"

"No, not at all, but I had to see a lady to her hotel, an acquaintance of mine in Rome, who's always been very obliging to me; out of politeness I think we ought to invite her round; she's told me she would very much like to meet you and the children. Let's see, one evening next week (she's here for about a fortnight); Monday or Tuesday are free; I'll ring her up to ask her which she'd prefer and I'll let you know her answer.

"I'm definitely not going to take this train again: it's too tiring and doesn't give you so much extra time in Rome (just one afternoon and evening); I've told them that next time, if they want me to have dinner in Rome, I shan't leave till the following day. By the way, I'll be lunching out tomorrow."

Through the increasingly transparent window you see the sky growing darker and darker, while among the mountains and over the countryside more and more villages light up, but the train goes into a tunnel and its noise is muffled again. Outside the window, the reflected light from the door beside you shines on black rocks rushing past.

Vespas and trams woke you early in your narrow noisy room in the Albergo Quirinale. You flung open the shutters and waited for daylight.

You hadn't a busy day at Scabelli's, and so it was easy to be at the little bar in the Piazza Farnese punctually at one o'clock.

You'd had one weekend devoted to Borromini, another to Bernini, others to Caravaggio, Guido Reni, late-medieval frescoes, early Christian mosaics; there had been weekends, in particular, during which you had endeavoured to explore the different phases of imperial Rome, the age of Constantine (his triumphal arch, the Basilica of Maxentius, the fragments of his colossal statue in the Capitol Museum), the age of the Antonines, that of the Flavians, that of the Caesars (their temples, their palaces on the Palatine, Nero's Golden House), during which you strove to reconstruct, from the vast scattered ruins, what these buildings must have been in their prime, what the town must have looked like in its full bold glory; and when you walked about the Forum together you were not only surrounded by the few forlorn stones, the broken capitals, the impressive brick walls or foundations; you were in the midst of a vast shared dream which grew more solid, more detailed and more authentic with every visit.

On one occasion your wanderings, your pilgrimages, your researches had taken you from one obelisk to another, and you were well aware that in order to keep up this systematic exploration of Roman themes you ought also to go, at least once, from one St Paul's church to another, from one San Giovanni to another, from one Santa Agnese to another, from one Lorenzo to another, to try to probe or encircle, to capture and interpret the images linked with those names, for this would undoubtedly lead to strange discoveries about the Christian world, which is itself so wrongly understood, that world which was even now in process of disintegrating, of rotting away, of collapsing about you, and from the ruins and ashes of which you were seeking to escape in its very capital; but you scarcely dared speak of this to Cécile, knowing that she would refuse to understand, through fear of contagion, through characteristically Roman superstition.

In your journeyings the month before, you had taken Pietro Cavallini as your guiding light, and last Friday, sitting in the little bar in the Piazza Farnese before going to lunch on the Largo Argentino (for on a weekday like this you couldn't go too far afield), you remarked how strange it was that you had never tried, like Isis and Horus collecting the scattered limbs of Osiris, to seek out what remained of Michelangelo's work, to reassemble the tokens of his activity in this city.

Then she broke into a laugh: "I see what you're getting at: the Sistine, of course; it's a ruse to force me to set foot in that detestable Vatican City, that cancerous growth clinging to the free and splendid Roman town, that stupidly gilded pocket of corruption.

"For all your protests, you're rotten to the core with Christianity, with the most idiotic piety; any Roman servant girl has a more open mind than you.

"Oh, I was expecting this to come, but I'm too deeply afraid of that insidious poison that has robbed me of so many things, and that's now robbing me of you, to be crazy enough to venture, particularly in your company, inside that accursed place, where everything would foster your faint-heartedness."

She looked wonderful as she spoke, laughing at herself and at her own fury, kissing you to convince herself of her power over you, and it was quite impossible, quite useless to explain to her that she was on the wrong track, to try and make her see reason.

"But we could go and look at Moses, if you want to, and do you know that at Sant'Andrea della Valle, close to my place, there's a chapel where they've collected old copies of his most important statues?"

You know you're coming out of the tunnel by the alteration in the noise of the train. Agnès, one hand tapping on the strip of metal that says "*e pericoloso sporgersi*", stifles a long yawn. The station of Oulx-Claviere goes past, with all its windows lit up and a lamp shining over the signboard.

Beretti, or Peretti, or Cerutti – no, Ceretti: it was "etti" that you made out on his passport – goes out with an apology, passing a woman in a long white fur coat, an unmistakably Italian woman wearing very delicate white shoes, and his friend Andrea picks up his bag from beside you and takes it on his knees, probably because he knows, he feels sure that the end of his journey is near, presumably because they're both getting out at Turin.

Agnès and Pierre take two tickets for the first dinner from the blue-jacketed attendant, and you one for the second, out of habit and so as to shorten the interval after dinner until the ceiling lights go out, until the little blue lamp in the middle sheds its dim peaceful beams. You're hungry, and yet you feel slightly sick; you're hungry, but you've got no appetite, and what you really need is a little wine or some spirits; your hunger is mingled with boredom and nausea, and you'd be wiser to wait until you're really hungry.

And Faselli, no, Fasetti, or Masetti, comes back with an apology and sits down again beside Andrea, then picks up his knapsack, which was lying between Pierre and Lorenzo; the latter hasn't taken a dining-car ticket this time, so he must be getting off at Turin, where his wife will be waiting for him, ready to throw the pasta into the boiling water as soon as she hears him unlock the door with that key he's holding in his hand, fastened to the same ring as the tweezers with which he's cleaning his nails; his wife must be about Henriette's age, and his daughter, who's waiting for him too, a little older than Madeleine (for he probably got married younger than you did) and already a bit of a problem.

This daughter's probably laying the table, or rather no, she's not there: she's pretended she was going to dinner with a girlfriend, whereas in fact it's with a boyfriend, and her mother told her: "Really, as soon as your dad gets back from his trip to France..." – which called forth a flood of tears.

Canetti or Panetti opens the flap of his knapsack, takes out bread, butter and a knife, and hands a slice to Andrea, who unwraps a small parcel containing thin slices of salami.

The Italians will go out, all three of them; they'll walk along the platform together at the same pace, as far as the barrier, and there the two workmen will say goodbye to Lorenzo as cordially and as noisily as if they were old friends, then their ways will part and they'll probably never see each other again, or if one day they meet in the street they won't notice one another.

Tomorrow morning at his office he'll have arrears of correspondence to deal with, and he won't get away for lunch till about one o'clock, having forced his secretary to stay and type his letters on an old-fashioned Scabelli, which she's been begging him to change for the past twelve months, both of them in a raging temper, and it must be this prospect, added to fatigue and hunger, that gives such a look of tension to his previously placid features.

Having examined his nails, he puts his bunch of keys back in his pocket and looks up at you rather anxiously, as though you reminded him of his boss, as though he were afraid of your verdict on this little operation (connected with something he's keeping secret? Something he feels he's given away? Has he been embellishing his hands for the sake of someone other than his wife, some other woman who'll be waiting for him at the barrier and whom he'll take out to dinner in one of the restaurants in the Piazza San Carlo?).

Suddenly you notice in the eyes raised towards you a look of surprise and almost of pity, as if your own face had altered, as if your features were drawn and your eyes strained, as if you had grown several years older since the last time he had looked at you at all closely; he turns away.

The dining-car attendant, shaking his bell, meets and passes a woman in a black dress, an Italian woman with a bent back like a lean Cumaean Sibyl, like old Mrs Da Ponte. Pierre shuts the book he had stopped reading long ago, gets up, straightens his tie at the mirror and steps over your feet.

Bussolino station goes past, lights ablaze, in the midst of the intenser darkness. Agnès goes out next. The train enters a tunnel and its noise grows deeper.

As you paid for the drinks, you turned to her and said: "Perhaps we've time to go there before lunch," but the door of the great church was shut when you reached the Corso Vittorio Emmanuele, so that you weren't able to go in until the evening, and then it was so dark in the chapel that you saw practically nothing.

The sun had already set; a cold wind had got up, sending flurries of purple dust flying over the tramlines; you hurried, anxious to visit San Pietro in Vincoli before dinner because it seemed to you a favourable time. You remembered having seen the statue (was it on that trip with Henriette?) in the midst of almost total surrounding darkness, lit up in solitary brilliance, so vividly that Moses's horns really seemed to be horns of light.

The main door was closed, night was falling over Rome and stars were appearing above the Vatican, above that sort of haze that rose from the streets in which lamps and electric signs were lighting up between the darkening roofs, above that great hum punctuated by the sudden screeching and grating sounds of traffic, while a different hum came seeping through the doors, a blend of organ notes and muffled singing, showing that a service was going on inside.

You went round the church and crossed the convent garden; it was the service of the Holy Sacrament, and the altar was bright with lamps and candles; there were clouds of incense, and in the depths of the nave kneeling women were muttering; several foreigners stood staring at the Moses, whose marble gleamed as though covered with oil or melting yellow grease like the statue of a Roman god of old.

Cécile tugged at your hand, and you were back in the dreary Via Cavour.

"We'll have to go back there tomorrow," she said.

"But we've got so many other things to see."

"Which ones, if we omit, as we shall omit, your prophets and Sibyls, your *Last Judgement* and *Creation*?"

"Well, Santa Maria degli Angeli for instance, in the Baths of Diocletian, and the Carthusian monastery."

"With that horrible statue of St Bruno by some French sculptor or other."

"Houdon – it's better to see his work in Paris. I must admit that Bruno is one of the more depressing saints as far as art's concerned."

"And in other ways?"

"I don't know; I've not much faith in him."

"That means you have faith in others; you ought to avoid these Holy Sacrament services like the plague, or else go to see one, go and revel in one in your beloved great St Peter's church, to cure yourself once and for all; but don't expect me to go with you, I shall wait for you in a trattoria to comfort you after such a horrible experience, and then I'll watch over you while you dream of crowds of huge St Brunos, but only for part of the night... Give me a kiss."

"Not here – in the pizzeria."

Some workmen were sitting at a table playing tarot, one of them quite tipsy.

"And then there's a Christ on a pillar, I believe, at Santa Maria sopra Minerva, the only Gothic church in Rome."

"One of the ugliest in the world; it's in our neighbourhood – we can go there straight from the Palazzo Farnese."

"And after that we'll go for lunch somewhere near the Porta Pia, although only one side of that is by him..."

"We'll check it all later in my pre-war Blue Guide; and then there's something else, something I've never seen, in a villa some way off, I believe, a *pietà* – does that ring a bell?"

And so, next morning, you took a taxi to the Villa Sanseverino, but when you reached the gate you saw that it was only open on Mondays from ten to twelve.

You thus had ample time to gaze at leisure at the statue of Moses in San Pietro in Vincoli, well before evening service, well before sunset, alone in the empty, icy nave, with no spotlight; the statue stood there like a ghost in a barn; above all you felt, as you went from one place to another, from one work of art to the next, that something essential was lacking, something that was within your reach but was denied to your sight because of Cécile, something about which you didn't want to speak to her, knowing all the while that she was thinking of it too, both of you haunted by those prophets and Sibyls, by that absent *Last Judgement*, both conscious that your walk today was pointless and absurd, both silent, not needing to express the disappointment you shared, to tell one another: "Yes, there's Moses, but apart from that..." since you both knew only too well what else there was to see in Rome besides Moses, conscious of the humiliating, painful bitterness of your common cowardice, for there's no other word for it, and even in front of the closed door of the Villa Sanseverino, if your first reaction was one of irritation, you soon fell silent, only too well aware that the *pietà*, however impressive it might have been, would not have put things right, could not have filled the void.

While she was cooking supper in the Via Monte della Farina and you lay on the divan looking through a copy of *Epoca*, she turned to you, wiping her hands on a striped dishcloth.

"Some days I feel utterly fed up with Rome."

"When is your next holiday?"

"Oh, of course, I'll only get away for a holiday; when you come to see me, it's only for a holiday; you only come to Rome for Scabelli's sake and presently you'll be going back to your Albergo. If only I could trust you, if only you could give me some proof..."

(it was to give her such a proof that you had taken the train this morning at 8.10); and when you were lying by her side with the light out, glancing down, from time to time, at the luminous figures on your wristwatch, and she whispered: "Don't be too late tomorrow morning; I'll make you tea and toast," you closed her mouth with a kiss, but next morning you'd forgotten all about it.

Outside the window, the earth's surface is as dark now as its depths (the train is making a different noise from when it was in the tunnel), and in the sky you can only make out a few greenish wisps of cloud, between which a few stars have begun to shine, like the lights of houses on the hillsides and the headlamps of cars along the roads.

In Paris, when Cécile was on holiday and you were not, about this time of the year, after endless minutes in your office longing for midday as if you had been a clerk and not the boss, you found her waiting for you in the rain, in a light-yellow hooded raincoat, standing squarely with her hands in her pockets.

"What weather!"

"Aren't you going to kiss me?"

"Not here, not in this neighbourhood, darling. I'm awfully sorry you've been waiting in the rain; next time..."

"Oh, what does it matter? Other times you'll have to have lunch with your wife..."

"Not every day."

"Almost every day."

"Not only with my wife; there'll be business lunches too, just as in Rome."

"There'll be all the less time for me."

"You're here for a fortnight..."

"I know – it'll soon be over. We'll take the train back..."

"Don't think about it yet. Where shall we go?"

"You're the guide here."

"There are only too many places to choose from. What would you like?"

"You lead me; it'll be more exciting."

"Right bank, left bank?"

"Right bank means your work, left bank means your wife – it's hard to decide."

"Well then, we'll go to one of the islands. I don't know what there is there, but we're sure to find something. Here's the car."

You drove through the Louvre gateway and, on the right through the rainy window, behind Cécile's profile, more relaxed now, you saw the triumphal arch of the Carrousel go by and the Concorde Obelisk, dim in the distance; then as you followed the Seine, the towers of Notre-Dame rising grey above the rooftops.

You sat down in a little restaurant overlooking one of the quays, with red-and-white checked tablecloths.

"I spoke to Henriette about you…"

"What?"

"Oh, I haven't told her anything, don't worry. I thought you wanted to meet her, to see my home and my children, and besides we'd agreed – hadn't we? – that since she'd have to know some day… For she will have to, won't she?"

"Oh yes, of course, she'll have to."

"That since she'll have to know some day, it would be as well to take advantage of this opportunity to prepare her gently, for we've always said we wanted to avoid scenes, haven't we?"

"Yes, yes, we've always said that."

"Then you'll obviously have to meet her. You'll get on with her, you'll see; it'll all go off all right; she'll realize what a fine person you are, so that some day, when she has to be told the facts, it'll all be much simpler."

"Yes indeed, it'll all be much simpler, for you."

"Why are you sarcastic? Was it my idea in the first place? I'd have been quite willing to keep your visit to Paris absolutely secret; it was you who kept telling me there was nothing to make a fuss about, that the whole situation was quite simple really and only needed facing up to, that it was essential that I should get rid of those old-fashioned ideas due to that bourgeois religious upbringing that I seemed unable to shake off. Haven't you told me so hundreds of times? So I said something about a lady from Rome, I told her your name (I can't remember if I told her your name) and that you'd been very helpful to me, that we ought to ask you round, out of politeness..."

"And what did she think about it?"

"I don't know what she thought about it. She said Monday or Tuesday, whichever suited you best. Of course she feels suspicious, but she also feels curious, and she's bound to imagine, with that bourgeois religious upbringing of hers... for she's the one who's had a bourgeois religious upbringing, and she makes no attempt to shake off its influence, which on the contrary has been growing more marked for years now, gloomier and more repressive; she wasn't like that when I first knew her, and that's why I can't bear her any longer and why I need you so badly, because you bring me freedom, as you well know; but on the other hand I must try not to hurt her more than I can help, because of the children, and because... oh, you know why, and if I love you so much it's because you understand it all so well, because you've told me these things yourself, because it all seems simple to you and to me, too, when I'm with you; whereas with her... oh, she doesn't say anything, particularly now, but she's no need to say anything... with her, everything is complicated, ridiculously and appallingly complicated; do you understand what I mean?"

"I understand perfectly."

"Then why do you force me to explain it all so laboriously? Of course if you don't want to come, it'll be perfectly simple – she won't take offence."

"Of course I want to come; I want to see that home of yours, those windows overlooking the Panthéon dome, and your furniture and your books, and your children, and your wife; of course I want to know what she's like, with her silent ways and that stiff, contemptuous smile which you've described to me, not often (for you didn't often talk about her in Rome; you left all your Paris life in a sort of remote distance as though you wanted it not to exist, at least as far as I was concerned, as though you wanted to be nothing else, as far as I was concerned, but the man I meet all too seldom), not often but with expressions and hints and a look of nervous tension that I can't forget; I want to see what sort of a woman she is, to have such a hold over you."

"Don't be jealous; you've absolutely no cause to be jealous."

"I'm not jealous; how could I be jealous when I'm well aware that I make you younger; it's quite enough to have seen you in Rome and then to see what you're like here in Paris. No, I'm not jealous, since I'm going to face her, to brave the monster in her den."

"A monster? Just a poor unhappy woman who'd like to drag me down into the depths of boredom with her."

"I'll go and see her, poor woman; you can tell her I'll go on Monday; she'll welcome me, I'll play my part well, I'll be gracious and unaffected, I'll watch her and she'll watch me: we'll be charming to one another."

"You'll be charming."

"We'll both be charming. You'll see how well I know her. I'll treat you like a rather distant acquaintance, like somebody to whom I have, in fact, done a good turn."

"Won't she guess?"

"She won't show it."

"We mustn't laugh."

"You'll have no desire to laugh. You won't have the least temptation to say *tu* to me, I'm sure of that. For all your directorship, you're just a boy, at least when you're with me, and that's why I love you, because I want to make a man of you, which she's been unable to do in spite of appearances. She's only succeeded in half turning you into an old man, and that's only natural, though you won't admit it. You leave it to us. It'll all go quite smoothly. We'll know how to behave. I'll get on all right with her, and she'll realize what a fine person I am. While you'll be on tenterhooks, we shall be saying polite things to one another. At the end I shall tell her how much I've enjoyed her party; then she'll invite me to come again, and I shall accept. You see that, in spite of all you seem to believe, I don't hate her in the least; have I ever given any signs of doing so?"

"Monday evening's all right then?"

"Perfectly."

You had nothing left to say to one another. You had to wait for their meeting. You had to make a start on those hors-d'œuvres which had been set before you ages ago. You had to hurry, for time was getting on. You nibbled olives and stared through the window at the water pouring over your black car, with the apse of Notre-Dame in the background.

On the iron floor-heater, the diamond-shaped pattern seems to ripple like the scaly skin of a great serpent. Now only the lights of cars and stations and houses scattered over the countryside pierce the reflections on the window panes, fleeting pin points spangling the mirror image of this compartment behind the profile of the younger of the Italian workmen.

At last the sky grew lighter after that grey cold dawn over the Mediterranean just before Genoa, after that uncomfortable night which had left you stiff and aching, during which you crossed the Campagna di Roma under pelting rain, in pitch darkness except for occasional stations which were invariably deserted, their only sign of life a bustle of trolleys and a few shouts from people who were either invisible or who wandered along the rainy platform swinging lamps; a night during which you got practically no sleep, constantly consulting your watch and reckoning the hours that remained before dawn, before crossing the frontier, before the following evening, before you reached Paris and were able to go to bed in your flat at 15 Place du Panthéon, intoning to yourself the list of stations which you'd already begun to know by heart, the most important ones at any rate, those at which the train stopped, and a few others made noteworthy by some trivial incident on your journeys or by some historical event, some famous monument, watching Henriette in her uneasy sleep as she gradually drew closer to you, huddled against you for warmth and let her head drop against your shoulder, stroking her hair, as you hadn't done for a long time, since the war maybe, as you had dreamt of doing in a Rome ablaze with sunshine when first you planned this journey, several years ago, saying to yourself, as you caressed her, that from now on, perhaps, it was only in her sleep that you could really possess her, come really close to her, and that, whereas Rome was to have brought you together, now, after this disastrous trip, this fiasco of a second honeymoon, Rome stood between you, an enormous barrier – Rome, to which you had become so desperately attached (never had you felt its attraction so strongly as on leaving it this time, after having been deprived of it and debarred from it by this woman whom you caressed with hatred in your heart), Rome, which now you longed to know more fully and more deeply since your incapacity to speak about it had been revealed to you by this woman tossing in her sleep, muttering plaintively against your shoulder, plaintively expressing her bitter disappointment, who had been quite incapable of helping you in any way because in this sphere she was utterly dependent on you, in this sphere from which she had come to feel herself excluded and to which she longed for you to admit her, so that you might be restored to her as you once were, on your first journey together before the war.

At last the sky was growing lighter and the clouds were dispersing, for although it had not rained since Pisa, they still hung heavy and low as they do over Paris at this time of year, altering the character of the landscape and the colour of the smooth sea, and all the travellers in your compartment – which was silent save for the constant bass kept up by wheels on rails, the constant rattle of all metal objects – began to open their eyes, spread out their hands, stretch their necks to right and left and run fingers through their dishevelled hair.

At last the thin winter sun had pierced through that layer of drab prickly wool; at last you had begun to talk to one another; she had said to you: "We chose a bad time to go to Rome."

And you knew that this was an attempt to forgive you, a way of avoiding telling you that you had chosen such a bad time on purpose, so as to make sure you'd never be bothered with her there again; that she was trying to obliterate these last few days, knowing in her heart of hearts that this was impossible, since the failure of this journey, the rift it had made between you, merely served to confirm and accentuate the failure in yourself of which she was reproachfully conscious, the rift between you which, as she knew only too well, had been growing for years and which she had hoped to stop through the medium of that city in which, as she guessed, your old, your enduring self had taken refuge – but only in a dream, and therein lay the tragedy; a dream, it was now self-evident, which did not even seek to be interpreted, so that her scorn for you was fully justified.

At last, out of the depths of her gaze, a smile reached you; she was trying to cross the abyss at one leap, to heal the gaping wound; she talked about Paris, about the children, who were waiting for you at her parents'; contact was resumed, your habitual contact which no longer satisfied either of you, but still it was something, and just then it was essential that this, at least, should be resumed, for you had nothing else, absolutely no alternative as yet.

You had left Turin behind; you were crossing this very region, now hidden in darkness, but then lit up by a brief interval of sunshine, these snow-covered hills, and soon the mountains, but as, passing through successive tunnels, you gained altitude, the windows grew thick with steam that turned into frost, and all the wide expanse of valleys and villages which you have just seen disappearing into the dusk was hidden behind a dense white forest in which a child's nail scratched letters and figures.

And beyond the border, after the customs check, when the windows had recovered their transparency, there was snow, then rain over the Jura, then darkness already at Mâcon, all these kilometres following one another at such a slow pace, tiredness regaining its dominion, Henriette's face its hardness and worry.

Crossing through the woods of Fontainebleau – where the Great Huntsman called out to you: "Are you mad?" – how you longed to be back in Paris at last, in your own room, in your bed! And when you were stretched out there together she murmured: "I'm very grateful to you, but I'm so weary; that journey was so long!"

She turned over on the pillow and fell asleep immediately.

And you're well aware that she was thanking you not for taking her to Rome, for you never really took her there, but for bringing her back to Paris, where, even if henceforward she was going to drift further and further from you, she had at least got these children, this flat and furniture, these habits, her bedrock.

A man in the doorway, an old bearded man like Ezekiel, looks right and left with a jerky movement and stares for a minute at his own face clearly reflected in the vibrating window pane, with only a few distant fleeting lights shining through it.

There was Saturday, when you met and kissed with genuine delight.

"Are you getting used to your Paris again?"

"I was used to it by the second night. I walk about the streets feeling as if I'd never left them. Of course everything's changed since I was here; the shops look different, and are different; where I'd left a black-and-grey haberdasher's I find a red bookshop, but it's just as if they were dressing up to welcome me."

"And I was hoping to show you about, to help you discover it all just as you've been helping me to discover Rome."

"That's what I expect you to do."

"But if you know it all already?"

"I've forgotten everything, I shall have to see it all afresh; I only remember things when I've got them in front of me, looking older or newer. I'm sure you know hundreds of interesting places where I've never set foot..."

"How can I tell which?"

"What a ridiculous question! Take me round; wherever you lead me I shall discover something I've once loved, something of which I've dreamt vaguely in Rome, or else some fresh reason to be sorry I'm going back there so soon, for when you're not there I'm so lonely, now that I've been crazy enough to get fond of you."

You were walking down the Avenue de l'Opéra on a lovely late-autumn day.

"There are those new rooms at the Louvre which you certainly don't know, but we don't really want to spend this afternoon in a museum."

"Why, aren't we regular visitors at the Villa Borghese and the Palazzo Barberini?"

"But that's in Rome."

"Shouldn't I behave in Paris just as you do in Rome?"

"Then we ought to study Paris just as seriously."

"I ought to come here far more often and stay here far longer, I ought to settle down here. That's why I leave it to you – whatever you like, whatever you fancy. How long is it since you saw these rooms?"

"A year at least, maybe two, I'm not sure."

"And today you'd like to go back to them because I'm there, and because I'm there you daren't go back for fear of boring me; yet you know I'm not devoid of artistic appreciation; why these doubts, this sudden anxiety, as if I'd all at once become a stranger to you? Haven't we got much the same tastes? When you're in Rome you tell me, with a voice throbbing with enthusiasm, eyes shining as though you were promising me the greatest of treats, and an earnestness that brushes aside all trivial objections: 'We simply must go and see such and such a church or ruin, such and such a stone standing in the middle of a field or embedded amongst houses'; haven't I always followed you not merely with docility but with passionate excitement?"

"It's just that you could so easily go and see them without me."

"And why do you want me to see them without you? Why should I be a burden to you?"

"Why are you being so cruel when I'm only anxious to please you? Do I really need to tell you that you could never possibly be a burden to me?"

"Never? Nowhere?"

"Everything else is a burden, including Henriette who comes between us when you're with me in Paris. So if you're going to start making things complicated too, how can I behave naturally?"

And so, after your meal, you walked through the Louvre scarcely speaking a word to one another, except in front of the Roman statues, the landscapes of Claude Lorraine and the two Pannini pictures, which you scrutinized with affectionate delight.

Long after you had left her, that night in your bed beside Henriette, who was already asleep, you realized that you had forgotten your earlier proposal to drive her out into the country next day, and had merely said: "I'll be seeing you on Monday."

And on Monday she did not refer to it. She was dressed with great elegance. As she came into the drawing room, the two women eyed one another up and down like two wrestlers about to grapple and, in expectation of the clash you so much dreaded, your hand was shaking so hard as you poured the wine that you had to hold the glasses to fill them, as instructed on dining-car menus, as if the whole room were vibrating, as if some violent jolt were imminent, some sudden jarring of brakes at the entry to a station.

Madeleine and Henri, alone at table with you (Thomas and Jacqueline had eaten in the kitchen and had gone to bed), were looking at the lady and looking at you, admiring her, not breathing a word, making great efforts to behave properly, cutting their meat into tiny pieces, eating slowly, wiping their lips carefully before drinking a mouthful, disconcerted by your unwonted clumsiness, feeling that there was something about this guest that affected you in a peculiar way, that it was she who reduced you to this state, realizing that you were anxious, on edge; without understanding the reasons for your dread they shared it all the more acutely.

Henriette alone seemed to notice nothing, all smiles as she rang for the maid and gave her orders, never making a blunder, displaying as much charm as Cécile and, since you were silent, talking nearly as much and nearly as well as she, about Rome and her journeys to Rome, asking her all sorts of questions about her family, her home, her job, and getting her to tell things that were still unknown to yourself.

And the clash you dreaded so much never occurred. You came to realize that their conversation was not merely artful, that their smiles were not entirely feigned, that the interest they showed in each other was not just a matter of policy, that in fact they did not hate one another now that they were face to face, that the two opponents appreciated one another's merits and that what their glances now revealed was a genuine mutual respect, since they had no other cause for hatred than your wretched self, sitting there almost paralysed in anguished silence, so that gradually their attention was diverted from you, and they stopped thinking about you, and drew together, forming an agreement, an alliance against you.

With a kind of horror you watched the unbelievable happen: Cécile, your rescuer, was betraying you, was going over to Henriette's side; a sort of shared contempt was beginning to emerge through their jealousy.

Then you intervened, hoping to put an end to this dreadful partnership. Oh, the real danger was not that the two of them, unable any longer to endure their mask of politeness, should join battle, but that this mask should become Cécile's own face, her true self!

Henriette, safe in that citadel of hers, your flat, would renounce none of her prerogatives, and yet that was what you had hoped for when you brought in her rival – that she should yield ground, acknowledge her defeat, admit its justice when confronted with that rival's beauty and her enduring youthfulness, her life-giving power. No, she despised you, but she would not agree to relinquish you.

What was going to become of you if she succeeded in convincing Cécile that you were not worth rescuing from her clutches? And that was what had begun to happen, imperceptibly so far, just a nascent shadow, but one which would grow inevitably, irremediably, if the two women were left together. Henriette would eventually triumph not in battle but by infecting her adversary with hatred, not for herself, but for you; they would overpower you together, an unhappy, disappointed pair; in league together they would get the better of the living corpse that you'd be, the ruin of your former self, going about your insignificant and odious duties, while both wept in silent hatred over the collapse of their hopes and the falseness of your love.

What agony when, on the landing, Henriette calmly begged Cécile to come back three days later and the latter accepted with an enthusiasm which, alas, was undoubtedly sincere, whatever she may have believed herself! But you couldn't shout to her: "Don't accept! I don't want you to come back here!" And when, a few moments later, you drove her back to her hotel in the Rue de l'Odéon, the thing was settled; there was no going back on it.

"Please don't think you've got to come on Thursday night; we can quite easily find some excuse."

"Not at all: we haven't so many opportunities of meeting here, and this plan is one of the simplest. You see, didn't I tell you: everything went smoothly, we parted the best of friends, and I even succeeded in getting a second invitation out of her, which I consider a minor triumph."

"You were wonderful."

"So was she, wasn't she? She's far more broad-minded than you, and you can stop deluding yourself: you're no longer all-important to her. It's not you who have invited me, it's she herself, and she's not doing it to please you, oh no; it's not that she worships you so much that she's willing to give you up and grovel before her supplanter – no, it's a perfectly straight-forward invitation. But don't you realize that she's leaving you quite free?"

You had stopped the car at the hotel door.

You wanted to tell her: "Cécile, I love you, I want to spend the night with you", and then you couldn't, it was impossible; you weren't in Rome: you'd have had to take a room…

She kissed you on the forehead. She came back to the flat several times. You grew accustomed to seeing her with Henriette. You said to yourself that it didn't really matter. You had no time to think about it. Things were going fairly well for the moment, and that, surely, was the important point. During the last week of her stay you did not meet once in private: she had renewed acquaintance with some of her relatives and you had a great many engagements at mealtimes.

On the iron floor-heater the diamond shapes seem to waver and come apart, with the grooves between them looking like cracks gaping over an acrid furnace; they curve and writhe and taper; then it all turns black again, with crumbs jumping about and dirty marks, splashes of mud, crushed fragments of food, the quivering edges of old newspapers lying under the seat. The reflections on the window panes are broken up by many lights from outside: here are the suburbs of Turin. You catch sight of Agnès coming along the still deserted corridor.

Signor Lorenzo pulls on his grey overcoat, but the two other Italians, the two workmen, sit quietly with their closed knapsacks on their knees and their arms folded, talking and laughing.

You say to yourself: it was a year ago, just a year ago; I'd forgotten, not our journey, but exactly what had happened on it, because I was thinking only of the journey back, and on the journey back things had more or less settled themselves.

Signor Lorenzo takes his green suitcase, thrusts his papers into his coat pocket and stands back as Agnès comes in, smiling at you; Pierre, just behind her, waits to let him go out.

The crowded platform slows down, and the glittering rails, the lamps, the dark vaulted roof, the signboards announcing Torino, the shouting, hurrying porters, the woman pushing a trolley with refreshments.

You feel thirsty, but you'll be drinking later on; you feel hungry, but you must wait for the attendant's bell, which won't be long now since the young couple are already back.

You say to yourself: I don't know what to do; I don't know what I'm doing here; I don't know what to say to her; if she comes to Paris I shall lose her; if she comes to Paris everything will be ruined for her and for me; if I get her into Durieu's I shall see her every day from the window of my office; I shall have to leave her in the lurch, with a far worse job than the one she's got in Rome, where she knows plenty of people after all. I mustn't think about it. I must let things take their course. I'll make up my mind when I get there. Things will look quite different then. I must keep my eyes fixed on things that are actually there, on that woman in the corridor lifting up her cases to pass them out of the window to somebody I can't see. How cold it is. I must keep my eyes fixed on those two happy young people who've just come back from their dinner, glowing with food and wine, and holding hands again.

How are you going to sleep tonight, Agnès and Pierre? Are these two Italian workmen getting out soon? In that case you could stretch yourselves out if nobody else comes in, and I might even move into another compartment when I come back from the dining car, so that you can lie more comfortably. Are you going to stay in this train as far as Syracuse?

What wonderful days you'll have there! You'll go for walks along the seashore, and there'll be a perfect understanding between you day and night, and perfect mutual respect; you'll think, with ceaseless wonder, that the walls of loneliness have crumbled at last; but what shall I be doing during these few days, tomorrow, Saturday, while perhaps you're still travelling, exhausted but delighted, discovering Naples, looking out at the ruins of Paestum, and on Sunday when you'll perhaps already be settled in the city of Dionysius the tyrant, in an exquisite, unpretentious inn with a window overlooking green gardens? And on Monday, what shall I be doing then, to which saint shall I be devoting myself?

Where are you going to settle down when you come back after this holiday, when you're in Paris again, caught up in the relentless machinery of life there, which will inevitably crush you? In ten years' time what will be left of you, of that mutual understanding, that joy that denies weariness, that turns even weariness into a nectar that you're now just beginning to taste with delight? What will be left of you when children have come, when you, Pierre, have got on in your career, which may be as stupid a career as mine or worse, when you're the boss of a large staff whom you underpay because the business has to be kept going, a rule which of course doesn't apply to yourself, when you've got that flat you dreamt of, 15 Place du Panthéon? Will your eyes show the same tender care for one another, or will yours, Agnès, hold that mistrustful look which I know only too well, and yours, Pierre, that dread of self-scrutiny which I recognize in the mirror when I'm shaving, and from which you can only be delivered temporarily, for a few days at a time, a few dream days in Rome, by some Cécile whom you'll be incapable of bringing back to your permanent base?

An old man with a long white beard like Zachariah comes in, followed by an old woman with a slightly hooked nose like the Persic Sibyl.

So Agnès and Pierre will not be alone, and you'll come back to watch them sleeping in discomfort, while you yourself are struggling with the nightmares that you already hear panting and howling behind the doors of your brain, behind that patterned lattice on the floor which barely holds them in, which they're already shaking and beginning to pull apart; when you're lost amidst the tattered remnants of the plan you had thought so strong, so firmly knit, never imagining that all these cracks harbouring crumbs and dust and a whole insect-like swarm of interconnected incidents cunningly eroding the screws and screens of your daily life and all that keeps it steady, that these rents were going to split it irremediably, letting you fall a prey not only to the demons in your own mind but to all those that haunt your race. Why had this fatal memory recurred so vividly, when you might both have lived in ignorance, at least for a time?...

And what about Zachariah and the Sibyl? What are they doing in this train? What sort of life have they led? Where are they going? Will that sleepless stare of theirs be with you all the way to Rome?

They've got an old black case; they've taken off their hats; he may have been a schoolmaster or a bank clerk. They must have had children. They lost a son in the war. They're going to a granddaughter's christening. They're not used to travelling.

Oh, don't say they're going to start talking! Why can't they leave me in peace! Why can't that dinner bell start ringing!

They've stopped talking; they're sitting stiff and straight, dressed in black, with their hands folded in their laps.

Here comes the bell; the train hasn't moved yet. You put the book down on your seat. You steady yourself against the frame of the doorway as you leave the compartment.

PART III

VII

I T WAS MERELY A PASSING MALAISE; aren't you self-confident
and strong again now, with the glow of wine and spirits in you
still and the aroma of that last cigar, in spite of a certain welcome
drowsiness, however (because you drank no coffee, contrary to
your usual custom, just so as to be on the safe side, so as to avoid
any additional cause of insomnia, of being caught up in that
tangle of thoughts and memories which might lead to Heaven
knows what catastrophic change of mood and of plan), in spite
of that sort of inward dizziness which persists, which possesses
you again, in spite of that malaise, that sense of bewilderment
which is due to the journey and to which you would never have
expected to be still liable, which proves that you're not so old, so
worn out, so blasé, so faint-hearted as, a short while ago, you
were inclined to think yourself?

In the company of these six travellers still sitting calmly in their
places, all silent, none of them reading now – the old man, the
old woman, Agnès and Pierre, and those two Italian workmen
to whom you'd given names that you've forgotten – you can now
calmly settle down once more to examine the matter about which
you refused to think during your meal, tricking yourself into
imagining that this journey was like all your others, at Scabelli's
expense and in Scabelli's interests, thinking about your current
business as if you were going to have to talk about it tomorrow in
the office on the Via del Corso, or else concentrating your attention, like a cook or an ethnologist, on the Italian food which you
love and which you're going to get for a few days even if you should

get nothing else, listening to Italians talking at your table and the nearby tables (because there were hardly any French people left there, and those were mostly silent, tired out already by their day in the train), in that Italian language which you love, although unfortunately you don't speak it well,

to consider the problem of your journey, of the decision you have taken, of Cécile's fate, of what you'll have to say to Henriette, now that your hunger is satisfied and that you're feeling tolerably rested, and no longer in that state of panic which had swept over you and blinded you and driven you out of the path you had chosen into cold and shameful darkness, making a nonsense of your whole present existence and of the fact that you were here, in that place reserved by the unread book,

solely because of hunger, solely because of fatigue and discomfort, because at your age you couldn't indulge in a young man's whims (I am not old, I've decided to begin living, I've renewed my strength, I've got over all that),

because of that disintegration of your being, because of all those cracks that had appeared on the surface of your success, so that it was high time you took this step, so that if you'd waited a few weeks longer, you might not have found the courage you've needed, and the proof is that, a short while back, in this very compartment, everything seemed on the verge of collapse,

calmly, reasonably, to stop thinking about it, for the thing's done, the die is cast, I'm here, you must tell yourself again: I'm going to Rome, for Cécile's sake alone, and if I'm going to sit down in that seat it's on her account, because I've had the courage to make up my mind to this adventure.

But why are you still standing in the doorway, swaying about with the continuous motion of the train, your shoulder bumping against the doorpost almost without your being conscious of it? Why are you standing transfixed like a sleepwalker interrupted in his wanderings? Why do you shrink from entering that compartment as if all the same old thoughts were going to pounce on you again the minute you sat down in that seat that you'd chosen at the beginning as being your rightful place?

Everybody stares at you, and in the window opposite you see your own reflection swaying like that of a drunken man about to fall, until the moon appears through a rift in the clouds and obliterates you.

Why didn't you read that book, since you'd bought it? It might perhaps have protected you against all this. Why, now that you're sitting down and holding it in your hands, can't you open it, don't you even want to read the title? Why, while Pierre gets up and goes out, while the moon rises and sinks in the window pane, do you merely stare at the back of the book, the cover of which seems to grow transparent and the white pages underneath to turn over automatically, with lines of letters on them forming words which you can't recognize?

And yet surely in this book, whatever it is – for you haven't opened it, and even now you've not enough curiosity to look at its title nor the author's name – in the book which has not proved able to distract you from yourself, to protect your decision from the erosive power of your memories, to protect your apparent decision from all that was undermining and nullifying it, to protect your illusions,

surely in this book, since it's a novel, since you did not pick it entirely at random, since it's not just any book among all those that get published but belongs to a certain category of books, as you could tell from its position in the station bookstall, its title and the name of the author, which you've forgotten and to which you're now indifferent, but which, when you bought it, certainly conveyed something to you,

in this book which you haven't read, which you won't read now because it's too late,

you know that there are characters bearing a certain resemblance to the people who have successively occupied this compartment during your journey, that there are descriptions of places and things, words and moments of decision, and that the whole thing tells a story,

in this book which you had bought so that it might distract you and which you haven't read precisely because during this journey you wanted, just for once, to be wholly involved in your action, and if under these circumstances it had been able to interest you sufficiently, this would have meant that it bore so close a resemblance to your own situation that it would have set out your own problem before you, and consequently, far from distracting you, far from protecting you against this disintegration of your scheme, of your precious hopes, it would only have precipitated things,

in this book there must be somewhere, however lightly sketched, however unconvincing, however badly written, a man in difficulties who wants to save himself, who is making a journey and realizes that the path he has taken doesn't lead where he expected, as if he were lost in a wilderness, or a wasteland, or a forest that somehow closes up behind him so that he cannot even recognize the path that brought him there, for branches and lianas have covered his tracks, the grass has stood up again and the wind on the sand has obliterated his footprints.

You stare at the back of the book, and then at your hands and the cuffs of your shirt which you put on clean this morning but which is already soiled, and which you won't be able to change until you get there, until this night and this journey are over, when you'll be feeling utterly weary before the dawn of the new day which must inevitably be a blighted day, since you can indeed tell yourself that the die is cast, the step's been taken, but not the step you expected to take when you got into this train, a different step, the discarding of your plan in its original form which had seemed to you so clear and so secure, the discarding of that luminous vision of your future towards which, you had thought, this engine was carrying you, that life of happiness and love in Paris with Cécile; you must be calm and rational and stop thinking about it, while Pierre, who has come back into the compartment, sits down beside Agnès, gives her a furtive kiss on the forehead and looks around him while she drops her eyes sleepily (but the light will stay on for some time yet), then reopens his Italian Assimil and begins to read with her, their lips forming the syllables without letting any sound escape them, the Blue Guide jumping about a little on the seat beside them: while old Zachariah in his black coat pulls a big silver watch out of his waistcoat pocket, opens it, listens to it (how can he hope to hear it ticking amidst the noisy commotion of the train?), looks at it (and you too can see that it's only half-past nine), shuts it up and puts it back; while the two workmen make signs to their friend passing along the corridor, who's urging them to join him, winking and wriggling his whole body, then both get up, lay their knapsacks on their seats, go past you saying "*scusi, scusi*", start talking noisily as soon as they have crossed the threshold, move off and go into another compartment.

The old Italian woman next you still keeps her arms folded over her stomach, but her lips have begun moving now as if she were mumbling to herself some prayer to safeguard her against the perils of the journey, her worn features hardening from time to time as if she were uttering imprecations against the demons that haunt crossroads, her eyes widening suddenly in a sort of terror and determination, then she settles down, her eyelids droop, the movement of her lips becomes almost imperceptible, and you wonder if it's not merely the motion of the train that makes her jaw quiver and sends a slight tremor through the folds of her ancient skin.

As for her husband opposite you, his face too has begun to show emotion; he looks at you, smiles to himself, tells himself a story as if you reminded him of somebody, and suddenly a gleam of cruelty and vindictiveness passes through his old eyes, as if he had some bitter grudge against you.

Novi Ligure station has gone by. The electric bulbs are shaking inside the globe. On the further side of the corridor you see the reflected light swaying distortedly against black slopes patterned with small windows of brightness.

No, everything will not have been said; everything you would have liked to say won't have been said; you won't have succeeded in preparing things as thoroughly as you'd have liked; a few dates indeed will have been fixed, but not that particular date on which, according to your original plan, you were to leave Henriette and go and live with Cécile in that flat you were contemplating.

You'll be reconciled no doubt, since you'll have come to Rome expressly for her sake, and told her your discovery of the longed-for job in Paris, but this reconciliation will be apparent only, and terribly slender and fragile, and in spite of it you'll know, yourself, that you've drifted further from her; you'll still feel the same tormenting uneasiness, even more acutely, for you'll be wondering with a shudder what will become of your love when she'll have come to join you, seduced by the bright prospects you've held out before her, misled, ensnared by the vows and protestations which you'll undoubtedly have renewed and intensified in your keen delight at being with her, all hers, in Rome, in such freedom, for a few days, and all the more passionately because the future now appears to you so uncertain, so full of dangers and disappointments.

Somebody will have asked for the lights to be put out. After passing Civitavecchia station, while skirting the seashore, you'll already be experiencing beforehand all the fatigue of that journey which you'll only just have begun; but sleep will not come, and you'll try in vain to find a less uncomfortable position, you'll sit up with a start whenever the train stops, striving to banish the nightmares that will have pursued you with their sarcasms and their inky venom.

At Genoa you'll leave that third-class compartment for which you'll have conceived a loathing; dawn will not have broken, the blind will still be drawn in front of the window and the night light still shedding its blue gleam, tingeing the faces of the men and women who sit there breathing stertorously, open-mouthed, in the close, foul air.

When you go back to it, the sour light of a gloomy morning, cold and rainy, will force their eyes to open, and you'll gradually climb up the Alps, trying to read a book so as to avoid envisaging the outcome of the train of events you'll have started with your impassioned words during your stay, this very book perhaps, which you won't have finished, for your evenings will be quite otherwise occupied and because this time, for once, you won't have to drag your weary way, grumbling at your fate, back to the Albergo Quirinale at midnight, this very book which maybe you still won't have begun, or another which you'll have bought at the Stazione Termini; a book which, in any case, you'll shut when the customs men come round, and which might perhaps be about a man lost in a forest that keeps closing up behind him, so that he can't make up his mind which way he ought to go nor recognize the path by which he came so far, because his footsteps leave no trace on the piles of dead leaves into which he sinks,

(hearing the gallop of a horse that seems to draw near and then vanish, and at the same time a sort of howl as if the rider too was lost and calling for help,

suddenly running into a fence so that he can't go on, but has to keep alongside of it, drawing his breath more painfully, hardly able to keep his eyes open under the rain that has begun to fall, dense and deafening,

then an armed and muffled-up figure appears, pulls a torch out of his pocket, sends its searching light around through the innumerable raindrops till it falls on that haggard face, those trembling raised hands,

finds a book tucked into the man's belt and opens it while the rain streams over the pages which gradually dissolve and scatter, bursts into a hissing laugh, then creeps back into a little hut like a huge clod of earth, leaving the road open),

this book which you'll have shut when the customs men come round, so as to show them your passport, once you're through the tunnel, and which you'll then begin trying to read again, as you go down the French side of the mountain, in those boxed-in valleys full of glutinous darkness, in order to avoid envisaging with too painful a precision the life you're about to lead, the days of work in your Paris office when you'll see, across the Rue Danièle-Casanova, Cécile at her work in the Durieu travel agency, Cécile who imagined when she arrived in the city of her dreams that you were going to lead that wonderful exciting life together which she had made you invent, and who soon discovered that on the contrary you were infinitely further removed from her than when she was still in Rome, sleeping with her from time to time, but no longer able to talk to her, and who would look at you sometimes with so much hatred, such terrible disappointment in her glance that you'd have to get rid of her, you'd have to arrange to have her sent away, so painful would you find it, each time you saw her, to have flung in your face the ludicrous outcome of your supreme attempt to free yourself,

this book in which you'll bury yourself so as not to think about it, because it'll be too late to change anything, now that you'll be skirting the dreary lake, now that you'll have told her all the plans you've made for her and that she'll have been so happy in her ignorance these few days that it will have been impossible to persuade her to give up the idea, impossible to explain your reasons without her utterly misunderstanding them and trying to revive your courage, accusing you of faint-heartedness once again, impossible not to yield before her trustfulness, her gratitude, her wonder-struck surprise.

At Bourg dusk will have fallen, at Mâcon it'll be pitch-dark and you'll be going over in your head the happenings of the previous days, these days that lie before you, congratulating yourself on having concealed from her the fact that you'd found a job for her in Paris and that some friends had even offered to lend you their flat, on having concealed it from her although she kept asking you about it so many times, on making her believe that you had certainly been hunting, and had even thought you'd found something, and that was why you'd arranged this brief visit to Rome incognito, but that at the last minute it had all fallen through, that of course you would go on hunting, that you had something in mind which might quite likely come off, just so that she should be happy, so that she should have the joy of looking forward to this transformation which will not take place.

And so you'll have no need to prepare for your battle with Henriette, to think of what you'll have to say to her or to keep from her, since as far as she's concerned nothing will have changed, and you'll look out through black panes covered, maybe, with thousands of raindrops and see, emerging out of utter darkness as the windows of the lighted corridor flash by, the banks covered with rotting leaves, the innumerable tree stumps in the forest of

Fontainebleau, and you'll fancy you can hear above the noise of the axles the far-off sound of a galloping horse's hoofs and the ironical cry: "Can you hear me?"

Then, in the wet Paris night, worn out by your long third-class journey, you'll reach the Gare de Lyon at 9.54 p.m. on Tuesday, alone, and you'll hail a taxi.

Beyond the corridor, where the skyline splits into a gorge, above a little zigzagging road outlined by the lights of distant cars, the moon reappears, parting clouds like birds' heads crested with great plumes. Behind the head of the old man opposite you, whose eyes are not quite closed and who seems to be reciting to himself some long poem in regular verse, shrugging his shoulders at the end of every stanza, the photograph of mountains, partly hidden by his black hat, forms a sort of dark, spiky halo. Outside the window a long goods train goes past.

You hadn't stopped since Livorno – you were in the Rome-Express this time – you were crossing the Maremma, and the sunlight glittered on the canals between ploughed fields, between tawny-leaved trees outside the window of the dining car, on your left, and just as Grosseto was coming into sight you met a long goods train.

Then the Italian woman opposite you, a tall Roman woman travelling with her husband (who spent the time pulling out of his pocket a small notebook bound in pale-violet leather, in which he made notes, crossed them out and scrutinized them anxiously, while she stared round her with great dark eyes and smiled at all the strangers, including yourself) asked you whether she might pull down the blind, through which a thousand pinpoints of light then shone.

You admired her well-kept hands as you peeled your orange, and thought of Cécile, whom you had arranged to meet at half-past six in the Piazza Farnese bar, wondering where she might be lunching at this moment, at home or in one of her favourite little restaurants; she would be thinking of you no doubt, of what you would do together that evening, and hoping no doubt that this time you'd bring her the news she was waiting for, the news of that decision in her favour that she wanted you to make and of the discovery of that longed-for post in Paris.

Back in your first-class compartment, where you were alone, with an occasional glimpse of the sea, you took up once more the *Letters of Julian the Apostate* which you had left on the shelf, but you held the book in your hands without opening it, looking out through the open window which sometimes let in a whiff of sand on the cool breeze, and watching the station of Tarquinia go by and the town in the distance with its grey towers outlined against the arid mountains, then staring at the wedge-shaped patch of sunlight that was gradually spreading over one of the cushions.

The way lay open; on the farther side was a high meadow of immensely long grass through which a dry wind was blowing, at dawn.

As the tufts grow sparser, he descries on the horizon, through the veil of dust, a jagged mountain outline from which he is separated by a ditch that proves deeper the nearer he gets to it, a canyon at the bottom of which a river must be flowing; he starts climbing down the side, clutching at the rare thorny branches. But the plants to which he tries to cling become uprooted; the stones on which he tries to set his feet crumble away, break loose and go rolling down until he can no longer distinguish the sound of their fall amidst the general rumble from below, while night draws on and the ribbon of sky overhead turns violet,

that big patch of sunlight on the cushions opposite you had spread slowly from thread to thread of the coarse material, then at a bend in the railway line it began to creep down towards the vibrating floor, and gradually withdrew from the compartment.

You were well aware that you'd have to reach a decision some day or other, but you had as yet no inkling that the moment was so near; you felt no wish to precipitate things, preferring to let them take their course, waiting for an opportunity to arise, for your adventure to take a fresh turn of its own accord, and so without considering Cécile's future nor the organization of your life together, without pondering on your present relations nor brooding over the memories you shared with her,

holding on your knees the closed volume of the *Letters of Julian the Apostate,* which you had finished reading, you sat there, your thoughts chiefly occupied by your firm's concerns, cursing them indeed, trying to put them out of your mind but forced to revert to them continually by their urgency, by the shortness of the interval before your appointment at half-past three; so that Cécile's face only peeped out between figures, signatures, proposals for reorganizing the French branch and advertising campaigns, Cécile's voice and gestures could only be glimpsed furtively through the buzz of commercial voices, the screen of schedules and sales figures.

There would first of all be this barrier, this frontier to be crossed, and after that you would find that peaceful respite in her eyes, in her walk, in her arms, that leisure, that renewed youth, those fresh horizons.

You had not time to anticipate the misery of your midnight walk back to the Albergo Quirinale, for your mind was full of other matters, all that prosaic business, those absurd problems, that pointless conflict, all that toil on which you wasted your life, without any benefit to yourself other than greater security in your position and the hope of a rise in salary enabling you to make life easier for the wife and children from whom you felt so alien,

for it was not for Cécile's sake that you had gone that time, your journey was not undertaken, like today's, solely on her behalf, it had been decreed and paid for by your employers; the joy of seeing her was something stolen from them; it was your chief revenge for the servitude in which they held you, the degradation to which they had reduced you by forcing you perpetually to fight their battles, perpetually to defend their paltry interests rather than your own, to become so meekly a traitor to yourself.

But beyond that tract of busy humiliation, of enforced activity, which you try, under your warder's eye, to disguise as zeal, and under the eye of those whose warder you yourself are, as enthusiasm, mutely contemptuous of them meanwhile if they are taken in by it, to you Cécile stood for deliverance, for a return to your real self, for relaxation; she was a smile and a flame, she was pure water that scalded and healed and purified, with her gaze that enfolded you like an immense, gentle distance, severing you from all that; and it distressed you that you could not fix your thoughts on her, while turning over in your mind the phrases, the wiles you'd have to use in your forthcoming interview in order to protect yourself against all those envious people who coveted your job, to promote that cause which was not your own nor anyone else's really, and while you sought to recover calm of mind and courage, and self-possession and enjoyment of life by gazing at the pines gently swaying in the sunlight!

Outside the window, beyond that exact, quivering reflection of the compartment, in which by leaning your head forward slightly you could see yourself on the farther side of that old Italian woman sitting motionless with eyes half-closed, only a little beyond that image of yourself, there's something like a millstone about to crush you, a mountain cliff, a canyon wall down which you're falling, and you guess that it's the rock through which the tunnel is pierced. Agnès is asleep, Pierre watching her, and above their heads, so close together that their hair is intermingled, one of the boats on the photograph of Concarneau seems to be floating. On the iron floor-heater their feet scrape and sway.

But this time it was for her sake alone that you came away, this time you had at last taken that decision which has gradually weakened and shrivelled up during the journey till you can no longer recognize it, and whose continuing and hideous dissolution you are powerless to check; this time you haven't read that book which you've got in your hands, you haven't even opened it, you don't even know or want to know the title of it because this time you're on holiday, because the pressure of outside duties is in abeyance, because your work for Scabelli no longer comes, like a huge screen, between you and your love, because, without knowing exactly what you were doing, what was happening, now that the situation had by degrees reached a critical point and you were forced to make an upheaval in your existing arrangements, to break with the routine that had become established, you found yourself driven into a corner by your own actions; you had without delay to examine more closely, with an eye sharpened by shock, your projects for the life that lay ahead of you, which only this morning had seemed so meticulously, so completely and finally settled: to think over your present position, thus throwing wide the gates to all those old memories which you had so utterly forgotten and packed away, and from which something within you (it could hardly be called yourself, since you had not been thinking about it), that something within you which controlled what you thought about had imagined you so well protected, that something within you which has been overwhelmed by the rush of events, by the unfamiliarity of this journey, all its unusual features, that other aspect of yourself which hitherto had succeeded more or less in disguising itself and which is now unmasked even while it grows weaker and fades away.

And so now another memory forcibly recurs to you: the end of that ill-fated visit, your meeting in the train (the same train as this one because of the same cursed business of expense), a long way out of the Gare de Lyon, where you'd arranged to meet her on the platform, only rather casually because it was several days since you'd seen her, and she had kept her return ticket from the previous journey, a long way out of the station because you hadn't got up early enough, and it was five minutes past eight when you got out of your taxi, so that you'd no time even to buy a packet of Gauloises; you'd waited until the last minute on the platform, looking for her in vain, then you'd jumped on to the moving train, which was very full, far more so than today, you'd edged your way through the crowded corridors and looked into every compartment, saying to yourself that if you couldn't find her, if she wasn't there, if she'd put off her departure without even warning you, being sick and tired of you and bitterly disappointed at the light in which you and your whole setup had appeared to her in Paris, then you'd pay a first-class supplement so as to be sure of a seat at least,

you'd sat down in the dining car where they were serving breakfast (you'd already eaten, but you were quite breathless), saying to yourself: what shall I do in Rome without her now? I'll go to the Via Monte della Farina tomorrow to see if she's come home, and if not I'll go back there every day until I leave, and asking for a cup of tea as you sat by the rain-spotted window through which you stared at the rails and points and the rusty-looking stones between the rails,

then, suitcase in hand, resumed your exploration along the other half of the train towards the engine, until you suddenly heard her call: "Léon!" when you turned round and stood in the doorway while she told you: "I thought you couldn't be coming, that you must have changed the date of your journey; I'd kept a place for you, but as the train had been gone some time I thought it was no use."

You went on standing there in the corridor, without a cigarette, saying nothing, watching her as she started to read again, then leaning on the window as you wondered: "What can I do to put things right? If only someone would get out at Laroche or Dijon so that I could sit beside her!" staring out blindly at the wet dead leaves of the forest and its tall almost leafless trees.

Now, after he had lain for a long time prostrate, listening to the tumultuous roar of the river between its deep banks, its waves glittering with thin splinters of moonlight – for the moon was up now, shining in the full brilliance of its first crescent, its horns in the air like a boat in the narrow space between the two cliffs – he thought he heard on the other side of the river the sound of a horse's gallop and even a voice calling, a few syllables echoing from rock to rock as if somebody was aware of his presence and was trying to find him: "Who are you?"

He follows the stream seeking a ford, sliding along the increasingly narrow path at the foot of the cliff; he stumbles forward, sinks into the sand between the stones, while the echoing uproar grows louder, and then he is carried away, tossed by rapids, flung on to rocks over which he crawls as far as the mouth of a cave through which a cold blast whistles. He gropes around for a flat surface on which to lie, but he's reduced to crouching in a corner, not prone but with his forehead pressed against a vertical wall, a vein of marble probably, as cool and smooth as a window pane; then his breathing becomes regular once more, and he is conscious of a smell of smoke.

Staring out blindly at the dead leaves of the forest of Fontainebleau, and those others smouldering in heaps in flowerless gardens, reluctant to ask Cécile for a cigarette as she sat immersed in her book, although you knew she must have some in her bag, for you didn't want your first approach to her to be a beggar's, you drew from your pocket a box of matches in which there were only three left which you lit one after the other, leaning one elbow against the bar of the window; they went out immediately, probably because of a draught from the other end of the corridor, and when you looked up you saw Cécile watching you and laughing at you, and so you moved away a little, which soon brought her out of her compartment, a cigarette between her lips, to ask you for a light; but you showed her the empty box and she went back for her lighter.

"Do you want one?"

"No, thanks."

"Don't you want to sit down?"

"I'll wait till there are two seats."

"Somebody's sure to get out at Dijon."

She kept flicking off her ash with her little finger. Sens Cathedral passed slowly by, rising grey above its town; you were skirting the Yonne.

"What time shall you have lunch?"

"I hadn't time to reserve a seat. I only arrived at the last minute. I went to bed very late last night. I've been so very busy these last few days."

"We've both been very busy these last few days."

"The attendant will soon come round."

"He's already done so. I've bought a ticket for the first lunch; I'd have asked for two if I'd thought you were there."

"It must have been while I was drinking a cup of tea. I didn't think you could be on this train either; I'd already hunted for you along half of it."

"We'll go and try our luck together. Surely to goodness…"

"Particularly as the head waiter knows me. Go and sit down again; you're not going to stand all the way to Dijon on my account."

But nobody in that compartment got out either at Laroche or at Dijon, and you had to wait until lunchtime to sit beside her, and even then you couldn't talk openly because of the two other people at your table, a quarrelsome husband and wife.

"In Rome we shall be free; I shall have to be at Scabelli's at nine o'clock, and I was a fool enough to accept a lunch meeting, but from six onwards I shall be my own master; I'll come and wait for you in the Piazza Farnese."

"In Rome…"

"As though you didn't love Rome!"

"I love it chiefly when you're there with me."

"I'd like to be there always."

"And I'd like to be in Paris with you."

"Stop thinking about this visit; next time it'll be quite different."

"I won't ever mention it again."

Your book drops from your fingers on to the iron floor-heater. As you raise your head again, you catch sight of the turrets and battlements of Carcassonne, the photograph above one of the workmen's knapsacks, reflected in the mirror between the picture of mountains and the one of boats. A small isolated station goes by, with just a few lamps shining onto a seat, a clock and some packing cases.

Then the noise redoubles and a succession of lights flash in at the window, like hammer blows struck furiously at a stubborn nail: the lighted windows of a train rushing in the opposite direction, the Rome-Paris express which you'd taken on your last journey home.

The two old people, still motionless save for their quiet rocking, look at one another with a smile of complicity.

Groping in your pocket, you find you've only two Gauloises left, and you forgot to buy any Nazionali just now. You try a different position, shutting your eyes because you're beginning to find the light trying. Sleep is out of the question for the moment; sleep may be out of the question all night. You feel easier now, but you won't be able to keep your legs crossed like that for long.

That smell of smoke must mean that there's somebody living in the cave, and he gets up carefully so as not to knock against the roof and moves forward, keeping both hands pressed against the rock, while the smell of smoke grows stronger.

Round a corner, he comes upon a great mist-filled hall with walls oozing damp, in the midst of which a big fire is burning, glowing orange through the haze; drawing near to it, he hears someone else's hoarse and heavy breathing, and sees an old woman sitting motionless looking at a great book; without moving her head, she merely turns her eyes on him with a sort of mocking smile and whispers (but her whisper, enormously amplified, sounds like the noise of the train in a tunnel, and it's very hard to make out what she's saying):

"A weary journey through the woods, a weary journey over the savannah, over the stones; but now you're entitled to rest a little, so as to listen to me and ask me those questions that you must have prepared with such care and forethought, because one does not embark on so dangerous an adventure without maturely considered and well-defined reasons, which are surely written down on those two sheets of paper that I can see through the smoke and haze of my red fire, sticking to that odd garment which, by its battered shape and faded colour, tells of the distance you have had to travel.

"Why don't you speak to me? Do you imagine that I don't know that you too are wandering in search of your father, so as to learn from him the destiny of your race?"

He says, with a sort of stammering gulp: "No, it's not worth-while laughing at me; I don't want anything, Sibyl; I only want to get out of here, to go home, to get back onto the path on which I started out; and since you speak my language, take some pity on my degradation, on my inability to do you honour, to speak the words befitting you, the words that would call forth your answer."

"Are they not there, on those pages of the Blue Guide for lost wanderers?"

"Alas, they're no longer there, Sibyl, and even if they were I could not read them."

"I can provide you with these two cakes burnt in the oven, but to look at you, I very much doubt whether you'll ever again see the light of day."

"Is there not a golden bough to guide me and open the gates for me?"

"No, not for you, not for those who know their own desires so ill; you'll have to trust to the wavering light that will appear when this poor fire of mine is out."

Now there's only a thick cloud that spreads, and a kind of silvery gleam in the distance, through the acrid haze; he sets off once more.

Unable to keep your legs crossed thus, you stretch them out one after the other as though you were walking, and you hit the foot of the old Italian opposite you, who has been sitting as motionless as a sleeper, although his wide-open eyes have been staring at you for some minutes as if it amused him to watch the movements of your lips and as if, in some dream of his own, he were interpreting them.

How it's all beginning to oppress you, the motion, the rocking, the noise, the light; all the fatigue that has been accumulating through hours and miles, and which, so far, you have borne tolerably well, now hangs over you like an enormous threatening haystack, and you feel a terrible urge to stretch your limbs; only you cannot, you can't disturb that old lady, you don't want to appear less tough than Pierre over there, with his Agnès asleep against his shoulder; he must be far less used to travelling on this line than yourself, in fact he's probably doing this journey to Rome for the first time, and yet he's still smiling as he caresses her, watched by the old Italian woman whose gaze is somewhat gentler now, tinged with a kindliness that seems to have risen to the surface after being submerged for years and years by harshness and stubbornness.

You wedge yourself in your corner, half-closing your eyes, and peering through that slit as a drunk man peers through the sunblind of a tavern when he can no longer find in his pockets the few pence needed to turn his sullen intoxication into drowsiness, you see those four faces rocking, in the haze, amid the rumble, and that rectangle of darkness, varying in intensity, to your left – yes, surely to your left – and within its reflected light, on the other side, the corridor along which you hear the metallic sound that heralds the Italian ticket collector.

You feel as if a thin rusty needle were being thrust into your neck, between your two upper cervical vertebrae, the atlas and the axis (the terms come back to you, like the taste of a too copious meal, from some long-ago natural history lesson) and meanwhile here comes the man in his peaked cap, opening the sliding door and, from under his moustache, demanding "*biglietti, per favore*"; hampered by the painful stiffness of your neck, you rummage in the pockets of your coat and your jacket, and at last discover the thin slip of paper in your trouser pocket without remembering how it got there, for you should have put it back in your wallet as usual; a ticket collector must have come round earlier, this ticket collector, while you were in the dining car, but he didn't stare at you like this; he must have expected you to be in first class; he may perhaps be used to seeing you in first class; he may perhaps be astonished to find you here this time; he must wonder whether you're ruined; he touches his cap with his punch, and pulls the door to violently.

Between your second and third cervical vertebrae another long rusty hatpin probes and bores its way into you, and all down your back you feel them pricking you, and that sets you rubbing yourself against the back of the seat, and that in turn drives them in still further; a dozen of them have gone in now, preventing you from moving, like claws and fangs thrusting deeper and deeper, and still more of them, a jaw with fifteen teeth in a row, each digging in as if it functioned independently and then suddenly pressing tight, so that you start and stiffen.

You don't want to turn round: you are afraid of smelling the breath from that mouth, of seeing those pitiless glassy eyes, the scaly, prickly body of that serpent whose cold tail is wound round both your legs so that you cannot part them.

The old man opposite you gets up as if to say: "See how easily I move"; he seems to float towards the door, which opens almost without his touching it; his huge figure disappears.

In the lamp overhead, the bulb quivers and its light flickers as though it were suddenly going out. Agnès gives a start, opening her mouth as if all at once she had seen a hole in front of her; she remembers that she's in a train, passes her hand across her forehead, on which some of her hair has escaped from her scarf, looks at Pierre, who takes her fingers and gives her a little kiss on the neck, lays her head on his shoulder again, looks at you, smiles at you, surrenders to the rocking motion once more and lets her eyelids gently close; the boats on the photograph above her seem to be sailing on waves of gold and dark-blue silk, at evening, as the hot Roman sun goes down.

The pines were swaying gently in the light; there was nobody about in the fields; the peasants must have been asleep.

Alone in your compartment, holding in your hands the *Letters of Julian the Apostate* which you had finished reading, you had just caught sight of the city and the dome of St Peter's, and the nearness of it filled you with joy.

Then you got up, you put your book away in your case, you lowered the window and looked out at the houses going by, the streets, the women in their doorways, the traffic, the trams, the Tiber, the Stazione Trastevere, then the Tiber again as you crossed it, the beginning of the walls, the Stazione Ostiense.

How freely you breathed then, how eager you were to get back to Cécile, how impatient to have done with Scabelli's business affairs, and how you longed, at that moment, to visit Rome for once solely for her sake, you didn't as yet know when, you didn't know that it would be this time, that you'd have taken this decision so soon!

The Stazione Tuscolana went by, then came the Porta Maggiore with the tomb of Eurysaces the Baker, against which was leaning an old drunkard who got up and waved to the train as if he were welcoming you to Rome, and there were men at work on the roadway.

He started off again. The stones on which he tried to set his feet crumbled away, broke loose and rolled down until he could no longer make out the sound of their fall amidst the ever louder rumble from below.

A thick cloud was spreading, and in the distance through the acrid haze a vague silvery glow appeared.

He has reached the water's edge; he sees a few narrow gleams on the waves; he listens for a long while to their tumultuous roar.

Then over the muddy, turbulent river there comes a boat without a sail, in which an old man is standing, armed with an oar held upright on his shoulder as if to strike.

Above his stiff beard, full of purple glints, there are no eyes, but only two cavities that look like gas jets, full of hissing flames so dazzling that nothing else of the face can be made out.

The boat is a thick hulk of rusty metal, but its edges are as bright as rails, as sharp as the edge of a scythe.

It draws up, barely rocking, and the oar is pressed against the dark sand; a strangely gentle voice is heard saying:

"What are you waiting for? Can you hear me? Who are you? I have come to take you to the farther bank. I can see that you are dead; have no fear of capsizing: your weight will not sink the boat."

No, no, he cannot take that hand; and on his own palm, in the raw light from the gas jets, he sees a black corrosive oil trickling from all his nails, clinging to his skin, creeping viscously down into his sleeve.

He collapses on the shore, the muddy waves lick his whole body and the ferryman picks him up, flings him into the bottom of the boat and pushes off again; he feels the fiery breath of those eyes scorch him, he hears the voice shriek in his ear, as though amplified by a railway loudspeaker:

"You wanted to go to Rome – I know you did, I know you – it's too late to turn back: I'm taking you there."

Then he passed through the Porta Maggiore and you were in Rome.

Other trains were approaching yours, travelling at about the same speed, and at their open windows men and women were looking out at that high red rotunda, the temple of Minerva Medica, then at the station buildings and the platforms with their marble seats.

What ages have passed since then, and yet it was only just over a week ago; you had never before made two trips to Rome so close together; all of the previous time for years back, piled up and precariously balanced like a tall stack of bricks, seems suddenly to have started rocking during this journey, and will keep on rocking relentlessly until tomorrow morning just before dawn, until things have at last assumed a new shape and a certain stability.

Everything was then still in a state of expectancy; the whole future was still open, a future with Cécile, the chance of enjoying renewed youth in a life with her, your first real unspoilt youth. The sun poured into the Stazione Termini on the left; how lovely those few days were!

The boats go sailing over Agnès's head as she lies asleep, lulled by the noise the train makes as it goes through a tunnel. Just above Pierre's ear, in the mirror, the towers of Carcassonne are trembling.

Cécile had sat down again in her third-class compartment, in the very place you are in now, the corner seat next the corridor and facing the engine. What was the picture she could see above the head of the person opposite her, whose face is a blank in your mind?

In the corridor, leaning against the brass bar, you saw that great stone wall go by with its inscription: "In this village" (you've just gone through it, you noticed the stone and the writing once again, but you still don't know the name, familiar though you are with the names of so many insignificant villages along this line) "in such and such a year" (early nineteenth century, eighteen hundred and something of course, but what next?) "Nicéphore Niépce invented photography"; you thrust your head through the doorway to point out this detail to Cécile, who then immersed herself once more in that book of hers whose name you don't know, and you began thinking of those pictures of Paris that she has in her room in Rome, the Arc de Triomphe and the Obelisk, the towers of Notre-Dame and a flight of stairs in the Eiffel Tower, those four pictures on the two walls on either side of the window, like the four in this compartment, this temporary, moving bedroom in which you can't lie down.

It was raining over the Jura, just as it rained there today; bigger and bigger drops covered the window pane and trickled down jerkily, as though panting, in sinuous diagonals, and in the tunnels the reflection of your face made a sort of transparent dark hole through which you could see the rocks flying furiously past.

You told yourself: I must stop looking back at that disastrous visit, I must blot out the memory of those few days of folly; Cécile was never there at all; we shall never speak of it again; I'm going to Rome, I'm going to find Cécile in Rome, I know she's expecting me there; we didn't go to Paris together; it's just by chance that she's there, behind me, reading that book she bought at the Gare de Lyon before she left.

It was raining over the Alps, and you knew that up in the unseen heights that rain was turned to snow; everything was smothered in whiteness when the train stopped at Modane.

You were sitting (somebody must have got out at Chambéry or one of the small valley stations) opposite Cécile, who was immersed in her book and only very occasionally looked up to glance out of her window and say: "What weather!"

The snowflakes clung to the pane. The customs officials asked for your passports. She closed her book; you haven't read it, you never even asked her what it was called, but perhaps it was about a man who wanted to go to Rome and who went on sailing under a fine rain of tar that gradually turned white as snow and dry as a shower of torn paper, sailing in a metal boat in which he was not really lying down, but leaning his forehead against a vertical wall as cool and polished as a pane of glass, and who then became aware of a smell of smoke, and once again caught sight of the red glow of a fire through the darkness; little by little the rocking motion subsided, the sand grated against the metal hull which came apart like a pair of hands on the misty shore; he was alone, the ferryman having vanished into the night, no doubt gone back to fetch some other ghost.

He was still clutching in his hands the two cakes, now stained with black oil from his palms and with drops of blood, for he had hurt himself on the edge of the boat while sailing in his sleep.

He stared at three or four thick drops that trickled sinuously down as if they were trying to represent a complicated journey through a hilly wasteland.

There was the constant noise of the black waves lapping on the purple sand, and then all at once, in the region where the fire was glowing, a great stir of wings, a flight of ravens scattering in all directions, some passing over his head and flying on over the river, if it was a river, or the lake, or the marsh maybe, for there was a growing smell of rushes, mud and weeds mingled with that of the fire, which must be a peat fire, and towards which he would have to go eventually, for he could not stay much longer lying there alone, in that ruined craft, that boat of thin, treacherous metal which had split open like a pea pod, while little waves and their froth licked his limbs and eddies of sand and gravel crept all over his legs and back.

The ravens mistake him for a corpse, if indeed they are ravens, for in this light any bird would seem black and these utter no cry; two of them perch on his shoulders, and another on his head, clutching his hair.

He draws himself up very slowly, straightening his neck first and then his chest, then, leaning on his lacerated hands, he rises, unsteadily, to his knees; at last he stands up, trembling, with the three ravens still holding him fast, unmoving, their claws digging into him, while two others tear from him the two thin round bloodstained cakes.

The scraps of paper are still showering down, like blossoms or dead leaves; they lie on the surface of the water, almost covering it so that it looks like flaking paint; they cling to what is left of his garments, to his face and to his eyes, which are growing adapted now, discerning that this is not merely a shore but a port, that there is a jetty on the right, a quay a little farther on, and steps and rings, and that this glow comes from a lighthouse.

He goes up; he lets himself be led; the noise of the waves decreases; from time to time a distant sound like the breathing of a great crowd breaks on his ear; he knows he is skirting a brick wall, and that here is the Porta Maggiore, but there are no trams, no railway, no workmen, no people, nothing moving in the diffused light, and in front of the gate there is sitting in a curule chair somebody much taller than a man, with not one but two faces, and the face that is turned towards the wretched wanderer puckers into a laugh and calls out:

"You can never come back again,"

but the other, turned towards the gate, towards the town, in the same direction as his own, the unseen face, can be heard calling out too, a long-drawn-out muffled moan, emitting the very cry that he himself could not utter, which turns into a howl like a dog's, while the birds circle above that two-faced head under the rain of torn paper.

Then all falls silent; there is only that vast, indistinct sound of breathing seeping from the wall.

The customs officials, with snowflakes on their uniforms and in their hair, hurriedly gave you back your passports and closed the door behind them.

In that hot, crowded compartment, among those people whose faces you have forgotten, whose faces you had not even noticed, French people and Italians who were presumably talking, but to whose conversations you didn't listen (it was just a noise like that of the train which had started off again, which had plunged into the tunnel), you looked only at Cécile, sitting opposite you: she had picked up her book again; she was taking no notice of you; she seemed unaware that you had lost her, that you were trying slowly and painfully to find her again, to get closer to her and bridge the gulf that had been formed between you by her stay in Paris, about which you'd got to stop thinking.

She had begun to stop thinking about it, or rather to stop thinking about you in connection with her stay in Paris, for if she could succeed in putting you aside during that brief period, in pretending that you had been out of Paris, if she could avoid remembering her arrival, your meetings, her visits to 15 Place du Panthéon, then that holiday that she had so much longed for would seem to her to have been a success, that holiday during which she had so much enjoyed rediscovering her native city, without any help from yourself in that respect, just as Henriette had got no help from you in discovering Rome when you had gone back there together after the war.

Cécile's eyes were drifting inattentively over the last lines of her book; you felt that something complicated was going on inside her mind; you watched her changing expression, and she took no notice of you, as if she had not realized that you were there, because, if she was to set in order her recollection of the past fortnight, she had to exclude you from it, she had to pretend that it wasn't with you that she had travelled, and that it was by pure chance that she had met you in this train, that you hadn't even had lunch together a short while ago; smiling to herself, she made believe that you were absent, that she was thinking of you, that she thought she was going to meet you in Rome, and that suddenly she realized that you were there already, and that she was delighted and amazed because it was as if Rome had come to meet her and welcome her.

This was what you read on her face, what you deciphered of that unformulated dialogue behind the screen of her book.

Sitting in the very place you are in now, a closed book in her hands, her head turned to the right, she pretended that she was looking out, in your absence, at that gloomy landscape of Piedmont at which you, a frequent traveller, had so often gazed, pretended that she imagined you sitting opposite her and looking out at it with her, having taken the same train as herself without knowing it and without her knowing it, pretended that it would be wonderful suddenly to see you there, that she passionately longed to see you and that suddenly, in fact, you were there in the corridor, that you saw her, opened the door and sat down opposite her in the place you were actually in, looking rather furtively at her with a worried air, on account of Scabelli's no doubt, on account of that Henriette whom she had never seen.

Now she was looking at you happily, as the memory of those scenes in Paris in which you had played so sorry a part yielded to these more powerful daydreams, but she was well aware that this was all dangerous ground about which it was not safe to speak, that it would have been better to break the silence at dinner by talking about Rome, towards which you were both travelling and where each of you wished that the other had been waiting for you, or rather that the other had come from Rome, had travelled for you, or rather that the other had come from Rome, had travelled as far as Turin to meet you, welcome you and bring you the latest news.

How each of you dreaded hearing the other speak, lest some rash word might reopen the breach between you which, you felt, had begun to heal! You went back in silence to that third-class compartment, from which a few passengers had gone away meanwhile, so that you were able to sit down beside Cécile and lay your hand behind her back when she told you "I'm tired," but you had to wait until you reached Genoa for the light to be put out.

In the blue glow, she fell asleep against your shoulder and you caressed her, placing little kisses on her black hair, which gradually came loose, escaped from the restraining pins, slid down your neck, tickled your lips, your nostrils and your eyes.

In the mirror above Pierre's shoulder, the black towers are moving about. Through the window, through that other mirror reflecting the compartment, you see the lights of the countryside go by, the headlamps of cars, a lighted room in a gatekeeper's house at a level crossing, where a little girl is glimpsed for a moment, unfastening her school frock at a wardrobe mirror. And there's still another reflection, the unsteadiest of all, in the steel-rimmed glasses of the old Italian opposite you who's asleep already – the reflection of the photograph above and behind your head, which you know shows the Arc de Triomphe surrounded by old-fashioned taxis.

You had not yet acquired that secure position, those settled habits of which you had sought by today's journey to rid yourself; you were not yet living between those walls at 15 Place du Panthéon from which you hoped to escape to live elsewhere in Paris with Cécile, but from which you will never escape, to which you are doomed now until your death, because Cécile will not come to live with you, because you will not get her to come as you had so firmly intended when you left the Gare de Lyon this morning, as you still firmly intended until you got to... as you still thought you firmly intended until you got to... because you will not get her to come to Paris, knowing all too well now that it could only end, despite all the efforts you might make to deceive her and to deceive yourself on this subject, in severing you from her gradually but inevitably, gradually but in the most painful, most degrading fashion for both of you, and that, if you desert her (and you will desert her, despite the sincerity of your love, with all speed), this post that you've discovered for her in Paris will prove a mere mirage, and she will be unable to stay there without your help, which you will then deny her because you won't want to see her again,

so, then, you were not yet living in that flat to which you are condemned to the end of your days because there'll never be another Cécile, because it's too late now, because this was your last chance of renewing your youth, this chance which you've done all in your power to seize, you can at least say that to your credit, but which has come to pieces in your hands, which has shown that it had no real existence but was merely a creation of your own weak and irresponsible mind,

you had not yet acquired the furniture that adorns your drawing room, because it was all still at your parents' home or that of Henriette's parents, or still unbought,

you were not yet the father of Madeleine, Henri, Thomas and Jacqueline, because you had just got married, you were on your honeymoon, you were going to Rome for the first time, Rome, the city you had dreamt of ever since your schooldays and your earliest visits to the museums,

and in springtime, with the outskirts of Paris full of blossoming fruit trees, the delicious air wafting in through the half-open window, and Henriette by your side, radiant in her fresh-looking frock in the fashion of that time, ecstatic about every little hill, holding in her hands the Blue Guide to Italy in that old edition (you've still got it, on one of the shelves of the little bookcase next to the window overlooking the Panthéon dome, which is floodlit on Saturdays), while you tried to learn by heart the examples in your Italian grammar,

the forest of Fontainebleau full of young green shoots (and wasn't it she who told you, at that point, how she used to walk there as a child with her sisters, terrified as soon as dusk fell of meeting the Great Huntsman, who would challenge them and carry them off?),

showers ahead of you making roofs and pavements glitter, dazzling meadows on the mountainsides.

At the border the sun was already sinking, you could see the peaks glowing gold above the shadows, and the police officers asked to see your passports.

Then there was nothing but that vast indistinct sound of breathing, seeping from the wall. The customs official, with his old Italian face, began to smile and mutter: "Where are you, what are you doing, what do you want?"

"If I've come so far, through so many dangers and deviations, it's because I am in search of that book I lost through not even knowing I possessed it, through not taking the trouble to read its title, although it was the only thing of value I had taken with me on my adventure. I have been told that in this city, at whose gate you are so pitilessly standing guard, I might be able to procure a copy."

"But do you really think you know Italian well enough to read the translation which, perhaps, if there is a copy left in a fit state of preservation, might be offered you?

"Come in, the gate is wide open, and with my other face I will watch over your first steps; there's no other solution left you: I can only bar the way behind you and assure you that it is barred, and lend you one of my guides, a she-wolf whose coat is so much the colour of the earth and of this haze rising from it that, with your dim eyes, you'll only be able to see her from time to time, when you are quite close to her; only then will you be able to make out her claws and her shaggy hair, the rest of the time you'll have to trust solely to the sound of her sniffing and scratching."

The moon reappeared above the crimson and golden mountain peaks, and against this vast, clear, fiery background the faces of the customs officials gradually took on a violet tinge; they were as coarse-featured as those you've seen today, but with a greater arrogance and cruelty about them.

When the train started off again to dive into the tunnel, even the night light had not yet been turned on; there were a few moments of absolute blackness, then you emerged into emerald green, that patch of twilit sky over the dark, steep, vast valleys of Piedmont.

Italy was a police state in those days, intoxicated with her dream of empire, and there were uniforms in every station; but now you were breathing that hitherto unfamiliar air, you were discovering that authentic spring of which no spring in France had ever given you more than a feeble inkling, and it would have taken more than this appalling armed folly to spoil your delight in this experience; and when Henriette confessed her uneasiness, you told her, "They don't exist," which she tried, in vain, to believe.

At night you travelled alongside the sea, and the moon shone on the quiet waves, while she sat beside you like Agnès beside Pierre, your arm round her waist, her head leaning on your shoulder, her two hands laid on your knees; a lock of her hair, blown by the draught, brushed lightly against your eyelids, and you waved it aside like some gentle insect; in the heat, you had taken off your jacket, and through your shirt you could feel her breathing.

You have twisted round more and more, until now you are leaning not against the back of the seat but against the corridor window, so that you have a direct view of the photograph of the Arc de Triomphe surrounded by old-fashioned taxis. Opposite you in the window, behind the profile of the old Italian woman, the mirror image of this compartment is suddenly pierced, shattered, scattered by another train going past with lights in all, or nearly all of its windows, which you cannot count or see through because of the doubled speed, its noise all the more violent because you've just entered a tunnel; now the train has gone and the tunnel has ended, the face of the moon emerges from a mountain that had screened it and hangs for a few moments a little below the ceiling light.

The lights grow more numerous; here are streets with luminous signs and busy cafés. You look at your watch – yes, that's right, you're nearing Genoa; there'll be another long tunnel and then the Stazione Principe.

A tram rattles past, nearly empty. The two workmen come back to pick up their knapsacks. The Sibyl moves over to the corner next the window. Agnès watches the rugged walls file past.

Here's the town centre, the port on your right with boats lit up at every porthole, the famous lighthouse, the platforms, other trains, all the passengers waiting with their luggage, the tall houses piled up on the rock above you; the train stops, and Agnès gets up to open the window.

As for you, in the sudden complete immobility, you turn over and over in your hand the book which you haven't read, but whose presence suggests so forcibly to you a different book, that book which you've imagined and which, in your present state, you so badly need, that Blue Guide for those who have lost their way, in quest of which that traveller goes hurrying, swimming, creeping, that embryonic figure now fighting his way through a vague inchoate landscape, now standing silent before the customs official, Janus, whose double face wears a crown of ravens, each of their black feathers edged with a border of flames that spread so fast that soon all their wings are on fire, then their bodies, then their beaks and their claws, like white-hot metal, only their eyes remaining like cold black beads amidst the blaze,

and now he hears a hissing sound, and strains to see, but there is only a thick cloud spreading and, in the distance, through that great arch that is still visible, a vague silvery gleam like the first light of dawn,

and in the midst of that thick haze that is beginning to disperse he catches sight of the tail and legs and, so he thinks, the ears of a fox or a wolf, a she-wolf,

then starts off again, goes through the Porta Maggiore, behind which he finds not a street but a crack between rocks, hears the light steps of the she-wolf in the darkness while he makes his way through that sinuous defile, high up in which he sees a sort of light, looks behind him for the last time, and sees in the haze, which is slowly condensing into an impenetrable curtain of metallic dew, the eyes and lips of the customs official clearly outlined in slender flames,

then loses track of the she-wolf, hurries on and, under the silvery light which comes from that round opening aloft, gropes his way along the walls, which are no longer rock but earth, oozing moisture, whose trickling sound prevents him from distinguishing the sniffing of his animal guide, then, where his path divides, hears words and footsteps and catches a glimpse of torches, white-robed figures bearing corpses and singing hymns, while a new aperture overhead casts a cone of light, dimmer than the first (it must be the close of day),

then hears the sniffing again, louder and louder, like the snorting of a horse, like the neighing of a horse,

in a straight, uphill passage along which he starts running, at the end of which he sees the opening, green in the twilight, and through it there emerges a she-wolf as big as a horse, whose rider carries on his fists ravens with outspread wings, which soar spiralling between tall houses above arcades with little lamps shining in the windows, ravens with wings as wide as eagles' wings,

then comes to a little square where there are tables laid out under the trees, and decanters of wine, and two or three men come up to him (they're Italians, he says to himself, they're Italians whom I know),

rubs his eyes so that the last papery scales fall off, and listens to the words being spoken to him but cannot understand them;

as for you, sitting utterly motionless, you turn over the book between your fingers.

Somebody says to you: "*Scusi, signore*," and a young woman comes in, a very tall woman with very red lips in a beige woollen coat, with a small purple case for which she tries to find a place; is she going to take a book out too?

You put down your own on the seat; you wonder why the train hasn't started yet; you get up to go and look at the time on the station clock.

VIII

YOU HAVE COME BACK, your mind still full of that agitation which has been growing more intense and more obscure ever since this train left Paris, your body tingling with those stabs of weariness which every quarter of an hour makes more acute, which interrupt the course of your thoughts with increasing violence, distracting your gaze when you try to fix it on some object or some face, switching your mind abruptly towards some part of your memories or your plans which you were particularly anxious to avoid, towards those chaotic regions, seething and fermenting with that reorganization of your image of yourself and your own life which is taking place, implacably unfolding independently of your will – that mysterious metamorphosis of which, you are well aware, you perceive only a tiny section, and the details of which remain largely unknown to you, whereas you so urgently need to try and throw some light on them, for surely the most arduous study, the most meticulous patience would not be too high a price to pay for having the shadows pushed back, however slightly, for gaining some security, some freedom, however slight, from that fatalism which is now crushing you in the darkness – that powerful process at work within you which is gradually destroying your sense of personality – that change of lighting and perspective, that rotation of facts and their meaning – resulting from your weariness and from the circumstances, resulting from that decision of which you thought you had firm hold, and from your situation in the sphere of human conduct, and finding concrete expression in your weariness as though in a panting cry, coating your skin with that dryish sweat that makes your linen cling to it, attacking you with that sort of hollow dizziness, that disturbance of your digestive and respiratory system, that malaise, that sudden weakness, that unsteadiness which makes you cling to the doorpost, that heaviness of eyelids and head which makes you not so much sit down as collapse into your seat without even taking the trouble to move the book which you had left there, and which you now extract painfully from under your thighs, leaning against the corner, stretching out your legs between those of the old Italian opposite you, the only person whose eyes may perhaps still be open, although you can't tell behind his round glasses shining in the midst of the blue half-light, then pressing your chin against your collar and rubbing your hand on it to feel all the stubble that has grown there since this morning,

feeling thirsty, longing for some of that clear wine glittering, in decanters as slender as girls, on the iron, scarlet-painted tables, under the festoons of electric lamps that perforate the night, round which swarms of mosquitoes are humming, while an ever-increasing crowd of people gathers round to speak to you, whom you could understand perhaps if this hubbub would stop, if somebody would step forward and utter a few words distinctly,

then saying out loud: "I'm thirsty," without anybody hearing you, saying it again much louder, and by this disturbance causing a wave of silence to spread to the farthest ends of the square, under the windows of the tall houses from which heads are staring out at you, saying it over again without making yourself understood, while they foregather to question one another, increasingly uneasy and suspicious,

pointing with your finger to those decanters, so that one of the men, with highly hesitant gestures, conscious that everyone is staring at him, fills a glass halfway, spilling a lot of wine on his fingers and on the cuffs of his blue-and-purple check shirt, lifts it up and shows it you, turning it round and round in front of a lamp, then hands it you, seized with a convulsive tremor, raising the rim to your lips with a tremendous effort, succeeding at last in drinking a mouthful (then the glass cracked in your mouth), spitting out the sharp fragments and that horrible wine that scorches your throat and gullet so furiously that you utter a shriek and fling the glass against one of the house-fronts, where it breaks a window pane, and a huge patch of corrosive liquid starts crawling over plaster and bricks,

rubbing your hand over your rough, greasy, dirty chin, opening your eyes and examining your fingers under the blue glow.

Who put the light out? Who asked to have the light put out while you were wandering along the corridors in search of the dining car which, as you should really have known, had been taken off at Genoa, in search of cigarettes which would surely have helped you to stay awake, to protect yourself against these absurd fancies which only increase your anxiety and confusion, when you so badly need to face the situation very calmly, with detachment, as an outsider might see it;

for if it's now certain that you only really love Cécile in so far as she represents Rome to you, in so far as Rome speaks and beckons to you through her, and that you do not love her without Rome or away from Rome, that you love her only because of Rome, because you first owed and you still owe your acquaintance with Rome chiefly to her, and she is the doorway to Rome just as Mary, in Catholic litanies, is called the doorway to heaven; then it's imperative for you to discover why Rome casts such a spell over you, and also why this spell does not possess enough objective strength for Cécile to become, consciously and deliberately, its representative in Paris, and how it happens that Henriette, despite all that the city of cities inevitably means to her, being a Catholic, could come to consider your attachment to it as the very embodiment of all that she blames you for,

and so, just as your love for Cécile has shifted under your gaze and now appears to you under a different aspect, with a different meaning, what you now need to examine calmly and deliberately is the foundation, the solid content of that myth that Rome has become for you, all that lies about and behind the aspect under which this huge thing, Rome, appears to you, trying to see round it in the light of history, so as to know more about its connections with the behaviour and the decisions of those around you, whose looks, expressions, words and silences condition your gestures and your feelings – if only you could offer some resistance to sleep and to those nightmares that beset you, under this blue light that is betraying you to your monster-haunted weariness.

Who asked for the light to be put out? Who wanted this night light? The other light was harsh and fierce, but at least the objects on which it fell offered a hard surface, something to lean on, something to cling to, with which to try and form a rampart against that spreading crack, that insidious questioning which humiliates you, that contagious doubt which is shaking loose more and more pieces of that machine that protects you, of that plate armour which is proving so much thinner and more fragile than you suspected hitherto,

whereas that blueness that seems to hang in the air, making you feel that you have to go right through it to see anything, that blueness, combined with the ceaseless tremor, the noise and your consciousness of other people's breathing, makes things revert to their original uncertainty, and you no longer see them plain but have to reconstitute them from signs, so that they seem to be looking at you as much as you at them,

makes you yourself revert to that quiet terror, that primitive emotion in which, above the ruins of so many lies, the passion for existence and for truth asserts itself with such haughty power.

You look up at that insistent blue bulb, like some great bead, which is not really bright, but whose opaque subdued colour calls up whispering echoes on the hands and faces of all the sleepers, and you see inside the protective globe of the ceiling light the two thin transparent spheres, whose filaments, now cold, were a short while ago glowing fiercely like those of the lamps in the corridor, beyond which from time to time, but less and less frequently, you catch sight of some village street at the water's edge still showing signs of life.

On Monday evening, when Cécile comes out of the Palazzo Farnese, she'll peer round in the darkness looking for you, and she'll discover you waiting for her close to one of the bath-shaped fountains, waiting apprehensively, since that's the time, when you go to the Tre Scalini for dinner, when you'll have to face a confession and a painful reassessment of the situation, because, you're well aware, it will be impossible just to keep silence, to let her go on hoping that you're going to make that decision, imagining that you are still looking for that job in Paris, that you're just about to find something for her, whereas you're not going to look any more, and whereas you had already found something.

It will be impossible not to tell her at that point, when you're preparing to leave her, after staying there for her sake alone, after those few days during which she'll have been so happy because of the surprise that you'll have given her, that you're going to give her in a few hours' time, those days during which she'll have imagined that she's won the game at last, not to tell her that you had originally intended a further surprise for her – the news that you'd found that job for her at last, that she was going to Paris, that she could give in her notice at the Embassy and begin to get ready, begin saying goodbye to Rome, recapitulating for her own benefit all that you had learnt about Rome together,

that you had taken steps to find somewhere to live, that you had several possibilities in mind, that everything was ready and within your grasp, and that you'd given it all up,

impossible not to try and explain to her the reasons underlying your change of heart, so that she may give up all hope in that direction,

impossible just to keep silence, because under the circumstances, in view of this extraordinary journey which you've undertaken for her sake alone, which she's bound to interpret as a kind of promise, a solemn declaration in her favour, such a silence would constitute a lie of the utmost gravity which would poison all the relations you still hope to maintain with her, your relations with Rome itself, would even infect and cloud the atmosphere of your relations with yourself, which you are seeking to purify.

You ought then, on that last evening, since you want to wait till the last evening so as to be able to enjoy together at least the semblance of that happiness which is actually slipping from you, to experience in spite of everything a brief taste of that life which you imagined so near to you and which is drifting farther and farther off into the realm of illusion and impossibility,

to have the courage, as you sit in the Restaurant Tre Scalini and look out at the Fountain of the Rivers, while she's distressed at the thought of your imminent departure and yet happy at still having you all to herself for that evening, a foretaste, so she'll still be thinking, of a far more permanent possession elsewhere,

to strike this blow at her, to inflict this disappointment, to try to explain to her that everything was within reach and now everything is lost,

but you'll be incapable of such an explanation; even if you had the words all ready, her face, her amazement, her incomprehension would make you incapable of it.

All the circumstances, all your actions on the preceding days will seem to her to give you the lie; she'll refuse to believe you; she'll interpret it all as a noble gesture, a sacrifice made for Henriette, whom she'll envy and hate, as the heroic last-minute quiver of an old affection in its death throes, and she'll imagine that she's only got to wait a little longer (since, as you'll have just told her, everything's ready) for you to find the strength to break off those last remaining fetters which kept your decision from asserting itself.

And your confession will give her that certainty, that trust in you which she lacked, so that not your silence merely but your explanation itself will be a lie, since she won't understand it, since your behaviour will have prevented her from understanding it.

They'll turn round, they'll look at that stain, those fragments of plaster and brick raining down on them, the shattered glass that has wounded some of them, and they'll shrink away from you with astonishment and hatred, while their muttered colloquy grows fiercer and more agitated, and that's when the police officers will break through the circle and take hold of you, not brutally but with a certain pity, when they see that you can scarcely walk, that you shuffle along, your bare feet scraping against the rough burning soil through the holes in the worn soles of your shoes; they'll support you by the shoulders, and from time to time they'll prop up your head, which will sink wearily forward again, and even try to comfort you with unintelligible words of kindness,

leading you through the streets of the Trastevere, where the people sitting at tables in the pizzerie, in front of ovens glowing red in the depths of the dark vaulted rooms, will cast mistrustful glances at you as they refill their glasses with Frascati, and all the heat of a Roman night radiates from the stones and the pavements.

Through the doors of a temple, between pillars, you'll catch a glimpse of a gleaming idol with a smoky torch and clouds of incense, a waft of which will reach you, while at the windows of the square the whole Da Ponte family will watch you without recognizing you.

You'll go into a courtyard full of guns, crosses and swords, you'll climb up several flights of a narrow spiral stair to the top of the huge Palace of Justice fronting the Tiber, through the attic windows of which you'll see the dome of St Peter's and the monument to Victor Emmanuel all lit up, the Piazza dei Termini and the station, and you'll hear a confused noise rising from a newly built Colosseum; and you'll come to a small black door.

Even your behaviour that evening will prevent her from under-standing what you'll have told her, for you won't have to return to the Albergo Quirinale to fetch your suitcase, or hurry after your meal; you'll go back to spend the rest of the evening with her at 56 Via Monte della Farina, in her home which will have been your home for three days; and every step you take thither, dragging your feet because of your uneasiness, because of your desire to disillusion her, because of all the efforts to that end which you'll have made in vain during dinner, and which you'll still be making as you walk, because of the anticipated fatigue of your return journey, and the least of your caresses, and every pathetically lover-like inflection of your voice, will seem to her to contradict what you've told her.

She'll encourage you then, she'll sustain you, and in the darkness of a Roman night you'll make out on her lips, to your shame and despair, that smile of all too baseless triumph which she'll endeavour to conceal from you, thinking thus to help you by playing your own game.

Lying side by side on her bed, below the pictures, you'll caress one another while you speak, but if she's to be brought to understand that after having found her a job in Paris and a home there, however makeshift, for the two of you, you're giving it all up, driven to do so by the implacable evidence that your love is a frail thing and inseparably bound to a particular place, then you should certainly have set about it earlier.

She'll let you go on speaking, but she won't understand; she'll think: "I'd never have believed him so true, so honest; how glad I am that he's confessed all this! I know him better than he knows himself, I trust him more, now, than he trusts himself; now I need only wait a few weeks; I've rescued him from that morass of timidity; I am his strength and his youth."

She should have time to weigh these words of yours; you should have spoken them the previous day or the day before that, which is tomorrow, so that she could think over them while watching you sleep, and while working at the Palazzo Farnese on Monday, away from you, so that she could get you to repeat them several times to make quite sure that was what you had actually said and that there was no other possible interpretation.

So you'd have to spoil these two or three days during which you had still hoped to enjoy her presence and that liberty that you'd set out to gain.

Is your whole stay to be ruined by mistrust, by efforts on her part to break what she thinks is your last fetter, by tender sarcasms which you'll find it so hard, well-nigh impossible to resist?

But even if, no later than tomorrow, you tell her the whole story (and how can you tell it to her?), nevertheless on Monday evening, on the platform, in front of the third-class carriage on which there'll be written "Pisa, Genova, Torino, Modana, Parigi", she still won't have understood, she'll still imagine that you want her to force your hand, that you're not sincere in your renunciation, she'll fasten on to the things that seem to her so positive – your journey without the firm's knowledge, and that job which you'll have described to her in detail, since she'll have demanded full particulars of you, being afraid at first that you might have lied in this respect; and when, after putting down a book to keep, so you hope, a place just like the one you're in now, you go down onto the platform again to kiss her, no doubt she'll ask you once more: "Well, when are you coming back?",

hoping to take advantage of your emotion and the excitement of the station to make you at last fling off this unfamiliar mask which, so she'll think, you've assumed in order to test her and, above all, in order to resolve certain of your own inner conflicts by acting a part to yourself,

hoping to make sure at last that next time you'll come back with this wonderful plan even more fully worked out and definitely adopted, regretting that she's had to fight so hard these last few days, that they haven't been a foretaste of that happy life which she feels so close at hand,

and then could you really, will you find the words? And even if you found them would you really have the courage, when you're on the verge of leaving her, with that hard, long, lonely journey ahead of you, would you really be capable of undeceiving her?

No, it won't be within your power to do so, and there's only one way to prevent her from attributing to your visit and to all the steps and schemes that have led up to it, which you'd have to describe to her in detail, a misleading importance which might decide things in a very different direction from that which, little by little, they seem to be taking now – that she should only learn of your decision later, a good deal later, through some third person perhaps, or through hints, once her hopes of you, which in their present form are bound to be disappointed, have gradually faded or altered.

You ought therefore to give up entirely the thought of seeing her this time; not having been warned, she's not expecting you.

She ought not to know that you've been, that you'd found that job, made that arrangement, since in fact, for her, it's just as if you'd never found it, never looked for it; for her, but not for you, since now you'll no longer look for anything, since now you know that you won't find anything.

That would be the only way – you see a light appear in your mind at last, like the way out of a tunnel – not to see her, not to tell her anything, not to meet her again until your next trip, at Scabelli's orders and expense, as had been agreed, holding this secret in your heart like a clot on your tongue, keeping on seeing her of course, keeping on loving her of course, but with a terrible rift between you which will go on widening painfully every time without hope of healing, because of this very journey you're taking now, until the day when she'll be sufficiently detached from you, when she'll have lost enough of her illusions about you for you to be able to tell her everything without anything being a lie,

the only way to avoid seeing her (having lowered the window of the compartment, or the corridor, to look out) running and waving to you as long as she can,

to avoid seeing, for the last time, that look on her face as she dwindles into the distance and you guess, rather than see, that she's breathless, flushed with effort and emotion, in tears maybe: that fresh smile, that obstinate renewed confidence, that compelling gratitude, which you would no longer have any possibility of destroying before the slow, deplorable, stupid catastrophe, your inevitable private catastrophe, and which would drive you back into that adventure for which you left the Gare de Lyon this morning and which you know now is a blind alley.

You'd have to make your way alone to the Stazione Termini, your mind all the more obsessed by Cécile because you'd have spent these few days avoiding her,

you'd have to watch the crowded platform disappear into the night without recognizing anyone upon it.

You'll see the suburban stations go by: Roma Tuscolana, Roma Ostiense, Roma Trastevere. Then somebody will ask for the light to be put out.

Raising your head, twisting your neck, trying to straighten your spine, you open your eyes once more and stare, above the old Italian's open mouth, above his stiff moustache and his nostrils, above his glasses with their curved lenses seen sideways on, at the rectangle of glass under which you know there is a photograph of mountains, quite invisible now because of the yellow glints from the corridor; next to it, in the mirror, there appears spasmodically, reflected from outside the window on which the blind has not been drawn, the face of the full moon.

Outside the window there was the moon in its first crescent above suburban roofs and gasometers.

In the first-class corridor, behind where you were sitting with your pocket well stocked with Gauloises, people were passing on their way to the first dinner.

There was only one other passenger in your compartment, a fat man of your own age, smoking little dry, dark cigars, with two huge red suitcases above his head.

Outside the window, in the forest, the trees had already lost most of their leaves, so that you could see through their branches the young moon swaying, like a boat standing on end.

You leant back against the clean, white openwork cushion cover, you laid your left hand on the broad elbow rest, and while the people who had finished their meal were coming back along the corridor, you held your hand up against the pane to try and make out in the night the station of Laumes-Alésia with its shed for disused engines.

Over your head, there was not only the green suitcase you've got today, but also your light-coloured leather briefcase full of files and documents; you were holding in your hands the orange folder that dealt with your branch in Reims.

Outside the window, the waters of the Saône were glittering softly. Then the fat man asked you to put out the light, then he pulled down the blind, and you went into the corridor to smoke one cigarette after another; you noticed in particular the almost deserted platforms at Mâcon and the second hand moving jerkily on the clock face.

It was at Modane that they switched the light on; the customs officer was tapping gently on the window with his rubber stamp.

And the small black door opens on to a very dark room with a vaulted ceiling barely visible above shelves covered with boxes and books.

Behind a long table sits a man with thick hands, who speaks to you; you don't understand what he says; you look round you and see all your guards shaking their heads, with pity in their eyes – men and women, the latter dressed in black and white veils.

Then, gathering up your courage and closing your eyes, you lift up both hands to attract attention, and when you feel that they're all holding their breath to hear you better, you begin to explain, speaking Italian as correctly as you can:

"All this happened against my will, I'm ready to make amends, I'm only a typewriter salesman, I contribute to your country's commercial prosperity, I'm one of its servants, I'm known and respected in this city – you have only to enquire at Scabelli's,"

but you're well aware that it's useless to go on, for how could they understand when the words which you think you're speaking so correctly die away in your throat and all that comes out of your mouth is a whistling sound that grows so shrill and penetrating that, in spite of their desire to listen to your defence, they all rise up slowly and move towards you with clenched fists to put an end to that useless and excruciating noise?

The customs officer had just turned out the light, and as the train started off again and dived into the tunnel, you stretched out your legs and put your feet up on the seat in front of you, and you only woke on reaching Turin station, which was full of bustle, although it was not yet day; here two priests in plushy hats came in, put on the light and began talking, some of their remarks striking you from time to time and arousing your curiosity for a brief moment, tedious tales about some school in Genoa.

While you were shaving, the frosted glass began to let through a little light; day dawned while you breakfasted in the dining car on foaming *café au lait* and those buns filled with jam which are called croissants in Italy; the sky was perfectly clear save for two or three sharply defined clouds which changed colour as they floated above the villages, in whose streets the lamps were going out while milk carts rattled ponderously along and the first cyclists emerged from the shadows. All at once you saw the sun appear in a sudden sharp dip in the horizon, and its horizontal rays swept over the table at which you sat, throwing everything, the very crumbs, into splendid relief, emphasized with long shadows.

In your compartment the folds of the black cassocks were filled with golden dust, and the chatter of the faces above them had ceased momentarily. Tunnels cut short all this splendour. When you emerged from the mountainside at Genoa, you looked at the boats in the port with their white dinghies, the glitter of their porthole windows vying with that of the gentle waves, and the tall lighthouse in whose shadow the seagulls became briefly invisible.

All three got out at the Stazione Principe, the priests, with their capes over their arms, cheerfully swinging voluminous suitcases which must have been practically empty, and the fat gentleman, half-asleep still and unshaven, leaning out of the corridor window and shouting *"Facchino!"* while you stood by breathing in the fresh morning air, smoking your first cigarette of the day, laughing to yourself at his flustered air, his drawn features, the sour look of his mouth, helping him to get down his cases and hand them to the porter and saying to yourself: he can't be much older than I am; that's what I might turn into if I didn't take care.

Now the moon's image appears, not in the mirror but above Agnès's head, tingling it with quicksilver, a misshapen moon like the footprint of some nocturnal creature, in the glass over the now invisible photograph which, you know, shows sailing boats at a quayside. Viareggio station has gone by.

So you must have slept longer than you thought.

Oh, if you can't hold sleep at bay, prevent those horrible stubborn dreams, why can't it at least go on, instead of breaking off constantly like this, leaving your head and your insides full of its noxious fumes, its toxic taste?

Why can't you at least avoid this recurrent awakening, and since the nightmare won't loosen its grip, then leave it a clear field once and for all, so that you can get rid of it, cleanse yourself of it as of this film of dirt that's clinging to your skin, those bristles that have been sprouting on your chin ever since you left?

Why can't you settle down to sleep properly till just before day, like all these other people, even this young woman who got in at Genoa, and who's leaning over so far towards you that you think her head's about to touch your shoulder? She sags over gradually, then sits up with a sigh, her eyes still closed, lets her head begin to droop again and then her shoulder, her hand lying loosely on the seat beside her; her arm stiffens to take her weight (at every sudden jolt her elbow gives, and then straightens again), while her open mouth shows a gleam of teeth between violet-painted lips.

And now her fingers slide gently to the edge of the seat and along it; her whole arm bends and her whole body sinks over towards you; her shoulders have come away from the back of the seat; her left hand brushes the lap of her dress and then drops down until her nails trail against the floor-heater. Between her collar and her hair, the skin of her neck is a paler crescent.

If that was Viareggio you passed just now, you'll soon be coming to Pisa (now you must be going through the pine forest and moving away from the sea); you don't know exactly at what time; it's written down in the railway guide in the suitcase over your head, but you can't be bothered getting up to look for it. You glance at your watch; it's about a quarter past one; you don't know how fast your watch is now; you've forgotten when you set it right.

It's not worth going to sleep now because there'll soon be a jolt, and lights, and somebody may get in.

Isn't that the Arno, faintly gleaming?

Now you see walls, empty streets ineffectually lit by lamps strung on wires overhead, and green lights and red lights, and another train, a goods train carrying cars on its freight wagons; the station glides slowly by; on the deserted platform a man is pushing a trolley full of mailbags; another emerges suddenly from an office, leaving his telephone receiver lying on the table; the train stops even more abruptly than you'd expected.

The woman by your side raises herself to rest on her elbow, draws herself up, sits back, passes a finger over her eyebrows, leans against the back of the seat and closes her eyes again; her features twitch in a grimace, then gradually relax.

Agnès wakes next, with a start. Pierre withdraws his arm, flexes and stretches it several times, says: "We're at Pisa," looking at the time on his watch. "We've only got four and a half hours more before Rome," takes hold of Agnès's hands, draws her head against his shoulder, enfolds and caresses her as if they were alone.

A door opens behind you; you turn round to see a guard come in, hiding his face behind his forearm, followed by somebody whose features you can't make out clearly, wearing the same clothes as yourself but in better condition and carrying a suitcase like your own; he looks a little older than yourself.

The policeman says a few words that you still cannot understand, and as soon as he's finished, you hear the voice of the newcomer saying with amazing clarity:

"Who are you? Where are you going? What are you seeking? Whom do you love? What do you want? What are you waiting for? What are you feeling? Can you see me? Can you hear me?"

Then nothing is left but an opaque blue light pierced by the violet hole of the round window. All the guards along the walls throw back their heads and close their eyes.

When the train starts with a jerk, they all begin to gesticulate.

The old Italian opposite you, who had not woken when the train stopped, gives a cough, takes his handkerchief and wipes his glasses, then rubs his eyes and the bridge of his nose with his fingers.

The young woman by your side is moving her lips as if she were obstinately repeating something to herself, as if she were determined to convince herself of something, then shakes her head and meanwhile gradually swivels round; now her temple rubs against the back of the seat, her shoulder starts gently sagging and sinking again, her arm bends and her legs, which were straight and neatly parallel, begin to slide forward unevenly, and her dress hangs slackly over her knees in a trembling hollow.

The old Italian woman sits with folded hands watching her, then turns to the window, unfastening her fingers, raises them as if in prayer and then clasps them again, with a slight shrug, and lays them on her black lap as she turns her eyes once more on the young woman sprawling there, breathing so deeply that her shoulders heave, who almost seems to be creeping towards you, whose hair you want to kiss, towards whom, over whom you long yourself to sink limply.

The moonlight falls on Agnès's face, the whites of her wide-open eyes gleam like porcelain, and a moist arrowhead of light flickers on the black pupils.

You see Pierre's face in profile, as if he were murmuring something passionately to his beloved, but he's asleep; he's the only one asleep in this compartment just now; you've got to go to sleep, you've got to settle down to sleep.

You're a long way from Pisa already; you're moving back towards the sea; you'll soon pass through Livorno; you've forgotten if the train stops there.

Agnès moves Pierre's arm aside gently; his hand drops; now his wrists are resting on the edge of the seat, with the palms of his hands turned upwards and all the fingers slightly bent.

Agnès stretches up one hand to grasp the rim of the rail above you, picks up her skirt with the other and goes out.

You want to go to sleep; you pull down the blind over the window pane beside you, and the old Italian opposite you follows your example, and lowers the blind over the door too.

Now there's nothing but the blue light from the ceiling and the patch of moonlight on Agnès's empty place. Outside the window, the headlights of a car flash suddenly on pine trees in the night.

You were alone, holding the Emperor Julian's *Letters* in your hand, having left the suburbs of Genoa behind, while the sun began to climb above roofs and mountains, and its colour brightened, and your face was steeped in its warm brilliance,

you were sitting in a different place, near the window, the church spires still casting long shadows, the roads busy, women at work already washing linen in a rushing stream, and on the other side, between the promontory and the villas, a triangle of sea showed suddenly with a dazzling sail on it, and there were still a few flowers in the gardens,

(at La Spezia, long grey ships lay on the green water),

dark tunnels rhythmically broke into the brightness (the ceiling light and even the night light were out), you saw Viareggio station go by, you had left Ligurian country now and entered Etruria,

(the pines were swaying in the wind, the train moving farther from the sea),

then above the crust of rooftops made of Roman tiles, against a horizon of low hills, you caught a glimpse, as dazzling as sails or gulls in a deep-water port at dawn,

the dome, the Baptistery, the leaning campanile, which you long to visit each time you reach this station at this hour, in that characteristic light;

but you've never got off at Pisa; you'd never have had time.

It was always Rome you went to, without lingering at intervening stations, because business awaited you, because Cécile expected you.

But today she's unaware that you're travelling towards her in the night; today Scabelli's unaware that you're travelling towards Rome.

In the straight, sunlit streets of Livorno, through which you're about to pass without seeing them, a funeral procession worked its way along. On the platform, a newsboy was shouting (but there'll be nobody but railway men), thick smoke was rising from a little old-fashioned engine. The air was very soft and refreshing outside, with its smell of salt and ropes and coal; a shaft of sunlight fell on your smooth-shaven chin.

Then you felt your head drop back in the midst of the room, where nothing was stirring.

Through the violet hole of the round window came wafts of air loaded with dust and sand and decay.

There was nothing left but that blue light growing more opaque so that you could no longer make out even the faces of the guards sitting opposite one another on their chairs, along inner walls which they seemed to be trying to break down; but you heard their regular breathing growing louder, harsher and more metallic.

You felt that your feet had ceased to carry you or even to touch the ground: they were gradually rising, your whole body pivoting in space until it lay horizontally at a level with the closed eyes of the people sitting there.

You could see nothing but the vaulted roof, under which you began to move as though through a tunnel, and the guards moved along the walls at the same speed, without making a single gesture.

Now you know where you are; those traces of stucco and paint, that seeping moisture, those reddish lamps around which huge viscous patches are eating away the walls – these are the vaults underneath Nero's Golden House.

From time to time, round holes give a glimpse of the night sky. The tunnel widens suddenly; everything stands still.

The train had stopped (the train must have stopped, you must already have left Livorno), the sun was shining on Livorno station among all the smoke (there's somebody who wasn't there before, and Agnès has come back too; they never disturbed you), you were alone in the compartment, with the window down, leaning out over the platform; you bought some papers from the newsboy, then you left Livorno station, looking out in the broad sunlight, still steadily bright on that early November morning in Tuscany, at the bare fields, the villages, the hills, the deserted beaches with their rows of blue or white bathing huts, that very landscape through which you're passing now in the dark night, immersed in your painful intermittent half-sleep.

Beyond the corridor, beyond the sea, lay the promontory of Piombino and the Isle of Elba.

In the dining car, at the first lunch, while you were passing through the Maremma, you sat down opposite a very beautiful Italian woman, a tall Roman woman who made you think of Cécile.

Once more above Agnès's hair, in the glass of the invisible photograph of boats alongside the quay in a little port, the distorted reflection of the moon looks like the footprint of some nocturnal creature, not merely its footprint, but its very claws, stretching and slackening as though impatient to clutch their prey; it shifts towards the edge of the frame, towards the window, and disappears, but then through the window the moon itself appears before you, fastening tremulously to the middle of the pane, and all at once its light flows directly into the compartment, flooding it so that you can see, between your feet, the renewed glitter of the diamond-shaped scales on the floor-heater.

In the blue light, travelling on towards Pisa, you watched her sleeping as if she were some strange woman you had met in the train, as if this woman by your side, her fine back heaving and falling with such amplitude, her hair touching your hand which still clutches the unread book, had ventured to huddle close to you to sleep instead of sinking limply on the seat, as if you had ventured to draw her to you while she slept, without her having uttered a word, without having heard the sound of her voice,

saying to yourself: I don't know her name, I don't know who she is, or even whether she's Italian or French, or when she got into the train; I must have been asleep, and I've woken up to find this lovely face pressed against my neck, my hand clasping her hip, her knee gently caressing mine, these eyelids so close to my lips.

The blind was drawn over the outside window, but not over the pane against which your forehead was rubbing, and beyond the bespattered glass of the corridor window you knew that the autumn rains were raging.

Exhausted by those days in Paris, by this journey, by this effort to camouflage your memories and set things in order within yourself, you gave a shudder from time to time, and Cécile's body, echoing yours, quivered too, but soon grew calm again and resumed its deep breathing; it seemed to steep your aching limbs, your scars, the sour disorder of your digestive organs, your creaking bones and bruised nerves, in a soft, sea-fresh oil, in a soft secret light, warm and gentle, in a heady, soothing distillation of the air, the walls, the steps and words and names of Rome, towards which you were travelling.

You had not stopped since Livorno; you were crossing the Maremma; you were trying to fall asleep again; Cécile woke up as you came into Civitavecchia.

Everything had stood still; above you, exactly in front of your eyes, there was a picture of the Flood; all the men and women who had accompanied you were growing larger, rising up the sides of the walls, curving over as they reached the vaulted ceiling.

Alongside your body, on either side, passed a whole procession of cardinals with their hats and copes, all whispering as they came near your ear: "Why do you profess to hate us? Are we not Romans?"

Then appeared the *sedia gestatoria*, carried by four black marble giants with amber eyes, and swaying as they walked; on it, surrounded by huge feather fans, under a parasol of white and gold silk, sat the Pope, his gloved hands loaded with rings, his head crowned with a tiara, his features drawn, his eyes hidden behind thick round glasses, and just as his feet were almost touching yours he spoke in a voice that seemed to come from far-distant tombs, and echoed with a hissing sound from the living walls, declaring very slowly, very sadly:

"O you who lie paralysed in mid-air at my feet, unable to move your lips or even to close your eyes to escape my apparition, you who long to sleep and to feel beneath you the solid ground which is now denied you,

watched over by so many images which you can neither set in order nor identify,

why do you profess to love Rome? Am I not the ghost of the emperors, haunting through the ages the capital of their lost and longed-for world?"

His head turns grey first, then all his garments take on a blue tinge; he melts into the opaque light which forms a sort of clot in the middle of the room.

Somebody got out, turning on the light to take a suitcase from the rack. Cécile had just woken up, not knowing where she was, and stared at you without recognizing you all the time the train was standing still, looking as if she had just emerged from a bad dream which she was striving to forget, and yet she had seemed to be sleeping so peacefully.

Your face in the mirror, as you were shaving, looked pale and haggard.

Instead of going back into the compartment where she sat unmoving, with her eyes open, in the seat you had left, you stood watching the suburban stations go past under the rain: Roma Trastevere, then the river, with a milk lorry hiccuping over the bridge, its headlights reflected in the black surging water, Roma Ostiense, then the dark ramparts above which the glow from the city, slowly beginning to stir again, was just perceptible; then the Piazza Zama, the Via Appia Nuova and the Stazione Tuscolana.

She was standing with a pin between her teeth, trying to tidy her hair. People were dragging their cases along the passage. You had gone past the Porta Maggiore and the temple of Minerva Medica; you were in Rome.

The moon has left the window, but you can see a very faint reflection of it in the mirror between Pierre's head and that of the newcomer whose features you cannot make out, a reflection of the reflection in the glass over the photograph of battlemented walls and towers. Grosseto station has gone by.

How those nails dig into your flesh, how tightly those chains are fastened round your chest, how those snakes go gliding down your legs!

You raise your neck slowly, you clench your fists, you stretch your arms, but you've lost that book you were holding – it must have dropped down; you bend over and rake the iron strip between the shoes and the swaying ankles, without managing to find it.

It's there on the seat, with the woman's fingers resting on it, that woman whom you want to bite gently on the neck so that she'd turn her head towards you without waking and offer you her lips, to clasp tightly while your hand slid down the neck of her dress,

it slips from her fingers and moves away in little jerks; you catch it on the edge of the seat.

The man whose face you haven't even yet been able to see goes out, closing the door behind him, a ray of orange light on his tweed coat, on one of your hands and one of your knees; then blue dimness once more.

And when that clot had dissolved there appeared in the depths of the room the King of the Last Judgement with his hand raised, while all the huge figures that hung round the vault threw back their heads and closed their eyes:

"At the mere sound of my words your limbs are beginning to twitch convulsively, as if worms were devouring them already. It is not I who pronounce judgement upon you, but all those who are with me and their ancestors, all those who are with you and their children."

Then lightning streaked the wall against which he appeared and it began to fall away in great patches.

Looking through half-open eyes at those heads with their eyes closed, in the opaque blue light, all thrown back and swaying with the motion of the train, at the rectangle of darkness outside, growing slightly greyer perhaps, between the old Italian woman and the fair, silvery Agnès, at those luggage racks stretched under the ceiling and carrying the possessions of these men and women whom you had never seen before, whom in all probability you'll never meet again, while the man you call Pierre wakes up, pulls his shoulders away from the seat, leans his elbows on his knees and watches the dark, truncated landscape go by, and the woman you call Agnès emerges from sleep too, takes her husband's wrist and tries to read the time by the light of the moon,

("...before we get to Rome."

"Yes, just about, you've time for a sleep."

"I'm going into the corridor for a bit to stretch my legs"),

and both of them get up, trying not to disturb you, and he grasps the handle of the door and tries to open it as softly as possible, a bar of orange light spilling over his hands and yours and the loosened hair of the woman by your side,

you try to find an easier position, you lean your forehead against the blind, but you'd never be able to get to sleep like that; you throw back your head once more.

Your eyes fixed now on the blue bead glowing in the ceiling, you shuffle your feet about on the floor-heater so as to insert them more comfortably between those of the old Italian, and you feel the young woman's dangling hand caress your ankle gently, her fingers fumbling with it as though she were trying to recognize something.

The rain on the Stazione Termini made almost as much noise as the train had done, drumming in great waves on the transparent roof of the main hall, while standing in the bar you rapidly drank your cups of *caffellatte,* and on the square there were great puddles from which taxis sent showers of splashes flying; sudden squalls blew under the big penthouse where you were waiting together, motionless and silent, muffled in your coat collars, in the black night where nothing save the bustle of trolleybuses indicated the approach of day.

You took Cécile's cases up to her landing in the Via Monte della Farina, then you left her quickly without kissing her, only whispering, as though to salve your conscience: "I'll be seeing you tonight"; then you heard her turn the key in the lock and slam the door.

At the Albergo Quirinale, in a small room with a balcony, on the top floor, you set down your suitcases on the table and took out Volume I of the *Aeneid* in the Budé edition; you opened the shutters; daylight began to creep through the lashing downpour, then a bright rift in the cloudburst showed above the roofs of the Via Nazionale.

That evening, after an exhausting and tedious discussion at Scabelli's which went on far later than expected, long after the time for your rendezvous with Cécile on the Piazza Farnese, you walked slowly, pausing in front of shop windows, roaming frequently from one pavement to another, making a detour through the Piazza del Pantheon just for amusement, in the cool and still dampish air, while dusk still lingered in the sky,

as though you wanted to avoid going to the Piazza Farnese (but your feet kept carrying you thither, and you felt a sort of inward fury against this stupid compulsion), hoping that she would not be there, that she'd have tired of waiting, especially after travelling all night and going back to work all day,

saying to yourself: she won't have waited for me, it's nearly seven, she must have gone home to make herself a sandwich and go to bed early;

but on the contrary there she was, at her usual place, looking through a fashion magazine and showing no signs of impatience.

You wanted to ask her how she'd got on in Paris, as if the words with which you'd introduced her to Henriette had corresponded to the truth, as if she really was a lady with whom you'd had dealings in Rome and who had always been very obliging to you.

She told you: "I'm starving; I saw this morning that there's a new restaurant on the Largo Argentina: we might try it; after that I'll go home to sleep."

That time you didn't even go upstairs with her or fix a meeting for the next day. She waved goodnight to you, with a yawn. You buttoned up your coat and walked back through the cold to the Albergo Quirinale, where you read Virgil till nearly midnight.

The far wall was tumbling down in great patches and the central figure took on a bluish tinge and seemed to dissolve in the opaque light, forming a sort of clot in the middle of the urban landscape which was gradually revealed in the night.

The vast figures bending over you were muttering as their fingers turned the pages of their enormous books.

You thought about her, saying to yourself: it's been merely an adventure, I shall see her again later on, we'll always be good friends; but next evening, under a rather misty sky, you couldn't bear it any longer, and when you came out of Scabelli's you hurried, almost running, towards the Palazzo Farnese.

You didn't show yourself at first; you followed her into the Roman night as she hurried off, with an air of nervous excitement, not in the direction of the Via Monte della Farina; you wondered, as you caught up with her: is she going to meet another man? Then you drew level with her and walked beside her for a little while, your head turned towards her, unable to take your eyes from her; at last she saw you, she stopped, uttered a cry, dropped her bag and without even stopping to pick it up she flung herself into your arms.

You kissed her on the lips; you said to her: "I can't do without you."

"If I'd known I should meet you, I'd have prepared dinner at home."

All the memories of that trip to Paris, all the aftertaste of it died away. You became young again; you had regained her at last; you had reached Rome.

After your meal in a little restaurant overlooking the island in the Tiber you went as far as the round Temple of Vesta, you passed through the Arch of Janus, skirted the Palatine and the Park of Caelius, pressed close to one another, embracing frequently, uttering no word until you reached the ruins of Nero's Golden House (the Colosseum Square was still busy with motor cars and Vespas) and read the inscription saying that it could only be visited on Thursdays.

"That's why I've never been inside it yet."

"I'll go and see it for you tomorrow."

Now the moonlight is falling on the head of the old Italian woman and on the glass over the photograph of Carcassonne which you can see gleaming above her, a slender vertical rectangle of brightness. The handle you were holding in your hand begins to move; the door opens; a man looks in, then shuts it again.

The blind, its fastenings undone, began to rise in tiny jerks, leaving a slit of window which grew brighter and broader and gradually disclosed a strip of the Campagna di Roma that changed colour from early-morning grey to green, then to yellow; then above the fields and vineyards, in the crook of the hills, there were triangles of bright sky.

Then somebody uncovered the window completely, and at a bend in the line the sun thrust its brazen pincers in and covered the cheeks and brows of the sleeping travellers with a plating of hot luminous metal.

A whole flight of rooks rose up over a farm, and beyond the corridor there were the waves of the sea, painted in sharp detail. "Are we there already?" asked Henriette, opening her eyes. "We're just coming into Civitavecchia."

The town had not yet been destroyed. It was before the last war. There were black-shirted children on the platform.

You told her to go and tidy her hair and freshen her face with eau de Cologne, but she stayed there beside you, leaning her hand on your shoulder, blinking as she stared at the sun rising and scattering the baroque clouds behind pines and villas.

Outside the old Termini station, that heavy nineteenth-century building, there were no Vespas nor trolleybuses then, only horse-drawn carriages, and you drove off in one of these after breakfasting in the gloomy, closed-in station restaurant of those days.

Your knowledge of Italian was purely bookish then; you had not yet joined Scabelli. Everything seemed marvellous to you, uniforms and *viva il Duce* notwithstanding.

You asked her if she wanted to rest in your room at the Hotel Croce di Malta in the Via Borgognone, near the Piazza di Spagna, but she refused: she only wanted to walk about and see things, and you set off together through the hot streets to explore the famous hills.

The vast prophets and sibyls close their books; the folds of their cloaks, their veils, their tunics begin to stir, to stretch out, turn into great tapering black feathers; now there's only a huge flight of black feathers above your head, parting to reveal the hazy depths of the night sky.

You feel yourself sinking; you're touching grass. Looking to right and left, you see broken shafts of grey columns and bushes set out in orderly rows, at the far end of which stands a great half-ruined niche built of large bricks.

And now there come floating through the air, a few inches above your eyes, minute bronze figurines decorated with iron ornaments.

"I am Vaticanus, god of crying children."

"Cunina, goddess of their cradles."

"Seia, goddess of the grain of wheat sown in the earth."

"Of the first shoots."

"Of the nodes in their stalks."

"Of the unfolding leaves."

"Of the young ear."

"Of its beard."

"Of its blossom while yet green."

"Of its whitening blossom."

"Of the ripened ear."

"We are the meticulous little gods of ancient Italy, gods of the minute dissection of hours and actions, from whose ashes rose Roman law."

"Jugatinus, who joins the hand of a man to that of a woman."

"Domiducus, who leads the young bride to her new home."

"Domitius, who maintains her in that home."

"Manturna, who preserves her for her husband."

"Virginensis, who unfastens her girdle."

"Partunda."

"Priapus."

"Venus,"

who grows taller as she moves away, and whose body glows bright and golden as she stands, a vast figure, in the great niche, turning towards you and holding all her companions in the palm of her hand.

Above her head three great statues rise, one of bronze, one of iron, and the third, much more dimly seen, of black clay: Jupiter, Mars and Quirinus.

Then from all sides foregather men in togas, in armour or in purple mantles, increasingly laden with gold ornaments, crowns, gems and heavy embroidery on their cloaks. One by one you recognize them: all the emperors in succession.

You walked along the streets together, exploring the famous hills, holding your Blue Guide, which was new then.

In the afternoon you visited the Forum and the Palatine; in the evening, when they were shutting the gates, you climbed up to the Temple of Venus and Rome.

"Over there in that corner," you explained to her, "on the other side of the Colosseum, there are the ruins of Nero's Golden House, down there on the right Constantine's triumphal arch, and farther off you can just see through the trees the foundations of the Temple of Claudius, for the emperors were considered as gods."

There was a great deal of traffic all round the amphitheatre, but these cars were very slow-moving compared to last year's or today's. The Via dei Fori Imperiali had just been completed and opened, and this garden had been laid out in the ruins of the temple.

Suddenly, sitting on the bench, in the heady evening air, she asked you: "Why Venus and Rome? What's the connection between the two?"

You're leaning right back now so that you can see the gleam of the glass rectangle over the photograph of the Arc de Triomphe above your seat. The lights of a station go by; it must be Tarquinia.

You say to yourself: I've got to keep still, I've at least got to keep still, this restlessness is absolutely useless; isn't the rocking of the coach enough to set all your convictions shaking and jar-ring against each other, like the parts of a machine that's been too roughly handled?

But you can't help it, that arm has simply got to relax. As if you were bending a bow and had suddenly let go of the string, your hand drops, your fingers spread out; you brush against somebody's cheek with the back of your fin-gers, which you draw back sharply as if you'd burnt them – against the cheek of that woman by your side, who sits up suddenly, and at whose face, whose now wide-open eyes you stare.

You had laid your right hand on the door handle again, and you feel it move once more; the slit of orange light opens; a foot is thrust through, then a knee; this time they belong to Pierre, who hasn't been to shave since he's holding nothing in his hands, who edges his way in, his chin where it catches the light looking as dirty as though he were swimming through ink, groping with his hands, leaning forward and twisting one way and another, lifting his feet very high and very slowly, one after the other, finally turning over on himself before he settles down on the seat.

You see half of Agnès's dress, then her raised leg describing an uncertain arc, the tip wavering like the needle of a galvanometer above your crossed knees, and the piece of pleated skirt, reflect-ing the light from the corridor, unfolds just at the level of your eyes like a great pheasant's wing; she rests her hand on your shoulder, then on the back of the seat beside you. She turns round, pivoting on the heel she's managed to insert, the edge of her skirt spread out over your trousers, your knees gripped between hers, a brief grimace puckering her features, which are now almost entirely veiled by the blue darkness; then the other pheasant's wing folds up and she turns round once more, leans both hands on Pierre's shoulders and swivels round into her seat, where she sits bolt upright, only her head slightly bent forward, watching the blue-black landscape go past with a few lamps splashing a few walls.

She hasn't attempted to close the door behind her; the old Italian puts out his hand as far as the handle, keeps it there for a few moments and then withdraws it; your knees are in the orange light and so are those of the woman by your side.

"Emperors and gods of Rome, have I not tried to study you? Have I not succeeded, at times, in making you appear to me at street corners and among ruins?"

And now a host of faces draw near, huge and hostile, as though you were some sprawling insect, faces streaked with lightning, the skin falling away in patches.

Your body is sinking into the damp earth. The sky above you is streaked with lightning now, and great patches of mud fall down and cover you.

Your wrist is in the orange light. Sliding your hand along your thigh, you push your watch from under your shirt cuff; it's five o'clock. These streets in which a few windows are beginning to light up must be those of Civitavecchia. You lift the blind on your right, and then the face of the Roman woman beside you is revealed, pale against the shadows and her black hair.

You won't sleep any longer now. You've got to get up, take your case and lay it on the seat, open it, take out your toilet things, then close the lid.

You've got to get that door open completely, though your legs will hardly bear you up.

You've got to go out.

IX

INSIDE THERE, IN THE CLOSE WARM AIR and the unfriendly smell, holding in your hand, in their cool, damp wrapping of red-and-white-striped nylon, the shaving brush, razor, soap, blades, the bottle of eau de Cologne, the toothbrush in its case, the half-empty tube of toothpaste, the comb, all the things you had spread out on the shelf beside the little washbasin without a plug and with a tap that yields water only in driblets, you rub your forefinger over your chin, which is almost smooth, your neck which is still rough and has a scratch on it; you look at the tiny drop of blood drying on the tip of your finger, then you lift the lid of your case and slip in the toilet things, you close both of its two thin brass locks, wondering whether to put it back on the rack or to stay in the corridor watching for the outskirts of Rome; on second thoughts, no, for you've still got nearly half an hour, you look at your watch, twenty-five minutes exactly.

So you hoist it up again. Thrust deep into the cleft at the back of the seat is the book you bought on leaving, which you haven't read, but have kept throughout the journey as a token of yourself, which you'd forgotten when you left the compartment just now, which you'd let slip while you were asleep and which had gradually slid under your body.

You take it in your hand, saying to yourself: I ought to write a book; that would be the way to fill this hollow emptiness within me, now that I've lost all other sort of freedom, now that I'm being carried along by this train all the way to the station, wholly bound, forced to follow these rails.

And so I shall go on with that unreal, soul-destroying work at Scabelli for the sake of the children, for Henriette's sake, for my own sake; I shall go on living at 15 Place du Panthéon; and, above all, on subsequent visits, I know, I shan't be able to resist going back to see Cécile.

At first I shall tell her nothing, I shan't speak to her about this journey. She won't understand why there'll be so much sadness about my embraces. She'll gradually come to feel what in fact she had always felt: that our love is not a road leading anywhere, but is destined to lose itself in desert sands, as we both grow older.

Magliana station has gone by. Beyond the corridor, there are the suburbs of Rome already.

In a few moments you'll be arriving at that transparent station at which it's so wonderful to arrive at sunrise, as you can by this train at another time of year.

It will still be pitch-dark, and through the enormous windows you'll see the gleam of street lamps and the blue sparks of trams.

You won't go down to the Albergo Diurno, only as far as the bar, where you'll ask for a *caffellatte*, reading the newspaper which you'll have bought, while daylight appears and gradually gains strength, richness and warmth.

You'll be carrying your suitcase when you leave the station at dawn (the sky is perfectly clear, the moon has set, it's going to be a marvellous autumn day), and the city appears in all its deep redness, and as you'll be able to go neither to Via Monte della Farina nor to the Albergo Quirinale, you'll hail a taxi and ask to be taken to the Hotel Croce di Malta, Via Borgognone, near the Piazza di Spagna.

You will not keep watch over Cécile's windows; you will not see her go out; she will not catch sight of you.

You won't go and wait for her outside the Palazzo Farnese; you'll eat your lunch alone; throughout the whole of these few days you'll eat all your meals alone.

You'll walk about Rome quite alone, avoiding the district where she lives, and in the evening you'll go back alone to your hotel, where you'll go to sleep alone.

Then in that hotel room, alone, you'll begin writing a book, to fill the emptiness of those days in Rome deprived of Cécile, debarred from going near her.

Then on Monday night, you'll go back to the station, at the time you had intended, to take the train you had intended to take,
   without having seen her.

Beyond the corridor the big petrol refinery goes past with its flame and the electric lights decking its tall aluminium towers like a Christmas tree.

You're still standing there, facing your seat and that photograph of the Arc de Triomphe in Paris, still holding the book in your hands, when somebody taps you on the shoulder, the young husband whom you call Pierre, and you sit down to let him go out, but that's not what he wants; he stretches out his arm and turns on the light.

All the passengers open startled eyes and show flustered faces.

He reaches up over his young wife's head, takes down one of the cases and lays it on the seat, opens it and looks for their toilet things.

You say to yourself: if there hadn't been these people, if there hadn't been these objects, these images on to which my thoughts fastened, so that, during a journey unlike my other journeys, cut off from the habitual sequence of my days and actions, a kind of mental apparatus was set up, making the various regions of my being go sliding one over the other, tearing me apart,

if there hadn't been this set of circumstances, if the cards had not been dealt this way, perhaps this yawning fissure in my being would not have appeared during the course of this night, perhaps my illusions might have held for a little longer,

but now that it has occurred I can no longer hope for it to heal or to be forgotten, for it opens onto a cavern which is the cause of it, which has been there within me for a long time, and which I cannot attempt to block up since it is connected with an immense rift in the sphere of history.

I cannot hope to save myself by myself. All the blood of my being, all the sand of my days would run out in vain in my effort to achieve integration.

So then, the only possible way for me to enjoy at least the reflected gleam – itself so wonderful, so thrilling – of that future liberty which is out of our reach, would be to prepare the way for that liberty, to enable it, in however minute a measure, to take shape and substance, by means of a book for instance, although there could be no question of giving an answer to that riddle which the name of Rome suggests to our conscious or unconscious minds, of giving even a crude account of that prime source of marvels and of mysteries.

The station of Roma Trastevere goes by. Outside the window the first trams, their lights ablaze, cross one another in the streets.

It was pitch-dark already, and the headlights of cars were reflected on the wet asphalt in the Place du Panthéon. Sitting by the window, you were taking the *Letters of Julian the Apostate* from your bookcase when Henriette came in to ask if you'd be there for dinner.

"You know I prefer dining in the dining car."

"Your suitcase is ready on our bed. I'm going back to the kitchen."

"Goodbye. I'll be seeing you on Monday."

"We'll expect you; your place will be laid. Goodbye."

The rain had stopped and the moon was showing between clouds above the Boulevard Saint-Michel, with its lively crowd of students of all colours gathering at the beginning of term; in your haste to get away from that flat you took a taxi, which turned round the corner of the ruined palace attributed to the Parisian emperor.

At the Gare de Lyon, you bought cigarettes and reserved, on the platform, your seat for the second dinner; you got into a first-class carriage, you settled down in a compartment where there was already a stout gentleman of your own age, smoking small cigars; you deposited on the rack your suitcase and the briefcase of light-coloured leather full of files and documents, from which you extracted the orange folder dealing with the affairs of the Reims branch.

It was only the start of an ordinary journey and yet already, almost casually, you had made enquiries in Paris about the possibility of a job that might suit Cécile; nothing had as yet rent the texture of your well-regulated life, and yet already your relations with these two women were drawing towards the crisis of which this exceptional journey, now nearing its end, marks the conclusion.

When the train left, you went into the corridor to look out through the window at the moon in its first crescent over suburban roofs and gasometers.

Outside the window, the full moon has gone, but in front of Aurelian's ramparts the Vespas are more numerous, and many lights are already shining in every floor of the new blocks of flats.

The man you called Pierre comes back into the compartment, looking fresher about the face, more wide awake, smiling; the woman you called Agnès goes out next, carrying her big handbag; the woman beside you, with the Roman face, gets up, straightens her coat and tidies her hair, and takes down her little suitcase.

You say to yourself: what has happened since that Wednesday night, that last time I set off for Rome in the usual way? How can everything be so utterly changed, how can I have reached this point?

The forces that had been accumulating for a long time already exploded at last when you decided to make this journey, but the fire thus started had far-reaching effects, for while carrying out the plan you had dreamt of so long, you were compelled to realize that your love for Cécile was dominated by Rome as though by some enormous star, and that if you longed to bring her to Paris, it was in the hope that through her Rome would be with you all the time; but you find instead that when Cécile comes to the scene of your ordinary life she loses her mediatory power and becomes just a woman like any other, a second Henriette with whom, in that sort of substitute marriage which you had intended to set up, the same sort of difficulties would occur, only worse, because you'd be perpetually reminded of the absence of that city which you had hoped she would bring nearer to you.

Now it is no fault of Cécile's if the radiance of Rome which is reflected and concentrated in her fades as soon as she comes to Paris; it's the fault of the myth of Rome itself, which, as soon as you try to embody it in any definite way, however timid your attempt may be, reveals its ambiguities, and you stand condemned. You were trying to counterbalance your dissatisfaction with Paris by a secret belief in a return to the Pax Romana, a world empire organized round a capital city which might perhaps not be Rome but, for example, Paris. You justified all your acts of cowardice by reference to your hope that these two themes might be fused.

Another woman than Cécile would have lost her power too; another city than Paris would have deprived her of it.

And thus you are aware that one of the great epochs of history has come to an end, that in which the world had a centre, which was not only the earth set amidst the spheres, in the Ptolemaic system, but was Rome in the centre of the earth, a centre which shifted about, after the collapse of Rome tried to fix itself in Byzantium and then, much later, in imperial Paris, the black network of railways over France being a sort of shadow of the Roman roads.

The memory of the Empire, which dominated all the dreams of Europe for so many centuries, is now no longer an adequate image to represent the future of the world, which for each one of us has become far vaster and quite differently organized.

And that was why, when you tried to make closer contact with it on your own account, the image fell to pieces; that is why when Cécile comes to Paris she becomes like any other woman, and the sky that had shone on her is clouded.

You say to yourself: this book should show the part Rome can play in the life of a man in Paris; the two cities might be imagined one above the other, one of them lying underground below the other, with communicating trapdoors which only a few would know, while surely nobody could know them all, so that to go from one place to another there might be certain short cuts or unexpected detours, so that the distance from one point to another, the way from one point to another would vary according to one's knowledge, the degree of one's familiarity with that other city, so that every man's consciousness of place would be twofold, and Rome would distort Paris to a greater or lesser degree for each individual, suggesting authentic or misleading parallels.

The old Italian opposite you gets up, laboriously takes down his big black case and leaves the compartment, beckoning his wife to follow him.

A number of passengers, carrying their luggage, are already passing along the corridor and lining up beside the door.

The station of Roma Ostiense goes by, with the white tip of Cestius's pyramid showing faintly against the blackness, and, beneath you, the first suburban trains are arriving at the Roma-Lido station. On the iron floor-heater, with its diamond pattern like an idealized graph of railway traffic, you gaze at the dust and minute scraps of filth that have accumulated and become encrusted there during the past day and night.

The following morning, Thursday, you went to see Nero's Golden House, for Cécile's benefit; you had taken her home about midnight the night before, to 56 Via Monte della Farina, and she had answered your pleading look by saying that you couldn't possibly go upstairs with her then, because the Da Pontes would not have gone to bed yet, and on Thursday evening you dined with her in her room, surrounded by those four photographs of Paris which you tried not to see and which prevented you from speaking.

You only felt able to tell her about your visit when you were both lying on the bed together with the lamp turned out, the room lit only by moonbeams that came in through the window with a slight waft of wind, the lights from neighbouring houses and the headlamps of Vespas as they swerved noisily round the corner down below, sending orange gleams on to the ceiling.

You left her soon after midnight as usual; you went back to the Albergo Quirinale; the broken threads were joining up again; the wound had healed over very lightly; the slightest indiscretion would have torn it open again; that was why you never uttered a word to her about that time in Paris, and why, next day, Friday, despite all your fears, she never uttered a word to you about it, while you were lunching together in a restaurant near the Baths of Diocletian, nor while she was saying goodbye to you on the station platform, gazing at you and waving as the train moved out.

You had won her back; everything seemed forgotten. You never spoke of it again, and it's because of that silence that now the wound is incurable, it's because of that false, premature healing-over that gangrene has set in, in that inward sore that is festering so dreadfully now that the circumstances of this journey, the jars and jolts and the discomfort of it have torn off the scab.

"Goodbye," you called out to her as she ran, looking so lovely with her head held high and her hair forming a crown of black flames round it, smiling and breathless. You thought then: I nearly lost her, I've regained her; I've been skirting a precipice, I must never speak of it again; now I shall know how to keep her, I've got her safe.

You stare at your shoes, streaked all over with grey creases, against the iron floor-heater.

And that "goodbye, Cécile" now rings out in your head, and your eyes fill with tears of disappointment; you wonder: how can I ever make her understand and forgive me for the lie that our love has been, except perhaps by means of this book in which she would appear in her full beauty, adorned with the glory of Rome which is so perfectly reflected in her?

Would it not be better to maintain the distance between these two cities, all these stations and landscapes that divide them? But in addition to the normal routes by which one could move from one to another at will, there would be a certain number of points of contact, of immediate passages which would open at certain moments determined by laws that would only gradually become known to one.

Thus the principal character, walking in the neighbourhood of the Parisian Panthéon might one day, as he turned the corner of a familiar house, find himself all at once in a quite different street from the one he expected, under a very different light, with inscriptions in another language which he would recognize as Italian,

reminding him of a street he had already been through, which he would presently identify as one of those streets in the neighbourhood of the Roman Pantheon, and meeting a certain woman there, he would realize that to find her again he only had to go to Rome like any one else who has the leisure and the money to spare, by taking a train for instance, by giving up a certain amount of time and passing through all the intermediate stations;

and in the same way this Roman woman would from time to time visit Paris; having travelled far to find her he would discover that, no doubt involuntarily, she had come to the very place he had just left; he might for instance get a letter from a friend describing her,

so that all the episodes of their love affair would be conditioned not only by the laws of these relations between Rome and Paris, laws which might differ slightly for each of them, but also by their degree of familiarity with these cities.

The young woman you called Agnès, about whom you know nothing, not even her name, nothing but her face and her destination, Syracuse, comes back into the compartment, sits down beside her husband, watches the Vespas interlacing in front of the gloomy wall of Aurelian, which moves off into the distance, hidden by embankments and the buildings around the Piazza Zama.

The train dives between walls and under the bridge of the Via Appia Nuova.

The station of Roma Tuscolana goes by. A man thrusts his head through the doorway and looks about as if to make sure that he hasn't forgotten something (perhaps he's the man who, for a few hours last night, sat in that empty seat opposite you and whose face you never even saw, since he was enshrouded in darkness while you were sunk deep in your uneasy sleep, in the agonizing flow of your bad dreams, and those questions that torture you now were slowly and painfully taking shape and germinating within you, and a dizzy terror seized you at the abyss that was opening up before you, that rift which widens and deepens as you come nearer your journey's end – and your arrival in a few moments is the only certain fact, the only solid ground that's left you – that rift in which everything you had built up was gradually being engulfed).

Everything was fresh to you on that spring night in Rome, as you walked back towards the Hotel Croce di Malta.

There was no Metropolitana yet, there were no trolleybuses, no scooters: there were only trams and taxis with vertical lines and a few horse carriages.

Henriette laughed like yourself at the troops of priests, young and old, in their coloured sashes, rambling through the streets.

Clutching your Blue Guide, which was still brand new, which has grown increasingly inaccurate ever since, which you used to bring with you on every journey until you started seeing Cécile and making use of hers, that guidebook which you've left in your little Roman bookcase near the window at 15 Place du Panthéon,

both of you tireless (in your room in the morning, while you shaved and she did her hair, you repeated phrases from the Assimil),

you visited the Vatican next day, wandering all round the walls of the city, laughing at the pious frippery in the shop windows, hurrying through the galleries full of inferior antique statues and gifts from modern sovereigns,

you gazed lovingly at people, streets and monuments, both of you convinced that this was only a first contact.

Then after a few all-too-brief days of this delicious sauntering, both with one accord abusing under your breath the countless uniforms you met at every turn, you had to make your way back once more to the old Stazione Termini, a shabby, grimy building in those days and quite unworthy of Rome, and as the train moved out you whispered to her: "As soon as we possibly can, we'll come back."

Another man thrusts his head through the doorway and looks around (perhaps he's the one who spent a few hours on the seat next the newly married young man).

You say: I promise you, Henriette, as soon as we can, we'll come back to Rome together, as soon as the waves of this perturbation have died down, as soon as you've forgiven me; we shan't be so very old.

The train has stopped: you are in Rome, at the new Stazione Termini. The night is still pitch-dark.

You are alone in the compartment, with the young couple, who aren't getting off here, who are going on as far as Syracuse.

You hear the shouts of porters, the shrilling of whistles, the puffing and creaking sounds of other trains.

You stand up, put on your coat, take your case and pick up your book.

The best thing, surely, would be to preserve the actual geographical relationship between these two cities,

and to try and bring to life in the form of literature this crucial episode in your experience, the movement that went on in your mind while your body was being transferred from one station to another, through all the intermediate landscapes,

towards this book, this necessary future book of which you're holding in your hand the outward form.

The corridor is empty. You look at the crowd of people on the platform. You go out of the compartment.